PRAISE FOR THE WOMEN OF IVY MANOR

CARLY

"*Carly* is a high-quality story of chaotic experiences and strong characters . . . Lyn Cote has created her most memorable story yet."

—Irene Brand, award-winning author of
Where Morning Dawns and *The Hills Are Calling*

"*Carly* is a rich treat . . . as she goes through her own growth and faith journey during the turmoil of the 1990s. Lyn Cote never disappoints."

—Lenora Worth, author of *Echoes of Danger* and *After the Storm*

"Lyn's finale in the Ivy Manor series . . . takes you into the heart and mind of a young woman thrown into the uncertain world of the Gulf War . . . An engaging tale of finding the courage to be the person you have always known was hidden deep within you."

—Susan Meissner, author of *Why the Sky Is Blue*

"Reading *Carly* is like discovering an interesting neighborhood with great places to shop. You can't go home until you've seen what's around every corner."

—Patt Marr, author of *Man of Her Dreams*

"*Carly* is so real, so captivating, once I started read[ing] couldn't put it down! Carly is us . . . struggling to f[ind] prove she's strong enough to stand on her own. [You] you'll cry and you'll be reminded that noth[ing] when we place our trust in God."

—Valerie Whise[ll]
auth[

BETTE

"A powerful story of love, secrets, betrayal, [and compa]ssion during the tumultuous years of World War II. [Lyn's] unique blend of storytelling and dynamic characters brings this era of history to life."

—DiAnn Mills, author of *When the Lion Roars*

"Lyn Cote lured me into realistic, gripping, and sometimes heart-wrenching encounters with an era that has left an indelible mark on both history and human hearts. *Bette* is truly unforgettable."

—Kathy Herman, author of the
Baxter series and *A Shred of Evidence*

"Lyn Cote's craftsmanship shines in *Bette*. Her beautiful plotting includes textured settings that jet you around the world into the lives of characters so real we think we know them. Add a heroine we can all admire, and once again the ladies of Ivy Manor grab hold of your heart and hang on."

—Lois Richer, author of *Shadowed Secrets*

CHLOE

"A romance of epic proportions, absorbing and satisfying, that never lets you forget how the Father takes you just as you are and that His love can bring you home from the farthest journey."

—Deborah Bedford, author of
A Morning Like This and *If I Had You*

"Lyn Cote hooked me from the very beginning, then expertly reeled me across the pages . . . Pages full of romance, suspense, heartbreak, forgiveness, acceptance, and, ultimately, a satisfying ending."

—Sylvia Bambola, author of
Waters of Marah and *Return to Appleton*

"Lyn Cote's return to historical fiction is a delight! CHLOE is lyrically written, enhancing a plot that's teeming with zigs and zags. Compelling characters take a journey toward happiness reached only by plumbing the depths of despair. This one's a keeper!"

—Lois Richer, author of *Shadowed Secrets*

The Women of Ivy Manor
Book Four

A Novel

LYN COTE

WARNER
Faith®

NEW YORK BOSTON NASHVILLE

This book is a work of fiction. Names, characters, places, and incidents are the product of the author's imagination or are used fictitiously. Any resemblance to actual events, locales, or persons, living or dead, is coincidental.

Copyright © 2006 by Lyn Cote

Scripture quotations are from the KING JAMES VERSION.

Warner Faith

Time Warner Book Group
1271 Avenue of the Americas, New York, NY 10020
Visit our website at www.twbookmark.com

The Warner Faith name and logo are registered trademarks of the Time Warner Book Group.

Printed in the United States of America

First Warner Books printing: April 2006

10 9 8 7 6 5 4 3 2 1

Library of Congress Cataloging-in-Publication Data

Cote, Lyn.
    Carly / Lyn Cote.
      p. cm. — (The women of Ivy Manor ; bk. 4)
    Summary: "A young woman is wounded serving as part of Operation Desert Storm, and returns to the nursing care of three generations of women who have faced their own wars—personal or otherwise"—Provided by publisher.
    ISBN-13: 978-0-446-69436-0
    ISBN-10: 0-446-69436-3
    1. Women soldiers—Fiction. 2. Persian Gulf War, 1991—Veterans—Fiction. 3. War wounds—Patients—Fiction. I. Title.
    PS3553.O76378C37 2006
    813'.54—dc22   2005034263

To my son and daughter, the brave new generation

Acknowledgments

I wish to thank the following veterans and soldier for their help in providing the facts that gave my book authenticity—thanks for your service, honesty, and candor:

Former Army Ranger Chuck Holton
Major Deloris Lynders USA (Retired)
Staff Sergeant Laura Marston USAF (Retired)
Master Sergeant Pamela Trader USAF (Retired)
Captain Christine Valley USMC (Active Duty)

And I heard the Savior say,
Thy strength indeed is small,
Child of weakness, watch and pray,
Find in Me thine all in all.

ELVINA M. HALL (1820–1889)

Carly

The Carlyle Family

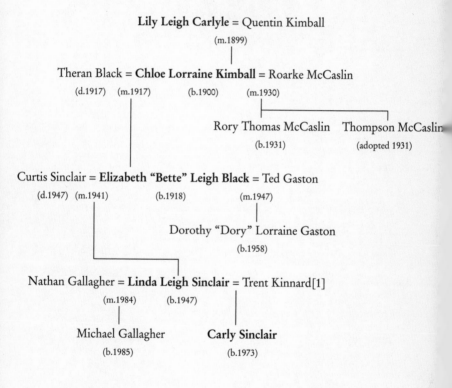

Lily Leigh Carlyle = Quentin Kimball
(m.1899)

Theran Black = **Chloe Lorraine Kimball** = Roarke McCaslin
(d.1917)   (m.1917)   (b.1900)   (m.1930)

Rory Thomas McCaslin   Thompson McCaslin
(b.1931)   (adopted 1931)

Curtis Sinclair = **Elizabeth "Bette" Leigh Black** = Ted Gaston
(d.1947) (m.1941)   (b.1918)   (m.1947)

Dorothy "Dory" Lorraine Gaston
(b.1958)

Nathan Gallagher = **Linda Leigh Sinclair** = Trent Kinnard[1]
(m.1984)   (b.1947)

Michael Gallagher   **Carly Sinclair**
(b.1985)   (b.1973)

---

[1] Birth father

CHAPTER ONE

Greenwich Village, May 1990

Can we talk about something, Aunty?" Carly Sinclair said, her dry throat making her sound hoarse. In worn, acid-washed blue jeans, she knelt on her aunt Kitty's kitchen floor and started scrubbing close to the baseboard. She'd tied her long black hair in a low ponytail so it wouldn't get into the bucket or drag on the floor. Her heart throbbed as she scrubbed. She glanced over her shoulder at her aunt.

In blue sweats, Kitty, who was really her great-great-aunt, shuffled slowly over to the table and eased down across from Carly, stifling a groan.

"Is your arthritis bothering you today?" Carly asked, pausing. Petite, silver-haired Kitty had always been a special person in her life. Carly had planned to use this conversation to prepare for the inevitable confrontation with her mother. But maybe this wasn't such a good idea. Kitty was really old—nearly ninety-three. *What if my plan really upsets her? What if she has a stroke or something?*

"Is that what you wanted to talk about? My arthritis?" Kitty grinned, her eyes crinkling up as they always did. "And can't I persuade you not to scrub my floor on your hands and knees?"

Carly shook her head. "You know you don't like the way Sylvia just swishes the mop around. Everything gets stuck in the corners." Two years before, Carly had been shocked to find Kitty on her knees trying to clean the corners herself. Carly had helped Kitty up and then taken over the job.

"Sylvia does her best," Kitty repeated for the thousandth time. "This getting old is for the birds. Just look at these hideous orthopedic shoes I'm forced to wear."

Carly half-smiled at her aunt's touch of humor. "Well, I've got young knees." Carly concentrated on swirling the scrub brush, ignoring the tension in her breast. "I'm sorry it's been so long—"

"What's on your mind?" Kitty cut in.

Carly took a deep breath and kept her head down. *Now or never.* "You know how Mom's been after me to decide what college I want to go to."

"Yes."

That's what Carly had always liked about her aunty. Kitty really listened. Unlike Carly's mother, Kitty didn't listen just long enough to start lecturing Carly. Nor did she just ignore what Carly said and go on as if she hadn't spoken a word.

Carly dropped the scrub brush in the bucket of warm wash water. She drew in a breath and began cautiously, "I don't want to go to college."

Kitty didn't answer right away. Then she said, "So, you know what you don't want to do. What *do* you want to do?"

Carly steeled herself for whatever reaction she might get. She sat back on her heels and looked up, meeting her aunt's eyes. "I've enlisted in the army."

Outside, just below the open rear kitchen window, Leigh Sinclair Gallagher, just arriving home from work, wondered if she'd heard her daughter right. *It can't be. She wouldn't do anything that stupid.*

"You've enlisted in the army?" Kitty's surprised voice floated out to Leigh.

"Yes, I got the idea last year at career day at school. They had recruiters from the navy, the army, the air force, and the Marines. I thought the army looked like the service that got things done."

Leigh felt as if the ground were moving under her like the earth tremors she'd felt almost twenty years before when she'd lived in San Francisco with Kitty. The army got things done? *Life* magazine images of the Vietnam War shot through Leigh's mind. She gripped the railing of the back steps.

"But why not go into service after you have your college degree?" Kitty asked. "Then you'd go in as an officer."

Leigh couldn't believe how calm her aunt sounded. Why wasn't she telling Carly how stupid this was? How ridiculous?

"I don't want to go to college—yet. I mean, I don't know what I want to do."

Leigh heard the clank of metal and the slosh of water and

fumed. What was Carly doing? Was she scrubbing Kitty's floor again? Why didn't Kitty let Sylvia retire and get someone younger who could scrub the floor the way she wanted it? Leigh started up the steps, ready to interrupt.

"But how do you know you want to join the army, then?" Kitty asked.

"It's just the only thing that's appealed—"

"Hey, Mommy!" Little Michael ran up behind Leigh. "Hey, you're home early! Look what I did in kindergarten today!" Her auburn-haired son waved a watercolor at her. "Look! We painted today!"

Leigh put on a bright smile and examined the mostly yellow painting while the two of them walked up the back steps, inside past Kitty's door, and up to the second-floor flat where Leigh, Nate, Michael, and Carly lived.

Leigh thought Michael's appearance had stopped her, fortunately, from barging in on her daughter and her great-aunt. Carly was a difficult child and she could be amazingly stubborn at times. Leigh needed time to think about what to do, and she didn't trust herself to go into Kitty's first-floor flat. She knew she wasn't a good enough actress to fool Kitty that she hadn't heard exactly what Carly and she had been talking about.

Michael chattered as she fixed him an after-school snack. Then she decided she needed to enlist her husband's support. Carly loved Nate, and Leigh didn't doubt that Nate could persuade Carly to drop this insane plan. *Please come home, Nate. I need to talk to you. I need you tonight.*

*   *   *

4

That evening, Nate walked into the apartment in the nick of time to help Leigh get their little son in bed and say good night. Then he headed straight for Carly's door to wish her a good night, too. But Leigh whispered to him not to and to follow her. Her expression was stormy, and he began to expect the start of another one of the endless circular arguments between his wife and himself. But he wasn't participating tonight. He was too beat.

"Okay." Nate leaned against the kitchen doorjamb, looking around for leftovers. His stomach growled. "What's put you in a foul mood?"

"Maybe if you'd come home earlier, you'd know." Leigh opened the refrigerator and then slipped a covered dish into the microwave above the stove.

Nate just stared at her. How could she make that accusation with a straight face? "You know when I'm working a case, I don't keep regular hours. When you have to work late, I don't nag you about it."

Leigh gave him her look that said, "Oh, really?" He hated that look. When had they started acting out this endless domestic drama, comprised of sharp words and unpleasant glares?

Then Leigh surprised him by holding her index finger to her closed lips and motioning him to join her at the table at the far side of the blue-and-white kitchen, farthest from the children's bedrooms. "Let's talk quietly. I don't want Carly to overhear us."

Concerned, Nate moved forward. He picked up a box of wheat crackers on the counter and then sat down at the table.

"What's wrong?" he asked in a subdued tone. "Did something happen to her at school?"

Leigh flicked away a few grains of salt from the oak table-top. "You won't believe this, but this afternoon I overheard her tell Kitty that she wants to go into the army."

"You're kidding, right?" As he munched a salty cracker, he leaned back and let his tired legs stretch out under the table.

"I wish I were. What are we going to do?"

Listening to the whir of the microwave made him even hungrier. "She must have a reason—"

"I know what the reason is," Leigh snapped. "Some army recruiter who wanted to meet his quota got hold of her at career day last year and filled her full of—"

"But Carly isn't the kind of kid who's swayed by sales-manship," Nate interrupted, not liking Leigh's spin. "Carly's got a good head on her shoulders."

Leigh gave him her superior expression—raised eye-brows and pursed lips—that always grated on his nerves.

"Don't give me that look," Nate snapped. "Our daughter isn't stupid. There must be more to this than we know—"

"Why do you always take her part?"

"Because you never do," Carly declared from the kitchen doorway.

Hearing the hurt in his stepdaughter's voice, Nate rose and opened his arms.

In an old T-shirt, cotton pajama pants, and barefoot, Carly hurried to him and hugged him hard. "I heard you come in, and when I finished the chapter I was reading, I came out to hug you hello."

Nate rubbed her slender back. "Thanks, sweetheart. I always count on your hello-hugs." *Because I never get them from your mother anymore.*

"I wanted to discuss this with your stepfather first," Leigh announced, "but we might as well get this out in the open."

Carly stepped out of his embrace and faced her mother. "We might as well. I don't know how you found out, but yes, I want to enlist in the army."

"You're a minor and I won't sign for you to enlist," Leigh said, folding her arms.

"I expected that." Carly raised her chin. "I'll just work a grunt job until my birthday next year and then enlist."

"Why are you doing this?" Leigh asked. "What can you be thinking?"

The microwave bell rang. Carly lifted out the warm plate of chicken and wild rice and set it on the table in front of Nate. "Here, Dad."

"That can wait." Nate pushed the dish aside. The conflict had tied his stomach into double knots. "Come on, Carly." Scraping the wood floor, Nate pulled out the chair between his and Leigh's and motioned her to be seated and then he sat down again. "We three can talk this over rationally and figure out how to work this out."

" 'Work this out'?" Leigh echoed. "She's not going to enlist. I forbid it."

Nate held up a hand to stop Carly from replying. "Leigh, Carly is a young woman now. Your days of forbidding her are over. Deal with it."

"She's only seventeen."

"You were only sixteen," Nate countered, "when you defied your mother and went to Dr. King's march in Washington."

"That isn't anything like this." Leigh's glance promised him open warfare. "That was just one day. This decision could change her life forever."

"From what you've told me, that day changed your life forever." He wouldn't let Leigh stonewall Carly. He'd seen her do it one time too many. "And any decision Carly makes about how to start out as an adult will impact her life, whatever that decision is."

"Don't you care about her?" Suddenly Leigh looked ready to cry.

"Nate loves me," Carly said, folding her arms in front of her.

"And I suppose that means I don't," Leigh snapped, blinking away tears.

"Leigh—" Nate began.

"Sometimes I don't love you." Carly leaned forward, her chin jutting forward, challenging. "You're always trying to keep everything under your thumb. I always have to be your idea of the perfect daughter to prove that you were the perfect single mother. I'm—"

"That's not true," Leigh objected. "I've never demanded that you get straight As or any of that kind of thing!"

"I don't think that's what Carly is talking about." Nate braced himself for heavy going. Why didn't Leigh use her good sense when it came to Carly, when it came to him?

Leigh glared at him. "What could you possibly be talking about?"

"I'm talking about the truth." Nate reached for Leigh's hand but she withheld it. "I thought that after we married and you told Carly about her father—"

"She didn't tell me anything about my father," Carly huffed.

"That's not true." Leigh slapped her palm on the tabletop. "I did tell you."

"You told me that you dated my dad but that you broke up with him. Big deal," Carly said with a sarcastic twist. "What did that tell me?"

Leigh clamped her mouth shut and her eyes blazed at Nate.

He tried another tack. "I thought after we married, and you told Carly about her father, that you would begin to loosen up. To be happy with me. To get closer to your daughter. But after a brief honeymoon period, you went right back to the grindstone. You're working your life and Michael's childhood away."

"Don't bring that up now." Leigh leaned toward him. "Carly isn't going to tell me that my successful career is what has caused her to entertain this ridiculous idea."

Nate wouldn't be deflected. "I urged you to tell Carly everything about her father and your relationship with him."

"You know why I didn't." Leigh wouldn't meet either Carly's or Nate's eyes.

"Why?" Carly gripped the edge of the table.

"I didn't want to hurt you," Leigh said in a haunting, forlorn tone.

Carly couldn't believe her mother could say those words with a straight face. "Not hurt me?" Carly felt her throat closing up. "What is he? An axe murderer? Don't you realize that not knowing . . . ?" Carly looked away, hiding the onrush of tears. "Who is my father? Why can't I know about him?" She couldn't go on.

"Nate is your father. He's the father who's raised you," Leigh insisted, sounding crushed yet defensive.

"He's not really my father," Carly blurted out. "You wouldn't let him adopt me." Admitting this shook her, but it felt good to let those long-suppressed words out.

"What do you mean?" Leigh swung around to face her. "I had a stepfather. He never adopted me, but I never felt he needed to."

"That's you. It's not me." Then Carly wouldn't look at either of them, fearing she'd gone too far. She hadn't meant to put Nate on the spot. Maybe he hadn't really wanted to adopt her. He might have just been being polite.

Nate gently took her hand. "Sweetheart, you are my daughter. And if you'd just let me know that it bothered you that I didn't adopt you, I would have. You know that, right?"

Carly blinked away tears. How could she tell him that when she was ten and had overheard them discussing this, she couldn't make herself say it? The yearning to belong to a father had been too deep, too crucial to be put into naked words.

As he had many times in her childhood, Nate tugged her and she slid willingly onto his lap. "You're my daughter, Carly. I still want to adopt you." He kissed her hair. "I love you. Never doubt that."

As always, Nate sensed just what she needed. Grateful for his arms around her, Carly buried her face in the crook between his neck and shoulder, frightened by the force of her reaction to this long-awaited declaration. Her feelings at the moment were too intense to face alone. As he stroked her hair, she grappled with them, with her lack of control. The lid had been yanked off her deep well of concealed emotions. Pain, loss, uncertainty, rejection whirled inside her, dark and thorny, tearing at her confidence, her peace.

She still couldn't speak, so in reply to his offer of adoption, she finally nodded against him.

"I'm sorry," her mother said quietly, touching Carly's back. "I didn't know it mattered that much to you. Why didn't you say anything?"

Carly lifted her head and faced her mother. "How could I tell you what was in my heart when you would never tell me the truth about myself? Who is my father? What is his name? Why did you break up with him? And—" Carly made herself ask the bedrock, most dangerous question. "Didn't he ever want to see me, talk to me?"

"I didn't want him to talk to you." Her mother stiffened. "Evidently you've made up some romantic image of him in your mind. By not letting him near you, I was protecting you."

"What was wrong with my father?" Carly held out both palms, pleading.

Leigh turned her head and looked away out the small window. She shook her head.

Instant, blazing anger consumed Carly. "What's so wrong with my father? What did he do that was so bad that I couldn't even meet him, know his name?" The molten lava of bitterness against her mother for keeping the truth from her overflowed its channel, spilling out into searing words. "How bad could he be? You liked him well enough to sleep with him."

Leigh slapped Carly's face. And then she stalked from the room.

Too shocked, too incensed for words, Carly clung to Nate, who rubbed her back and murmured soothingly to her.

Ivy Manor, May 1990

Tall oaks and maples shaded the summerhouse behind Carly's great-grandmother's ancestral home in the early evening. Being there gave her confidence. At Ivy Manor she was completely loved. Chloe didn't dole out acceptance based on performance the way Leigh did.

In her pale blue graduation dress, Carly sat in the white wicker rocker with the wide curved arms and pushed a bare toe against the floor. She closed her eyes and listened to the chatter of voices around her. The three older generations—the eldest, her frail, silver-haired great-grandmother Chloe and great-great-aunt Kitty, next her grandmother Bette, and then her mother Leigh—sat in a casual circle on venerable lawn furniture. Only Aunt Dory, her mother's younger sister, was missing. And Carly—the fourth generation—was getting ready to explode the quiet tranquility.

She opened her eyes. Across from her, on the love seat with dark green cushions, her mother looked cool and beautiful as usual. Leigh was wearing a stylish ivory linen suit. Nate sat beside her, his sport coat off and his tie loosened. All the other guests, extended family and friends, had left.

Much earlier that day, in the last second before the guests had begun arriving, her mother had hissed that she forbade Carly to bring up the subject of the army. Carly hadn't bothered to reply. Today, she would bring it up and hoped for support from her family. But whether she got support or not, she was going through with it. And they might as well all know that. She jittered with nerves, but she'd never felt more sure of a decision.

"Well, Carly, all day people have asked you where you're going to school this fall," Chloe commented. She was wearing one of her vintage designer dresses. "But you kept saying you didn't know. What aren't you telling us?"

Carly's little half-brother Michael, in his rumpled dress shirt and slacks, slipped inside the summerhouse and climbed into her lap. He laid his head against her breast. "Rock me," he murmured in a drowsy voice.

Carly said, "Uh-huh." She pushed her toe down again. The chair rocked back and forth. Michael made a sound of contentment.

"Maybe Carly doesn't want to go to college right away," Bette commented. In a fashionable purple sundress, Bette sat on a white Adirondack chair next to the love seat. Her long silver and black hair was pulled into a stylish bun at the nape of her neck.

"Why not?" Leigh snapped back, looking at Carly, daring her to bring up the currently forbidden topic. "Part of the reason she finished high school in three years was so she could get on with her life."

"Maybe she isn't as driven as you are," her stepfather said.

A tense silence swelled among them.

"This isn't the time or place to discuss that," Leigh said, her voice low as she gave Nate another warning glance.

He snorted. "It's never the time or place to discuss it."

"Nate," Leigh warned him, sounding in earnest now.

Wildfire blazed through Carly. She hated it when her mother bossed Nate around.

"It's a bad sign," Chloe said in a mild tone without any reproof in it, "when a man and woman open up their disagreements in front of others."

"You couldn't be more right," Nate agreed. "But your granddaughter has become a dictator, and it's nearly time for her overthrow."

"Me, the dictator?" Leigh shot back. "You're the one who's giving the orders, not me."

Michael burrowed more deeply into Carly's arms. "Make them stop," he whispered.

Carly stroked his thick auburn hair, so like his father's, and pressed her hand over his exposed ear. She didn't want him to have to hear the coming explosion. She looked pointedly at her mother, a look that said, "Here goes."

"Carly—" Leigh started.

Carly braced herself for her mother's outrage and entered the fray. "I'm not going to college."

Leigh sat up straighter and sent Carly a more urgent warning glance.

Carly lifted her chin as if to say, "I dare you, Mom." Her stomach quivered in unpleasant anticipation of the tide of angry words that were about to be unleashed. Carly hated turmoil. *Mother, I've always let you mow down my questions, but this is too important to me. You will not get your way.*

"You are going to college," Leigh insisted, moving forward on her chair, her face flushed.

"No," Carly said, proud of how cool her voice came out.

She kept her hand over Michael's ear and with the other, stroked his springy hair. "I've made other plans."

"What are those?" Chloe asked in a voice that bespoke only interest, but her gaze shifted back and forth between Carly and Leigh.

Carly took a deep breath. She might as well jump head-first into the deep end. "I've enlisted in the army."

Leigh made a sound like a woman being strangled.

Carly watched her dispassionately, suddenly feeling removed from the scene. Nothing her mother said would deter her, touch her. *Rant and rave all you want, Mom. But I'm going through with it.*

"Never," Leigh announced. "Never."

"I've already filled out the papers. I report for boot camp in three days."

Leigh surged to her feet. "You're only seventeen—a minor—and I told you I won't sign for you."

Carly shrugged. "Then as I told you, I'll just work some job till I'm eighteen next year. I'm not changing my mind."

"I absolutely forbid it," Leigh declared.

Kitty leaned forward and held out a restraining hand. "Foolish words, my dear. When did Bette's forbidding you to do things ever stop you?"

Chloe chuckled. "The apple never falls far from the tree."

Leigh glared at Chloe and Kitty. Carly watched her mother breathing hard and fast. She wondered where her own feeling of control, of calm, had come from.

"And we aren't asking the most important question, really," Bette said, turning to her granddaughter.

"And what's that?" Leigh demanded.

"Why does Carly want to enlist in the army?"

"I would think it's fairly obvious," Leigh replied before Carly could. "She's doing it because she knows it's the last thing I want her to do."

Bette looked to Carly. "Is that why you want to enlist?"

"No." But the larger question, why the military attracted her, still stumped Carly. It was something she hadn't been able to put into words. She'd never told anyone about the nightmares, afraid they would worry everyone. Then her parents might make her go back into counseling. But the day she'd spoken to the recruiter had been followed by two nightmare-free nights. "It's the only thing that's interested me," Carly mumbled.

"What about it interests you?" Bette probed.

"Why are you even taking her seriously?" Leigh asked her mother.

"Because when I was young, if I could have, I would have enlisted to fight Hitler."

"There is no Hitler in this world today," Leigh declared.

"Are you so sure of that?" Kitty asked.

"What's going on here?" Leigh demanded of her senior female relatives. "Why aren't you telling Carly that this is ridiculous, out of the question?"

"Maybe because," Bette said, "Aunt Kitty's right. In the sixties, whenever I forbad you to do something, you always did it anyway. Why do you think you have the right now to forbid your daughter to do anything?"

"I was right to do what I did. The march on Washington and the 1968 convention were two of the most important events of the century. You shouldn't have tried to keep me home."

"I was just trying to protect you," Bette said.

"And I'm just trying to protect Carly," Leigh added.

"I'd think you'd be pleased with Carly," Nate put in. "Didn't you write several articles about women in the military?"

"That has nothing to do with this." Leigh drew away from him as much as she could on the love seat.

"That's hypocritical, Mom," Carly said dismissively, "and you know it."

"You are not going to enlist in the army until after you finish college. It makes no sense to go in as enlisted personnel." Leigh looked ready to spit.

Feeling her anger flare again, Carly stared at her mother, reaching down deep to come up with yet another cool, calm reply. She might as well speak the truth. "You can delay me, but you can't stop me."

"Then at least I'll delay you for a year and maybe you'll come to your senses."

"If you won't listen to the good advice your family's just given you, I will. If Carly still wants me to," Nate said with quiet authority, "I'll adopt her and then I'll sign her enlistment papers."

Carly gasped.

Leigh gawked at Nate. "If you do that, knowing how I feel, I'll file for divorce."

CHAPTER TWO

Carly closed her eyes. How did her mother always manage to make herself the center of attention? *If you're stupid enough to divorce a great guy like Nate, don't try to blame it on me.*

"Have you lost your mind, Leigh?" Chloe's voice sliced through the stunned silence. "Carlyles don't announce ultimatums in public to their husbands, and we never argue in front of others."

"McCaslins don't either," Kitty added.

"It's time you sit down, Leigh," Chloe ordered, "and get your emotions under control."

Opening her eyes, Carly noticed that her grandmother Bette had pursed her lips so tightly, they were white. Carly rocked Michael again, keeping her hand over his ear. He felt warm against her. Even though it was evening, the temperatures were still in the low eighties. His eyes were closed and his breathing was steady. Carly hoped he'd fallen asleep.

Chloe nodded her head in the direction of Michael and gave Leigh a pointed look.

Leigh sat back down. She looked shaken but unrepentant.

Carly knew that her mother would bounce back quickly. And stonewalling was her favored tactic. *Well, I can stonewall, too, Mom.*

"I don't think it has escaped anyone's notice," Nate said in the uncomfortable quiet, "that Leigh and I are dealing with a stressful period in our marriage."

Leigh glanced at him sideways, but said nothing.

"I think . . . I've told Leigh that she needs to cut back on the hours she devotes to her writing career." He held up a hand to stop Leigh from breaking in. "We both need more time together and time with Michael. He'll be getting into more activities like Little League and music lessons. We need to be available more. And I've already discussed adjusting my work schedule with my captain at the precinct."

"Before I met you, I worked full-time and I managed to find time to do things with Carly," Leigh retorted. "I don't—"

"You didn't manage to pick me up on time that night at the dance studio," Carly said in a deceptively calm voice, referring to the life-changing event that had taken place seven years before. Inside, she shook with sudden emotion. She'd never voiced this accusation—though she'd wanted to for as along as she could remember.

Obviously stunned and uneasy, everyone turned to look at Carly. She stared back at them, waiting for someone to react, waiting for her mother to react.

"I can't believe you've brought that up now. Don't you know the guilt I carry because I wasn't there to protect you?"

Leigh finally replied, rising again. "Do you think you can browbeat me with my past mistakes and get your way?"

"We're getting far afield," Bette said, motioning Leigh to sit down.

Leigh complied but didn't attempt to mask her irritation.

"We were discussing why Carly wants to serve in the military." Bette turned to Carly. "Why do you want to do this?"

Carly still trembled, the aftereffect of finally voicing her deepest pain and grief. Stalling, she tucked Michael closer and chewed her lower lip. A gust of wind stirred the leaves of the tall trees. The sound reminded her of her vague but menacing shadowy nightmares. At last, she said, "I want to be on my own."

Bette nodded encouragement.

Carly searched for words. She wanted to sound logical and in control. But she didn't completely understand yet what drew her to the army. How could she say, "It makes me feel stronger"? So she said, "I want to be part of a group."

"That makes sense," Leigh said in derision. "Those are opposites."

Carly ignored her mother's uncharacteristic dig. "I want to see if I have what it takes." That final reason rocked her inside. She felt the old terror escalating, and she tamped it down. She faced bad dreams at night and sudden bursts of panic in daylight. At some level, she knew that to free herself, she must face and defeat her fears. Was that why she was enlisting? Was she testing herself, as she had in other ways in the past? Well, if that was her true reason, no one needed to know but her. "That's about all I can put into words."

Leigh opened her mouth, but Bette spoke up first, her

voice strengthening word by word. "I think each generation tries to protect the younger. And it never works. All it does is cause discord. Leigh, forbidding your daughter to start her life her way won't deter her. It will only put up a wall between the two of you."

"Thank you, Bette," Chloe said quietly. "Thank you."

Carly looked from face to face. She didn't like the feeling of being the only one present who didn't know what everyone was talking about or, rather, not talking about. Why were there always secrets? "What am I missing?"

Bette faced her. "When your mother was your age, I did a lot of forbidding, and it had the effect I just mentioned. I don't know if your enlisting in the army makes sense, but perhaps it's something you need to do. I don't know. I ran out of having all the answers several years ago."

Nate stood up. "Carly," he murmured, "is Michael asleep?"

She nodded. Michael's body against her had finally taken on that sensation of boneless, complete relaxation that meant deep slumber.

Nate scooped him gently from her arms. "Leigh, let's take him up and put him to bed. Then we're going to take a walk and do some talking. You're not divorcing me, so get that out of your head."

Carly expected her mother to argue, but instead she trailed Nate out of the summerhouse with only a backward glance, one filled with anxiety.

No one talked until the couple had disappeared inside Ivy Manor's back door. Then Chloe let out a long sigh. "I'm feeling every one of my ninety years right now."

Carly decided to push against the unspoken rules once more. "Why won't my mother tell me about my father?"

All three women stared at her but said nothing.

"Why?" Carly insisted. "And why won't you tell me?"

Kitty gave her an apologetic smile. "It's Leigh's story, her secrets—"

"They're my secrets, too," Carly cut in.

"We can't tell you, my dear." Chloe rubbed her temple as if in pain.

"Yes, it's important that Leigh do it," Bette added.

"Why?"

"Carly, remember," Kitty said, "unfortunately, the truth isn't always what we want it to be."

Nate led his wife into Ivy Manor. He'd come to love this place. It was a haven of peace. His everyday world dragged his mind through murder and other forms of cruelty he had a hard time stomaching. More and more he fought becoming completely hardened to life, to people. He'd talked to his father and grandfather enough to know that a completely cynical cop was not what he wanted to be, nor what God wanted him to be. And visiting Ivy Manor washed away the filth he brought with him and gave him hope again. Even about the woman he loved.

Leigh and Nate entered the quiet house with Michael fast asleep in his arms. Stacks of washed dishes covered the plain oak kitchen table. The housekeeper, Rose, would finish putting everything back in place the next day. They walked up the hardwood steps to the second floor and Nate laid their son on the antique trundle bed in Carly's room. Then they walked back down, out the front door, and between the ivied pillars of the front porch.

What am I going to do with this woman? He gazed at his wife of seven years. So beautiful. So proud. So ambitious. He said what he was thinking. "I thought I could balance you."

Leigh looked at him. "Is that why you married me?"

"I married you because I fell in love with you. Because you needed me and I needed you. Because I loved you, loved Carly, and wanted to be her father."

"Then why didn't you insist on adopting her?" Leigh sounded uncharacteristically petulant.

"It was early days for us." Even though the evening breeze was rising, he unbuttoned his cuffs and rolled them up a turn. "I was feeling my way, getting to know you and Carly."

"Why didn't she tell me?" Leigh folded her hands under her arms.

"Carly isn't like you." Nate tugged one of her hands free and clasped it. "You bubble up and explode. You declare what you want and expect the world to snap to attention. Carly is still waters, deep waters. I should have taken time to dig out what her opinion of being adopted was. But our marriage came only a couple of months—"

"After I didn't get to the dance studio on time, after Carly had been snatched," Leigh snapped and then burst into tears.

*   *   *

"What do you mean—the truth isn't always what we want it to be?" Carly couldn't keep the anger from her voice. She felt her pulse speeding up.

"We mean," Chloe said, "that you may have some unrealistic idea of who your father is or what he's like."

"Do you know my father?" Carly demanded.

"No, dear," Bette replied, patting Carly's arm, "none of us have ever met him or even seen him."

"But you know who he was—I mean is—right?"

"I know his name," Kitty confessed.

"I know what kind of man he is," Chloe added.

"I know that he hurt your mother as much as a man can hurt a woman," Bette said.

"Your mother trusted him with her heart and body, and he proved himself to be unworthy of that trust," Chloe said.

"But I'm his daughter." Carly heard her voice rising with her indignation. Why were they all protecting her mother? "That means that I'm like him. I have his genes. What about me is like him? Not like him? Don't you see? I need to know."

"It was unkind of Carly to throw that up to you," Nate said, cradling Leigh in his arms, stroking her hair, silk against his palm. "But . . ."

"But what?" his wife asked tearfully.

"But this conflict is bound to unearth the past, stir up muddy waters."

"Why? Why is she doing this?"

Nate was heartened by Leigh's diffident tone. If nothing

else, Carly's rebellion had shaken her mother out of her own righteous vision of things. "She is trying to find her feet as an adult. I know you think that Carly's done this just to insult you. But I don't see her doing that. Carly is very much self-directed. I think this may have something to do with . . ." He struggled with the words circling in his mind. "Somehow this is tied up with her kidnapping and her birth father."

Leigh pulled away from him. "So this is all my fault. And I deserve it."

"Stop that." He jerked her back to him, holding her against him. Her heart beat against his chest. "You're important. But right now the spotlight is on our daughter. This is all about her. She needs to . . . I think she's trying to face the future and be strong."

He shrugged. "I see it all the time with new cops right out of the academy. They all want to become cops for different reasons and for the same reason. They all are facing life and want to take a strong stand." He shook his head. "That's as clear as I can make it. Maybe that's why I understand what's pushing Carly. I felt it once myself."

"Yes, we see that you need to know your father's identity even if you never choose to meet him," Bette said. "We love you, Carly, and we'd like to help you."

"But you won't." Carly turned her face away from them. How could they hold back the information that meant so much to her?

Bette stood up. "We can't. All of us have learned through hard experience not to meddle, not to interfere. I tried to, and

I nearly lost your mother, nearly lost my relationship with her, with you. I'm . . . I'm afraid of saying the wrong thing, crossing some line that could break our family apart. Our family is strong and fragile at the same time." She shook her head and began pacing.

"Someday I'll find my father." Carly rose, confronting her grandmother. "Someday I'll know everything."

"And your mother will be the one to tell you," Chloe spoke up. "I have confidence that she will. She's going through something now." Chloe shook her head. "The past is still strangling her. But I have faith that she will make the right decisions when the time comes."

"I do, too," Kitty agreed.

Carly grimaced. "Well, I don't. I'm her mistake. She'd be happier if I weren't here, if I'd never been born." The familiar desperate feeling rushed through her. She ran from the summerhouse down the lane toward the stream. Silent tears washed her face.

Later, after everyone was in bed, Chloe shrugged into her cotton robe and slippers and crept down the hall to Nate and Leigh's room. Bette and Kitty were both staying in the little cottage so Nate and Leigh could be near Michael and the children's room. Chloe knocked.

Nate opened the door. "Do you need something?" he asked with concern.

"I need a few private words with my granddaughter."

He gazed at her a moment, then nodded. "I'll go downstairs and get a glass of milk." After squeezing Chloe's shoulder, he walked around her and headed down the staircase.

Chloe entered the spare bedroom, lit by the soft glow of the bedside lamp.

Sitting on the edge of the colonial four-poster, Leigh was wearing a pale cotton nightgown. She didn't look up.

"I haven't come to scold or argue," Chloe reassured her as she sat down at the little empire-style desk in the corner. "I've come to make a suggestion."

"What's that?"

"I think you've overlooked someone who could help with this problem."

Leigh looked up. "You mean Frank?"

Chloe nodded. "Since he's made a career in the military, he could give you advice and a different perspective on the army. And he's known you since you were a teenager. He understands you."

Leigh buried her face into her hands. "Why can't life ever be easy?"

"It never is. We're strong people, a strong family, or we wouldn't still be here in this house that's nearly three hundred years old. I can remember when Daddy had electricity installed." Chloe glanced around. "It wasn't a pleasant experience. Mother had a fit when the workmen had to open up walls. But candles and oil lamps no longer were sufficient, and we had to move with the times."

Leigh looked up. "And you think I'm acting like your mother? Trying to hold back progress?"

"You are now the previous generation. A chilling thought, no doubt." Chloe smiled. "But remember, I'm the *oldest* living generation, even more chilling. It gets very lonely when you outlive all your friends and relatives. I'm so fortunate that Kitty is here with me. But there isn't a day that I don't miss my Roarke." Chloe paused.

"You want to talk about Nate and me," Leigh prompted. She wouldn't make eye contact.

Chloe walked over and sat down on the soft quilt beside Leigh. "Honey, good men who love us are rare. I'm afraid Nate's right. You've been burying yourself in work, and it's showing in Michael. I can see it."

"I don't want to hear that." Leigh turned her head away.

"I don't want to say it. But I also need to say that you should never have linked divorcing Nate and Carly. You should not have made it sound as if you were putting the blame on Carly if you divorced Nate."

"I didn't mean that." Leigh swung back and turned her face into her grandmother's shoulder. "Whatever problems Nate and I are having, Carly didn't cause them."

"I know, dear. But you need to say that to your daughter and make it right." Chloe rubbed Leigh's tight back muscles through the thin cotton gown. "Call Frank. He can help."

"Don't you think he might be prejudiced in favor of the military?" Lifting her head, Leigh gave a twisted smile.

The next morning at Ivy Manor, Leigh sat beside the telephone in the den downstairs. She could hear Rose talking to Chloe in the dining room. No more delay. She forced herself to dial Frank and Cherise's number in northern Virginia. Frank worked at the Pentagon now, so he'd moved back from

Georgia about three years before. A young female voice answered, and Leigh asked for Frank.

"Hello," Frank's rich, familiar voice came on the line.

"Hi, Frank, it's Leigh."

"Leigh! What a great surprise. We were really sorry that we couldn't make Carly's graduation party."

"I know. We felt sorry we couldn't get to Lorelle's party." Frank's second-born, his eldest daughter, had graduated that year, too.

"What can I do for you, Leigh?"

"I couldn't have called just to talk?" she asked, delaying the conversation she did not want to have.

"No, we're both busy people and we've never had much time just for chatting. What's up?"

After what her grandmother had said the night before about Michael's being neglected, Leigh didn't like that response. But she drew in breath, readying herself. "I need to talk to you about Carly. She wants to enlist in the army."

There was a brief silence. "Your daughter, too? Did they plan this together?"

Leigh wrinkled her forehead. "What do you mean?"

"Lorelle intends to enlist as well."

"No." Leigh was shocked. "Why wouldn't she go to college first, then go in as an officer?"

"Wants to make it on her own and wants to pay for college on her own."

"Why?"

"I don't know. Maybe it's the middle child thing. Cherise thinks Lorelle's trying either to get our attention or stand out from her brother, James, who went dutifully off to college but

29

doesn't plan a military career. Or maybe it's generational. We boomers, we're the 'Give peace a chance' generation. Maybe our kids are reacting to that."

Leigh tried to juggle this unexpected development. *Who would have thought?* "This is really weird."

"I know. We've had a few lively discussions here with Lorelle. I bet you're as thrilled as we are."

"Then you don't think I'm wrong in refusing to give my consent."

"Give your consent?"

"Remember, Carly is almost a year younger than your Lorelle, still a minor."

"That's right. I'd forgotten. Your girl finished high school early."

"Yes, and I refuse to sign for her . . . but Nate says he will sign for her."

"Ah." Frank sounded smug.

Irritation prickled through her nerves. "Ah, what?"

"Leigh, Carly's enlisting in the army isn't the end of the world. She'll still have a lot of years left when her enlistment ends."

"I just don't see Carly in the military," Leigh declared, putting all her will into it.

"Why?"

Leigh paused, marshalling her reasons. "She's so slight, you know. She's not one of these strapping young women who could play football. She could get hurt."

"Recruits rarely get hurt beyond bumps and bruises, and the army takes in all kinds. If I remember correctly, Carly lettered in track all three years of high school. That means she's probably in better shape than most recruits."

"I just don't want her to do this," Leigh said, feeling rising desperation.

"Don't you remember how my family had a fit when I went in for officer candidate school?"

"But you went in the military as an officer."

"I know, but our daughters don't want to go through college first. They want to do it their way. Just like we did."

"You're not much help." Leigh couldn't argue. She remembered all too well the way both of them had pushed against their parents' restraints.

"Leigh, Carly sounds just like you at seventeen. She has her own agenda and will do it with or without your consent. I mean, she just has to wait until she turns eighteen, and then she won't need your consent."

Leigh frowned and twisted the phone cord. "That has been pointed out to me. Repeatedly."

"Step back, Leigh. They have to grow up sometime. We want to protect them, but we can't. Remember, I survived two tours in 'Nam and," he teased, "you survived tear gas and rioting at the '68 convention in Chicago. Your daughter is tough enough to make it through basic training."

"I wish you'd sided with me," Leigh scolded. "It would have given me something to hang on to."

Frank chuckled. "Hey, there's a good chance that our two girls will end up on the same post for boot camp. There are only a few posts where women companies go through basic training. They probably won't end up in the same platoon, but at least they'd have someone on base that they know."

"I thought the army had gender-integrated basic now."

"No, we tried that from 1978 to 1982. And some people are talking about bringing it back. But we had too many people thinking that the female recruits were getting injured at a higher rate."

"That's a reassuring thought."

"I didn't say it was fact. It was just the prevailing idea. And it should reassure you if you're worried about Carly's safety."

"Frank, you're not helping." Leigh felt a little sick. Her daughter on an army base? In a platoon?

"I'll tell Lorelle so she and Carly can chat about it."

Leigh tried to hold on to her stand. "I don't want this to happen."

"Leigh, I'll tell you what I told Cherise: 'Mom, it's time to let go.'"

Chapter Three

May 28, 1990

In the large, crowded, but oddly silent reception hall at the army base, Carly fingered her earlobes, touching the tiny diamond earrings that had been Kitty's graduation gift. She'd worn them daily since receiving them. Now she stood in line, waiting to enter the amnesty room, trying to think what to do.

She knew she wasn't supposed to bring anything valuable on base—especially not jewelry. Now they'd been told that they must leave whatever they shouldn't have brought onto base, and that they would never see what they left there again. *Why didn't I take them off?*

Carly almost raised her hand to ask if she couldn't send the earrings home. She stopped herself. Nate, who had done two years in the army when the peacetime draft was still in effect, had told her to remember two things to survive basic training. First, she shouldn't take anything said or done personally. Second, she should never call attention to herself. In an effort to follow number two, Carly had dressed in a plain navy blue T-shirt, jeans, and worn Nikes to arrive on base.

So now, if she raised her hand, she'd be calling attention to herself, negating her effort to blend in. But she couldn't bear to part with the earrings. Kitty was nearly ninety-three. How many more gifts would Carly receive from her?

"Rich witch," the female recruit closest behind her hissed into Carly's ear. This slur was followed by a string of vulgar insults.

Caught off guard, Carly merely glanced at the girl whose name was something like Alexa or Alex. Then the line moved forward.

It all went down so fast that Carly didn't realize what was happening until it was over. Alex-somebody, the name-caller, hooked a foot in front of Carly's ankle. Carly felt herself losing balance—smoothly she turned and executed the response she'd learned in years of tae kwon do lessons. She used the other girl's momentum to propel her down onto the floor. Then, breathing fast, Carly stood above, gaping down at her.

Suddenly another woman's nose touched Carly's. "What in the heck do you think you're doing?" Spit from the drill instructor's mouth splashed Carly's face.

"She tripped me," the girl on the floor accused.

"I don't give a whoop who tripped who. Drop and start push-ups. Both of you!" she roared, spitting in Carly's face again. "Now!"

Carly dropped and began performing push-ups. The girl beside her started doing the same. Carly felt her heart pounding, not from the physical exertion but over the unexpected attack by a stranger and being yelled at about it. What was this girl's problem?

But Carly's more pressing dilemma—how to keep the earrings—popped up, nagging more insistently. What could she do in the amnesty room to conceal the earrings on her person? If she could hide them, in three weeks when they were allowed to write letters, she could send them home.

Perhaps she could hook them to some part of her clothing. But she was still wearing her civilian clothes, which she would soon surrender for a military uniform and dog tags. But she wouldn't be changing underthings, would she? No, because she'd been told what kind of underwear and how much to bring to basic. *I'll just hook them into the cleft in the front of my—*

"Little Miss Show-Off," the drill instructor barked above her.

Carly paused and looked up.

"You think you're going to impress me?" the woman demanded.

Carly glanced over at the other girl, who lay gasping on the floor beside her. Suddenly Carly became aware that her arms were tired and she was a little winded. "I beg your pardon?"

The DI reached down and pulled her to her feet. "Get back in line."

Carly stumbled slightly as the sergeant thrust her backward. The sergeant dragged Alex-somebody to her feet and shoved her behind Carly. "Any more trouble out of either of you, and you'll regret it!"

Carly didn't doubt her. She felt herself gasping for breath, not from the exertion but again from the shock. She'd never been manhandled or verbally abused like this in her whole life. Nate repeated in her mind, "Don't take anything personally." That hadn't sounded difficult when he said it, but now tears were coiled right behind her eyes, ready to spring forth. She drew in breath slowly and let it out, gathering her composure. Breaking into tears wouldn't bring any sympathy here.

Finally, Carly's moment of decision arrived. She entered the amnesty room. Hiding herself by bending slightly forward and toward the wall behind her, she quickly took off her earrings and fastened them into the interior front of her bra. Mentally, she inventoried the rest of her belongings but couldn't think of anything else she needed to leave behind. She walked swiftly from the room, doing her best to look innocent.

After the amnesty room, all the recruits were herded into two rooms, one for males and one for females. Inside the females' room, Carly looked down at the folded camouflage uniform, called a basic drill uniform or BDU, she'd been handed. She shrugged out of her T-shirt and jeans and with an arm shielding the contraband earrings, she slipped on the new cotton uniform and put her dog tags around her neck. She was now not Carly Sinclair, but 89236108. Flipping her long ponytail out of her collar, she glanced across the room and glimpsed Lorelle Dawson, buttoning her shirt.

Just before Carly waved, she caught herself. She'd almost done it again, called attention to herself. Lorelle's eyes connected with hers, and it was enough. According to the initial entry training or IET handbook, each recruit would be assigned to a platoon of fifty, which was part of a company four platoons strong. So Lorelle would be at least within the same company of two hundred. Probably not the same platoon—that would be too much to ask. Carly sighed. Carly had entered the base gate after nine o'clock that morning, just an hour before, but the day seemed long already.

"I know what you did with those earrings, rich witch." Alex-somebody had slipped up beside Carly.

Carly gave her a sideways glance. Her self-appointed adversary was tall, thin, olive-skinned, reasonably pretty, but really young-looking. Carly bet that the girl was just guessing about her earrings, playing mind games for some weird and unknown reason. Carly turned her back and hefted her heavy khaki-green duffel of possessions. She took her place at the door, ready to march to the next station. Alexa or whatever her name was stuck close as a burr. Carly felt like telling the girl to get a life. What was with her?

Late in the evening of the second day at the reception hall, Carly and her platoon finally finished all the shots, physical exams, forms that had to be filled out exactly right, and the military haircuts. Carly hadn't slept much in the cramped quarters in a nearby reception barracks. She needed a shower and a good night's rest, but she had no way of knowing whether she would be allowed either of the two luxuries. The army was making her completely dependent on those in command and methodically stripping her down to the bare minimums of life.

Again, she fingered the tight short braid at the back of her neck. Earlier, under cover of the buzzing clippers, the military barber had whispered that he loved long hair on a woman and that he hated to cut hers. Then with one click of his scissors, he'd cut away nearly a lifetime of growth. But he'd left her hair long enough to pull into a tight braid that just cleared her collar.

The other female recruits had come out with short bobs similar to what her great-grandmother Chloe still wore. Their male counterparts came out bald, looking like newly hatched chicks. With a surreptitious but warm glance, Carly had silently thanked the barber who'd left her a vestige of what made her feel like herself. Now she let her hand fall. She didn't want any of the DIs that hovered to note that some of her hair, something of herself, had been left to her.

Then they were processed and ready to officially start training. Carly's platoon DI shouted and all fifty recruits jumped to their feet and lined up to leave the reception hall. Just before Carly left, she glanced back quickly to say a silent good-bye to Lorelle. Their gazes met and then Carly was outside in the muggy darkness. If the base were a normal place in the universe, she would assume the recruits would be transported to their permanent barracks for a good night's sleep. But only two days in the army had taught her to assume nothing.

Their drill instructor began shouting rapid orders. Carly tried to catch them all but gave up, deciding just to watch and mimic the other recruits. The shouting overwhelmed her senses, and she couldn't process the words. DIs evidently had only one volume; their consistent decibel level was close to that of a heavy metal concert.

The DI started shouting numbers. One by one, recruits grabbed their heavy duffels and sprinted to what looked like a cattle car and jumped inside. Carly strained to hear her number called. She'd memorized her dog tags and fingered them now as if reading them in Braille. The DI called her number next. Hoisting the weighty duffel onto her shoulder, she charged the few feet and jumped up inside the vehicle. She sat down beside a petite blond recruit who reminded Carly of Dolly Parton. "Dolly" gave her a quick nervous grin in the low light.

One by one, the other recruits crowded inside. Soon everyone was sitting thigh to thigh, and still more squeezed in. Carly began feeling claustrophobic and breathing became a struggle. She hugged her duffel to her and tried to ignore the press of hot bodies all around her. She closed her eyes and forced herself to breathe in and out, slowly and evenly.

Of all things, she despised feeling out of control, of being overwhelmed by something. It brought back the panic left over from her childhood, from those two days when she'd been taken from home and mother. Carly fought the tide of breathless fear. *What have I gotten myself into?*

Kitty's voice played in her mind, telling her how homesick she'd been in 1915 when she left Maryland to go to Columbia University. Aunt Kitty had told Carly this to prepare her for her first time away from home, but Carly doubted that Columbia University was anything like boot camp. Still, Carly made her mind picture Kitty, Chloe, and Bette, the images of those strong women helping her to resist giving way into the claustrophobia.

Finally, they were packed three-deep and Carly turned her head sideways and stuck her nose up against one of the holes in the side of the cattle car. The vehicle lurched to a start and Carly was bumped about by the movement of the vehicle and crushed by the swaying of the bodies inside. She clung to the metal behind her and tried to think of other things, other places. Anything but the bodies pressing against her, smothering her.

At last, the vehicle lurched to a stop, throwing them against each other and back and forth. Angry German shepherds barked and lunged against the sides of the cattle car. The DIs began shouting unintelligible threats and orders. The tailgate was thrown open and the first few of the fifty in Carly's platoon literally fell from the vehicle. Black-shirted military police restrained the dogs that surged toward the recruits who were scrambling up off the ground. Following orders, the new soldiers left their duffels behind and started grouping into the tight formation they'd all been taught.

When it was finally her turn, Carly leaped from the back. As she hit the ground, a ferocious German shepherd with teeth bared leaped at her face, barking as if it were going to tear out her throat. Its hot breath and spit made her jerk her head back and she bumped into the recruit who'd leaped out after her. It was "Dolly" who caught her by her shoulders and steadied her so she didn't stumble. The DI screeched at them. Carly rushed forward and took her place in the tight formation.

On and off for two days, Carly felt her heart pounding like a war drum. She felt weak, as if she were a thin rubber band that had been stretched too far too often about to snap. Again and again, tears lurked just behind her eyes as she stared straight ahead, blocking out the noise and the queasy feeling in her stomach.

As of that night, it was no longer a question: had she made a mistake by enlisting? It was now a certainty. She had made a very bad decision. *I'm stuck. For four years, no less. I got what I wanted. And now I don't want it.*

Suddenly the yelling ended and Carly snapped back to the scene. The dogs were sniffing the duffels. When one paused by any of the duffels, the MP dumped everything out and let the dog sniff it again. Carly couldn't believe that they actually thought someone was trying to bring drugs onto the base. Who would be that crazy?

Evidently, this was just another of the gestapo tactics that the army used to break platoon members down individually so they would form a team. Nate had warned her that indoctrination was the whole idea of boot camp. And right now Carly sensed she was near a breaking point. Her hands knotted into fists at her sides. *Please, God, don't let the dog pause at my duffel. Please.* Her tension tightened inside her like a wire being twisted again and again.

Finally the MPs led the dogs away. Carly felt the tautness leave her spine. Three of her compatriots followed orders and in the dim light, scrambled to gather up their possessions and stuff them back into their bags. Then with their duffels shoulder high, they all began running to the barracks. At the entrance of the barracks, the DI pointed which way the recruits, in pairs of "battle buddies," were supposed to go—left into one side of a barracks or right into the other. Carly groaned when Alex was paired with her as her "battle buddy."

After all of them were standing beside bunks, the DI stood in the hallway between the two halves and ordered them to unpack, make their bunks, and get into them. They had five minutes, and the DI stood there gazing down at her wristwatch.

Carly gave Alex-somebody a dirty look. Battle buddies—

they had to be kidding. This girl was a total nutcase. *Why should I be surprised to get her as my buddy? Everything else that could go wrong has.* Carly stuffed her possessions into the nearest locker, snapped shut the lock, then quickly made her bed.

"Lights out!" And the room went dark. Carly lay down and realized then that she hadn't even shed her clothing. She was too tired. After untying her shoes, she laid her head on the lumpy pillow and closed her eyes. No one made a sound. A kind of stunned, exhausted silence held sway over them all. What could any of them say? *Let me out of here?*

Carly felt the soothing fingers of sleep unknotting her tension, claiming her. With her last bit of energy, she unfastened the diamond earrings from her bra. She felt through the sheet that her mattress was the old kind with buttons in it. She slipped one out and slid the earrings into the mattress stuffing and then put the button back in place. With her fingers, she counted the buttons from top and side edge so she'd remember which one concealed her contraband. Her last conscious thought was, *Who would look for something under there?*

At seven o'clock the next morning, in the nearly silent mess hall, Carly looked down at the full tray of food and cup of murky coffee that had been handed her in the food line. Her touchy stomach clenched and warned her not to eat anything. Too little sleep, too much anxiety, too much noise, too much everything—except privacy, time to think, and basic human respect—had taken its toll.

"There will be no talking!" a DI yelled. "And you will

not be allowed to leave the mess until you have eaten everything on your plate."

Everything? Carly felt her mouth drop open. *I never eat breakfast.* The petite blonde who'd helped her stay on her feet the previous night sat across from her. "Dolly" gave her a commiserating look. In return, Carly sent her a trace of a smile. But unfortunately the girl, Alex-somebody, who hated her, sat right beside her. It must have been on purpose. What was with her? And how could Carly avoid her, especially since they were "buddies"?

"Start eating now!" a DI yelled. "You have fifteen minutes."

Carly picked up her fork and wished she were anywhere but there. Tentatively she forked up a bite of runny scrambled egg and hash browns. She put it in her mouth and chewed. Her stomach gave her another warning. Would she be sick? What would they do to her if she were?

She tightened her resolve and began forcing food in, forkful by forkful. The only sounds in the room where two hundred people ate breakfast were flatware touching plates and coffee cups being put down on the Formica tabletop. With one eye on the clock over the door, Carly worked her way through the plate of food. The clock hand ticked around toward the quarter-hour and the sergeant shouted, "One minute. Finish now!" Unfortunately, she was standing right behind Carly. The DI was so close that Carly could hear her breathing.

Carly looked down, gathering her courage to force down the last of breakfast. Without warning, Alex-somebody spat onto the remaining few bites left on Carly's plate. Carly gasped with surprise.

"Clean up those plates now!"

Carly stared at her plate in shock, horror. Then, her fork in midair, she turned to Alex-somebody and stared in disbelief.

"What's wrong with this table?" roared the DI right at Carly's shoulder. "Why is this table just sitting here when everyone else is ready to go?"

Carly looked around and realized she wasn't the only one who'd seen what Alex-whoever had done. Horrified faces looked back at her.

"Eat!" The sergeant shouted into her ear. "Scrape that plate clean, recruit!"

Carly stared down at the last two bites of food. Should she say something? In the normal universe, she would know what to do. But here, anything might happen if she told the truth. Carly closed her eyes and scooped the remainder of the food into her mouth. A shudder of pure disgust went through her like a wild jet of green slime. She gagged and gasped for breath.

"Attention! Outside! Into tight formation!"

Carly staggered to her feet and along with the rest of the company, she deposited her tray on the kitchen counter on her way out the door. Outside, the summer sun was already beating down. At the bottom of the short flight of steps, the combination of the bright sunlight and her revulsion hit her. Carly doubled over and vomited. She vomited until everything that she'd just eaten poured out onto the ground at her feet. Cold sweat dotted her forehead. Finally, her stomach was empty. She tried to straighten, but weakness made her lightheaded; she slid to kneel on the ground.

"What in the heck did you do that for?" her DI yelled into her ear.

Carly couldn't even look at her. The world was still kind of undulating beneath her. And the sour taste in her mouth threatened to push her into the dry heaves.

"Someone spit onto her plate, and she ate it anyway."

Carly opened her eyes and saw that the blond recruit with a bashful face had spoken.

"What did you say, recruit?" The DI switched her wrath to "Dolly."

"Someone spit onto her plate, and she ate it anyway," the blonde repeated.

"You expect me to believe that?" the DI demanded.

The blonde recruit shrugged.

The DI turned back to Carly. "Did someone spit onto your plate?"

Carly didn't know whether to say yes or no. Again, all the rules of conduct had changed. In the reception hall, she'd been punished when Alex-somebody had tried to trip her. What would the sergeant do to her about this?

"I asked you a question, you piece of garbage!" the DI yelled an inch from Carly's face.

Carly nodded but refused to look up at her. Caught between conflicting impulses, she stared at the ground away from the reeking contents of her stomach.

"Miss Stick-My-Nose-into-Other-People's-Business, drop and give me twenty!" the DI ordered.

Carly watched in shock as the sergeant punished the blonde for telling the truth. What would the DI have done if Carly had pointed an accusing finger at Alex-somebody?

The DI dragged Carly up by her collar. "Get into formation! In the army, you may have to do something worse than eat someone else's spit! Don't you dare faint on me or I'll drop the whole platoon!"

Feeling drained and desperate, Carly walked as if moving through Jell-O to her place in formation. She reached deep down inside herself and dragged up strength and will. Over and over, she silently chanted, *You can do this. You will not faint.*

The blonde finished her push-ups and was ordered back into formation.

The DI glared at all of them. "Now whoever spit into 89236108's food, step forward."

Silence. No one moved. Carly found she could barely breathe. Waves of nausea still buffeted her.

"I said, whoever spit into 89236108's food, step forward!"

Again, no one moved. Carly's heart pounded in her ears and a cold sweat covered her. She stiffened her quaking knees.

"The army is all about the team, all about becoming a unit. Now, for the last time, whoever spit into 89236108's food, *step forward!*"

No one moved. Carly stared straight ahead, willing herself deeper into self-control.

"All right, then," the DI said in a voice pregnant with malice. "We were going to take just a short eight-mile hike this morning, but I think this refusal to speak up means that you're all ready for a ten-mile. About-face!"

Carly wondered if she would last for a ten-mile hike. Normally that wouldn't be a problem. And as problems went, the main one before her was not merely how to survive today; she had an unexpected enemy. Why was this stranger, Alex-somebody, targeting her? What did Alex-somebody think she could gain? What was she trying to prove?

Chapter Four

*I*n the dark and quiet night, a thread of sweat trickled down Carly's back as she struggled to keep her eyes open. *Exhausted* didn't even come close to describing how she felt. And she wasn't alone. Nearly three weeks of basic had pretty much mowed down all of the recruits. That night they'd been awakened after about an hour's exhausted slumber to do perimeter duty. They'd been ordered to don full combat gear within ten minutes—all to guard baked dirt and rocks. Or that's what it seemed to Carly. After an hour's duty, they'd been marched back to their barracks, where they undressed and climbed back into their beds, ready to sleep the night through.

But within an hour, they'd been yelled awake for a second hour of perimeter duty. Carly trembled with fatigue. The 8.8-pound M-16 she clutched had never felt heavier. The breezeless, muggy night pressed close and wrapped around her like warm, wet papier-mâché. How long would this torment last?

Carly felt herself sway as her knees tried to fall asleep on their own. A bead of sweat slid down her nose and dripped to the ground. She made no move to wipe it away.

Not just her platoon, her whole company had been called out for this ridiculous, mind-numbing torture. In the ranks across from her, Carly could just see the top of Lorelle's helmet under a yard light. She tried to make herself recall everything she could about Lorelle's family—a mental exercise she hoped would keep her awake. It failed.

Someone nearby cleared her throat. Carly knew everyone in her barracks so well that she easily recognized the sound. It was Alex Reseda—the girl who hated her for no discernible reason. Alex's pursuit of her and vendetta had continued. With all the trouble Alex had caused Carly, she couldn't collapse now, couldn't call more attention to herself.

In one of their few free moments, Carly had discussed Alex with Francie Rains, the petite blonde who had told the DI about Alex's spitting in her breakfast. Francie hadn't been able to come up with a reason for Alex's nastiness either. Ever since that morning, whenever possible, Carly made sure to put as much distance as she could between her and "Crazy Woman," her private name for Alex.

Over the intervening days after the memorable first breakfast, Francie stuck protectively close to Carly, which was a little funny since Francie didn't look as if she could do more than shout for help. Now, in the hushed darkness filled with human silence and the clicking and droning of insects, Carly's mind brought up Francie. A country girl from Kentucky, she possessed an endearing cheerfulness that made her stick out. So far those precautions—keeping away from Alex and Francie's hovering as a witness—had worked. There hadn't been another incident between her and Alex. The DI still watched both her and Crazy Woman more closely than the other recruits. But so far the sergeant had had no reason to punish them more than the others. She dished out plenty of that for everyone.

Carly figured she could do a hundred push-ups now without much sweat. What an accomplishment. She'd written a paper in high school about treatment of POWs in the Vietnam War, and she had noticed an unpleasant correlation between the methods used by the Vietcong—intimidation, sleep deprivation, public humiliation, total loss of control—and those of her drill instructor.

Carly's eyes slid shut of their own volition. She took in a deep breath and forced them open again. *How much longer, how much longer? Dear God, don't let me fall asleep and collapse.* Her M-16 started to lower, and she straightened her spine. *Don't give in. Don't give in.*

Again, she turned her mind back to the one who hated her. What would Nate tell her to do in this situation? What would Nate do about Crazy Woman? She asked him in her mind, and she heard his answer loud and clear. *Don't make waves—whatever you do.* And that seemed to sum up her total lack of control. She was no longer in the ordinary world; she was in the army, a GI, government issue.

"Atten-tion!"

Carly, along with all two hundred of their company, snapped to attention.

"About-face!"

Salvation had come. They could go back to bed—for at

least another hour's sleep. *Dear God, don't let them make us do another hour out here. Please make them let us sleep.*

Two afternoons later, Carly sat at one desk in one row of desks in a crowded classroom, staring ahead at the most boring film ever made and trying to stay awake. Failing to do so was a fate not to be contemplated. And to make matters worse, though she'd tried to maneuver herself away from Crazy Woman, Alex sat right in front of her. But then Alex hadn't looked very pleased to have Carly at her back. *Good. Let Crazy Woman feel exposed.*

Carly's mind wandered to another unpleasant shock that had come just before dawn that morning. She'd wakened before the DI and since everyone was still snoring, she'd counted the buttons on her mattress and pulled up the one over her earrings. Since that first night in the barracks, she'd been so busy, and never alone, that she hadn't checked on them. So, just making sure, she'd felt around in the predawn gray for the tiny diamond earrings. They had not been there.

Then the DI had shouted them all awake and she'd popped the button back into the mattress and leaped to her feet. Had someone come in and switched their mattresses around? Why? Had someone seen her put the earrings into the mattress? That didn't seem possible.

Carly's eyelids slipped down and shut. She blinked rapidly, fighting her body's deep fatigue. Once again, she was fighting the sleep demon. Two nights in a row, she'd been allowed around four hours of sleep, but not four consecutive hours. An hour here. An hour there. How could sleep become such a huge thing in a life?

On the screen, the nondescript man with a mesmerizing voice in the ancient black-and-white 1950s film droned on about how to read a topographical map. *Map! Just set me free, and I don't need a map to lead me to my bed!*

Carly glanced sideways at Francie, who sat at the desk just to her left. Her head was nodding, nodding. Carly slid her boot sideways. As soundlessly as possible, she tapped the side of Francie's combat boot—once, twice. The DI was walking around the room, looking, looking.

Carly bumped Francie's boot hard. *Wake up, Francie!* Francie's chin snapped up, her eyes blinked open.

The man in the film began discussing what could happen to a soldier who misread a map. This was slightly more interesting because it actually talked about something that sounded as if it might be important someday. When a squad of ten soldiers was out on its own during a battle, bad stuff could happen if no one knew how to read the map—especially with night maneuvers. Soldiers could die. Carly listened with interest to the experiences of soldiers in World War II and Korea.

Then she heard it—nearby incoherent mumbling. She glanced around, then realized the sound was coming from right in front of her. Crazy Woman must have fallen asleep and was having a dream. Fear for Alex zinged through Carly. *But why do I care? Crazy Woman hates my guts.*

From the corner of her eye, she caught Francie nodding her head toward Alex. *No, no way am I waking her up.* Francie gave that little nod again. *Not a mean bone in her body.*

Not a brain in her head. Carly gave the slightest shake of her head. When she saw Francie lift her hand as if she were going to actually lean over to prod Alex, Carly poked Crazy Woman's back once, hard.

"No!" Alex shouted, jumping in her desk. "Don't touch me!"

The lights snapped on, but the gray, nearly invisible man droned on. The DI glared at Alex. "What in the heck?"

"She poked me!" Alex accused, spinning around to face Carly.

Carly glared at Alex, hoping that Francie wouldn't speak up in her defense.

"You two separate!" the sergeant roared.

Carly leaped up and hustled to the front of the room where a vacant seat remained. She waited for the punishment to come. But the lights clicked out and the film hummed on. Was this over or was punishment just delayed? For a moment Carly pondered Alex's nightmare and the fact that her own bad dreams had become few and far between. Was it because of sheer exhaustion or something else?

The June Sunday afternoon sun shone clear and sizzling. At the end of week four, Carly and her platoon had been given a blessed three-hour break. So she hefted her duffel, filled to bursting with every piece of clothing she wasn't wearing. With the letter in her pocket, Carly took one last longing look at her bunk and then staggered out of the barracks and down the few steps on her way to the laundry. Having to wash her own clothes had been an unpleasant surprise.

There was a centralized laundry where they could turn in their clothing, pay, and then later pick up their clothes. But the laundry was sent off base to a contracted laundry service, and the DI had suggested they keep their clothing on base. The service was famous for sending back single socks without partners and for losing laundry. It wasn't as if Carly didn't know how to do laundry, but this chore seemed just one more thing the army hadn't included in its attractive, glossy enlistment brochures. She headed off for the laundry.

Arriving there, Carly saw two of the eight heavy-duty washing machines were empty and raced to them. She stuffed her whites in one and her colors in the other, poured in powdered detergent, and slid quarters in. She sighed happily as the warm water gushed in. She shut the lids with contentment. She planned to go and sit in the corner and read the letter again. But she turned to see a special surprise walking in the door. "Lorelle!"

They met in the center of the long narrow room and in spite of the other recruits looking on, the two hugged. "How are you?" Carly asked.

"The same as you." Lorelle, with her creamy tan complexion and her short curly hair, grinned back. "I figure it will probably take us one full week of sound, uninterrupted sleep to make up for all the hours we've lost in the past four weeks."

"Oh," Carly moaned, "let's not talk about it. Talking about sleep makes me tired."

Grinning, Lorelle led her outside onto the shaded top steps. Carly sat down beside her friend and sighed deeply. It felt so good to have a little time off and to talk to Lorelle, someone she'd known all her life and who would understand what she was going through. "Four weeks down and four to go."

Lorelle nodded. "We'll make it. I hear you have some ditz in your platoon that's always on your case."

Carly made a face. "Let's not waste any time talking about Crazy Woman." The unexpected letter in her pocket seemed to call to her. "Who wrote you?" Carly asked nonchalantly, referring to the first permitted mail delivery the previous week.

"Dad, Mom, Great-Grandma Minnie, my brothers and sisters. Even my Grandma Lila, who is still marching for peace." Lorelle shrugged. "I think my dad made everyone write me."

Tension clicked through Carly. Should she tell Lorelle about his letter? Could she? "I heard from everyone, too." She gazed down at her feet. The desire to tell someone who would understand clutched at her, squeezing her until she couldn't bear the tension. "And I mean *everyone*."

"You sound strange," Lorelle prompted. "What do you mean by 'everyone'?"

She knew Lorelle from family occasions over their lifetimes and the summer weeks they'd spent together at Ivy Manor, whispering to each other in the room with the trundle bed. They were friends, but this topic felt touchy. Still, she had to tell someone. And Lorelle was the closest thing to family there and then. Carly drew in breath and said, "My father wrote me."

"Nate? What did he say?"

"Not Nate. My . . . *birth* father." Carly suddenly was breathing hard.

Lorelle sat up straighter and turned to fully face Carly. "No."

Unable to speak, Carly nodded. Yes, Lorelle understood.

"Wow." Lorelle stared at Carly, openmouthed.

Carly looked away, trying to hide all the emotion that was flowing up from inside her like some uncapped geyser.

"What did he say? Did he tell you who he is? Give you his address?"

Lorelle's rapid questions made Carly feel a bit nauseated. She drew the letter out of her pocket. Her hand trembled sharply as she said, "Here. Read it." Her voice sounded thick and unnatural.

With wary eyes on Carly, Lorelle took the envelope as if it might explode. She slowly slid out the one crisp sheet of vellum. After reading the brief note, she looked at Carly and then back down at the page. "Weird. Sounds like he's been keeping track of you."

"I know." Carly had memorized the brief note:

Dear Carly,

I have waited until you graduated from high school to write you. I am your father. I'm hoping that some-day soon we will be able to meet face-to-face. How-ever, I will understand if you don't want to. I am the guilty party and your mother had every right to keep you from me. But don't ever think that I didn't care or want to see you, be a part of your life.

With love, T.L.K.

Masking her confusion, Carly rubbed one moist palm on her thigh and looked off into the distance. A heat mirage floated on a far-removed post street. "It feels really strange," she said. "He knows where I am, right down to my boot-camp address. But I don't know anything about him." The old, restless curiosity curled inside her.

"Do you think your mother told him?"

"No." Carly's denial came swift and strong. "She hates him—or she must. Whenever my birth father has been mentioned or I've asked about him, her face just freezes in anger."

Lorelle gently touched her shoulder.

Carly took back the note and slipped it into her pocket.

"I overheard my mom and dad talking about your natural dad once." Lorelle paused as if asking permission to go on.

Suddenly alert, Carly nodded encouragement.

"It wasn't much. Just that it was a shame that Leigh had made such a . . . big . . ." Lorelle hazarded a glance at Carly. "Mistake, but they were happy that your mom had married Nate. And they said something about your dad being involved in . . ." Lorelle cast her another worried glance. "Your kidnapping."

Jolted, Carly shoved her spine back against the step. Her pulse raced. "Can you remember exactly what they said?"

"Just that the man was trouble and he'd better stay away or my dad would do . . . something." Lorelle's voice dropped. "About him."

It couldn't be true. Why would her birth dad . . . ? Carly's face twisted with a frown. "Did they think my dad kidnapped me or paid someone to?"

Lorelle shrugged. "I've told you all I heard. But if he had, don't you think he would have come to where you were being held and told you who he was?" Her friend's voice trailed off, thin with uncertainty.

Carly breathed in and out, holding off tears. Thinking about it, trying to remember every detail of those two horrible days always gushed fresh terror inside her. "I wouldn't think that my father . . . any father would treat his child . . . like the kidnappers did. They didn't abuse me, but it was cold and scary." Carly rubbed her eyes and her fingers trembled.

"Sorry I brought it up."

Carly looked into Lorelle's pretty, brown, very concerned eyes, taking strength from her sympathetic reaction to the topic. *I'm not overreacting. And maybe my dad was the one who helped me get home.* "No, you did right. Someday, I will meet T.L.K."

"No return address, right?"

Carly shook her head. "Yeah, evidently he can only handle one-way communication now. Or maybe he thinks my mom would do something if she found out he had contacted me without her permission." Did T.L.K. know how much Carly wanted to see him? Did he expect her to be angry at him? Is that why he'd not included his name and address? Or was he still keeping his distance from her because of her mother? "At least I know that Mom told him to stay away from me." *He'd said he'd wanted to be with me.* Hope sprang to life—followed by the same old bitter disappointment. *How would I feel if I saw him for the first time?*

Lorelle shrugged and looked down.

"Well, if it isn't Ebony and Ivory," said the sarcastic voice of Crazy Woman.

Carly looked up at Alex, who had her duffel over one shoulder. She had just run out of patience with Crazy Woman. *Get a life*.

"Come on, Carly." Lorelle rose, obviously wanting to put distance between them and Alex. "Your stuff should be ready for the dryer, and I can get mine started in your washers."

Carly didn't hesitate. She went inside. Pointedly ignoring Alex, she emptied her wet clothing from the two washers into a large wheeled cart, and then Lorelle quickly stuffed the washers with her clothing. No dryer was free, so Lorelle and Carly sat along the wall opposite the dryers, watching Carly's cart and waiting to see someone's clothes spin to a stop behind the large, round glass doors. They didn't dare leave; they'd been warned that people might steal uniforms to replace those they hadn't laundered. Alex hovered in the doorway with her bag of laundry.

Lorelle leaned over and whispered in Carly's ear, "Everyone's trying to figure out why she's on your case."

Carly cocked her head. "How come you have the time to gossip?"

"Because you're one of the main topics of conversation in our company. I, on the other hand, keep a low profile."

Carly leaned closer to Lorelle. "I can't help it if Crazy Woman picked me as her target."

"Did she really spit in your food?"

Carly nodded.

"Gross."

"Are you two talking about me?" Alex demanded, suddenly appearing in front of them with arms crossed.

"What we're doing is none of your business," Lorelle snapped.

Carly rose, her back against the wall. "What is your problem? Stay away from me."

"You gonna make me, rich witch?" Alex raised her fist.

"Are you out of your mind?" Lorelle jumped up. "Starting a fight in the laundry? Get away from us."

The others in the large room had stopped speaking and stared at the trio. Carly held her temper. She wasn't going to let Crazy Woman provoke her. "I would like to know," Carly said in the calmest voice she was able to manage, "what you have against me. You've been on my case since day one. What is it with you?"

Alex stared at her. "You're the kind of witch who makes me sick. With your Calvin Klein jeans and T-shirt, your Nikes, and those diamond earrings. What are you doing here? You know you don't belong here."

Carly tried to take this in. "You're mad at me about my clothes? Are you out of your mind?"

"You didn't have to enlist in this frigging army like I did, just to get away." Suddenly Alex's eyes filled with tears. "You could have gone anywhere, done anything."

Carly recognized on one level that Alex was acting out the total exhaustion they all felt; the recruits carried it around like a huge load on their backs and their emotions. But Alex hadn't been exhausted when she'd chosen Carly as her target in the reception hall. "You are wacko."

"You don't belong here," Alex said, wiping her tears away with her fingers. "Rich people have all the money, and they get all the breaks."

Carly watched with horror as the young woman began sobbing right in front of her. Obviously boot camp had drained Crazy Woman, and she was coming undone. Carly didn't want to be there watching it.

Across the room, one dryer stopped. Carly steered her cart around Alex and headed for it.

"Don't you walk away from me!" Alex shouted.

"You don't like me. We all get that," Carly called over her shoulder. "But I have laundry to do, and I'm *not* fighting with you." Carly met another soldier, a stranger, at the dryer who quickly unloaded her clothes and headed for a folding table like a woman running from a storm.

"I've had it with your too-good-for-the-rest-of-us attitude!" Alex yelled. She charged Carly from behind.

Carly turned in time to meet the attack.

Alex went berserk. That was the only way to describe it. She pulled Carly's clean clothes out of the cart and threw them on the floor. She moved as if to stomp on them with her dusty combat boots. The final insult.

Carly went on autopilot. Without planning to, she assumed her fighting stance and launched herself at Alex.

CHAPTER FIVE

*L*orelle's voice penetrated the roaring in Carly's ears. "Carly, listen to me. *Stop it. Stop.*"

"Is she gonna kill her?" an unfamiliar voice asked.

"No," Lorelle snapped.

The word "kill" got through to Carly. She blinked, dissipating the red haze that surrounded her.

Then she realized that she was sitting astride Alex. She had Alex's shirt collar twisted in her fist. Carly realized that she'd just banged the girl's head on the floor. Shocked, Carly released her grip and slid backward till her seat hit the hard linoleum floor. Her breathing was a deep, frantic heaving.

Alex didn't move. She lay still, faceup, as if stunned.

Lorelle was kneeling on the gray linoleum beside Carly. "Take it easy. Calm down. It's okay. Everything's okay."

Carly felt sick. She rubbed her forehead. "What happened?"

Lorelle began stroking Carly's back like a mother comforting a child. "You'd finally had enough of her. You started out with that martial arts stuff you do but once you got her down . . . you went a little berserk."

"Is she hurt?" Carly nodded toward her opponent, feeling a fluttery, panicky regret. "Did I . . . hurt her?"

One of the soldiers that ringed the trio in the center of the room knelt down at Alex's side. "She's breathing. Man, we thought you were going to kill her."

Carly hid her face in her hands. How had it come to this? A shiver shuddered through her. "I've never lost control like that before."

Feet pounded up the steps and into the laundry room. "What's going on here?" a sharp feminine voice demanded.

Carly twisted around and saw that a DI, though not her platoon's, had arrived.

A private Carly didn't know also entered the door but hung back. It was obvious that she had run for help. Carly didn't blame her. If their places had been reversed, she would have done the same.

"What's going on here?" the DI repeated.

"She was askin' for it," another private said.

The DI glared at the speaker.

"I heard you try to get away from her," another private said, looking at Carly. "We all did." Others murmured in agreement.

The DI swept the room with her gaze, taking in all the faces present. Then she stared at Carly and Alex. "Fighting on base is strictly forbidden. You're both on report. Tomorrow morning after breakfast, report to the company officer." The DI left without a backward glance.

Carly felt the tears that she'd held back for weeks well

up inside. She could hold them back no longer. She began sobbing.

Lorelle helped her to her feet and led her back over to the avocado-green plastic chairs where they'd been sitting. She pulled Carly close and Carly buried her face in Lorelle's shoulder. The sobs wracked her body in heaving, pounding waves. Through her tears, she glimpsed someone helping Alex to her feet. Alex looked dazed and wandered outside, leaving her laundry bag on the floor where she'd dropped it.

Another soldier picked up Carly's damp laundry from the floor, shoved it into the dryer, and fed it a quarter. Still casting glances toward Carly and Lorelle, everyone moved back to what she had been doing before the fight. An unnatural quiet hung over them all. Only the sound of the washing machines agitating and the dryers spinning accompanied Carly's waning sobs.

After her clothing dried, Carly went through the calming motions of folding her dry clothes into the neat little piles their DI had taught them. When she was done, she wordlessly hugged Lorelle and headed back to her barracks, her duffel on her shoulder.

She felt flattened—unable to get more upset over what had happened. Someone had told a sergeant about the fight, and she was on report. So what? She didn't have enough strength to care. She couldn't change what had happened, didn't want to change what had happened. She defiantly told her conscience that Alex had deserved what she'd gotten.

Francie met her at the entrance of the barracks. "I heard there was trouble at the laundry."

Carly closed, then opened her eyes, trying to clear her

head, trying to shake the disorientation she was experiencing. Well, this made it a certainty. If it had already gotten to Francie, everyone must be broadcasting it loud and clear.

"I'm bushed. I have to lie down." Carly walked past her.

Francie squeezed her shoulder but didn't try to stop her.

As Carly lay down on her bunk, she wondered what the punishment for fighting on base would be. She laid her head on her pillow. Her last conscious thought was, *I don't care.*

But after breakfast the next morning, Carly admitted to herself that she cared very much. After turning in her empty tray, she approached her drill sergeant. An ingot of solid lead was slowly sinking through Carly's stomach. Was she supposed to tell her DI that she had to go to the company commander's office? Or would the drill sergeant order her to go?

Her drill sergeant stared at her. "Do you remember where the company commander's office is?"

So she did know. Carly couldn't speak through her dry mouth, so she nodded.

"After your appointment," the DI said, "you will be brought out to join us at the firing range. Be sure to bring your weapon and be prepared for practice."

Stiffening her spine, Carly refused to be intimidated. No matter what the outcome was, she had done nothing wrong. Her chin up, Carly turned on her heel and marched out of the dining hall. Operating on pure bravado, she headed for the company commander's office, which lay in the center of their area of the base. She heard footsteps on the sidewalk behind her but did not turn her head. *Alex must be behind me.*

Unhappily, Carly thought she could predict what would happen at the upcoming meeting. She had heard of Article 15. It was what the army used first to discipline soldiers who failed to obey their drill sergeants—without advancing all the way up to the military justice system. The injustice of having to report to the company commander and perhaps be threatened with an Article 15 punishment galled her.

It's not fair. I've tried everything I could to fit in and to succeed. What could I have done differently, when it was always Alex who started something?

Frustration burned inside her breast as she approached the company commander's door. Up three steps, Carly opened the door and entered. Alex had caught up with her and went through the door right behind her. The company commander's secretary greeted them and asked them to sit on the black upholstered chairs along the wall in the wonderful air-conditioning until the commander could see them.

Carly kept her eyes straight ahead. She didn't trust herself to look at Alex's face—no doubt Alex's sneering face. Certainly her self-elected tormentor must be gleeful now. What she had evidently wanted since the very first day was happening: Alex had finally gotten Carly into deep trouble.

The door to the inner office opened. A tall woman wearing the insignia of a captain stared at them. "Gallagher, Carlyle? Reseda, Alex?"

Belatedly Carly jumped to her feet and snapped off a salute to the officer. Beside her, Alex did the same.

"Inside, please."

Carly entered the room, tightening her defenses, prepared to face and survive a humiliating interview. *I will show no emotion. I will not disgrace myself.* The two of them, she and Alex, stood at attention, facing the commander who had taken her seat behind an imposing, absolutely neat desk. The first sergeant of their company, a thin, middle-aged woman, also stood beside the commander's desk.

"This is an unpleasant task," began the commander, an attractive woman with red hair pulled back in a tight bun. "You two have been under close scrutiny since you arrived at the reception hall. Your drill instructor has discussed both of you with the first sergeant repeatedly and a certain disruptive pattern has become evident. Your drill instructor tried to force the two of you to make peace by making you battle buddies. This strategy has failed. Both of you have also been punished with extra physical training in an attempt to persuade you to cooperate. This, too, has failed."

Carly was a bit confused. She had expected to be reprimanded over the fight the day before in the laundry. Learning that her drill instructor had been discussing her behavior in the past four weeks was distinctly disturbing. The awful thought that she might be facing more than an Article 15 breathed through her like a cold chill. Perhaps she faced military charges or being discharged from the service. The thought brought a cold sweat to her brow. She'd survived four grueling weeks of boot camp. Would it all be for nothing? The thought made her nauseated. *No!*

"Private Reseda," the captain said in a stern voice, "for some unknown reason you have chosen to carry on your own private war against Private Gallagher. This must end."

Carly felt her mouth drop open.

"But yesterday she jumped me in the laundry!" Alex accused.

"Quiet!" the first sergeant ordered.

"Private Reseda, among many incidents," the commander said, looking down at a list in front of her, "you have spit into Private Gallagher's food. You have tripped her on various occasions. And yesterday you threw her clean clothes to the laundry room floor—direct provocation. Do you think we did not see what was going on here?"

Carly closed her mouth. She tried not to look too happy. Gloating, Nate had taught her, was always unattractive. Besides, it was still too early for gloating. Time after time, she had been disciplined for situations Alex had created.

"Private Gallagher, it has been noted that you obviously have had track and serious martial arts training."

"Yes, ma'am. Nearly seven years."

"It would appear, Private Reseda," the commander said, looking directly into Alex's eyes, "that you chose the wrong individual to harass. Private Gallagher can outrun you, outfight you, and has displayed extraordinary fortitude in the face of your harassment."

"The rich witch wins again," Alex sneered. "I'm not surp—"

"Shut that smart mouth, soldier," the first sergeant snapped.

The company commander tapped a stack of papers on her desk top. "Fighting is not permitted on base. And for violating that, Private Gallagher will be disciplined. But Private Reseda, you will be scheduled for counseling sessions over the next four weeks. Also you will be encouraged to visit the chaplain to discuss how you can change your self-destructive behavior. It is not our goal here to end military careers. Our goal is to train soldiers for successful military careers."

"But—" Alex objected.

"Silence!" the officer commanded. "This meeting is finished. If there are any further incidents between the two of you, Private Reseda, you will be facing an Article 15. You two, return immediately to your barracks, get your weapons, and join your platoon. Dismissed."

Both Carly and Alex saluted, turned, and exited the room. Carly didn't want to speak to or look at her adversary. She began jogging toward their barracks. Alex began running too. Carly increased her speed. Alex followed suit. Carly poured on the gas. She left Alex far behind.

"You witch!" Alex called after her, "I hate you!"

Carly raced to the barracks, intent on reaching the firing range before Alex. Even though she still faced punishment for fighting, vindication was sweet, very sweet. But it left a sour aftertaste. Why did any of this have to happen in the first place?

A week after the incident at the laundry, Carly, along with her platoon, waited in a large gymnasium to go into the gas chamber. She couldn't remember a time when the mood of the whole group had been this tense and somber. Even Alex, who always tried to appear unconcerned, looked petrified. And why not? They'd just endured a full-day training session on biological and chemical warfare. Carly hadn't been aware of all the horrible means people had devised to kill other humans.

Each of them in the platoon had been given an NBC—a nuclear biological chemical defense suit. It was a two-piece suit that felt rubberized, with gloves, boots, and a gas mask that made her feel as if she had been trapped in a nightmare. Fortunately, they hadn't been ordered to wear the full defense suits there in the heat of the day. Each of them carried merely the mask. That was bad enough. Carly tried to keep a distance between Alex and her. She didn't want to think what Alex might try if they hit the gas chamber at the same time.

"Now," the DI barked, "in small groups each of you will enter the gas chamber. The door will be shut behind you. Tear gas, CS, will be released in the chamber. On command, you will remove your gas mask—"

Carly's mind stuttered at this. *Remove my mask?* They were going to gas . . . to gas them?

"You will remain in the chamber until the door opens and you are ordered to leave."

Well, even though Carly had scrubbed her whole barracks bathroom with a toothbrush, her true punishment for fighting had come. And in a way, it was more dreadful than she could have predicted. Surely the gas chamber test was intended for more than instruction; it had been designed to defeat her. Just donning the gas mask panicked her. She tried to think why this was true, tried to protect herself. *Get a grip.*

The first group, the one in front of Carly, was herded into the room that had windows so she and everybody else could see what was going to happen to them. *Great.* Panic reared its ugly spiked head. *I'll go crazy.* Wouldn't that look good on her record? What would they do if she just ran out of the room screaming? She clenched her fists at her sides, trying to stiffen her resolve to conquer this new test of her fortitude.

Carly stared with unbelieving eyes into the small chamber ahead of them as another drill sergeant, also wearing a gas mask, leaned over and uncorked a canister. She saw the gas, like a white angry cloud, begin to fill the chamber. She heard the muffled command to take off masks. The brave souls inside obeyed. Within seconds, they were all coughing and gasping.

Carly's throat tightened sympathetically. *Open the door. Open the door.* Her pulse raced in empathetic panic. Now she knew why the gas mask and chamber were shaking her so much. The scene was so similar to the amorphous, shadowy menace of her nightmares. The door opened and the first group staggered outside, coughing, gasping, sobbing, gagging.

"Next group," the DI ordered from the doorway through her gas mask, "don masks." Each group in turn went in and came out, and Carly kept working her way to the back of the platoon.

"Last group, don masks."

Carly froze in place, but the remaining group around her moved her forward, crowding together as if for protection. She stumbled and caught herself. With numb fingers, she pulled on the mask, positioning it so that she could see what she was going to suffer. The group carried her along into the gas chamber.

Why is this so frightening? she asked herself. It was just a rubber mask and a few moments of tear gas—nothing more. But Carly felt as if she were smothering and gasping already. In her mind, she felt again the sensations that she had felt the day she had been kidnapped, pulled into the car by strange men. Someone bigger had roughly taped her mouth shut and her eyes shut. The gas chamber exercise stirred the same horrible helplessness she relived in each nightmare. A scream, a plea for help stuck in the middle of her throat. She was ten years old again—without her mom and without hope.

"Masks off!" the DI shouted.

Carly tried to pull off her mask, but she couldn't force herself to obey. Her arms felt like overcooked spaghetti. The DI reached over and yanked off her mask. Carly gasped for air, and suddenly her lungs were on fire. She wheezed and choked. She pushed her way toward the door that the DI barred. Her last bit of control and caution stopped her—just before she screamed incoherently, before she shoved the DI out of her way. Then the DI stepped aside and opened the door. Carly charged out and fell to the ground, gasping, shaking, tears pouring from her eyes. Her skin tingled and her throat burned.

All around her, her fellow soldiers swiped their streaming eyes. Most were still standing, but they were bent over with their hands braced on their knees. Carly looked up into Alex's red eyes. "That was awful."

Bent over, Alex nodded, wheezing.

"Now," their DI explained, "you can have confidence that your gas mask will protect you from whatever poison might be emitted into the air. Those of you who kept your heads, stayed calm—you minimized your contact by breathing as little as possible. Those of you who are experiencing a marked reaction to the CS should learn from those who handled the situation better."

Carly stared at the woman and hoped that never again would she be in the situation where she would have to put on her gas mask. It was too much like all her childhood fears tied up into one terrible lump. But pride flickered for a moment. She hadn't had a bad dream for weeks, and today, she had survived. Once again she'd survived.

Carly couldn't believe that basic training was coming to an end. In another week, she and her fellow soldiers would take their end-of-cycle tests. If they passed, they would go through their graduation ceremony and become E-2s—real soldiers. The big event they all looked forward to now was seeing their families at graduation and having a few days off before they reported to their MOS, military occupational specialty. But first, they had to survive their final test, night infiltration training.

Two days before, they'd moved out of their unair-conditioned barracks into the sweltering field for their bivouac—setting up tents, eating field rations or MREs, and sleeping on the ground. Deep summer with its muggy heat, mosquitoes, and chiggers had done its part to make it a challenging expedition.

The final night of the bivouac, the air began to cool down. While standing in tight formation, the recruits listened to their drill sergeant's instructions: "Tonight, you will work together in ten-person squads. You will be in full battle gear, carrying your weapon. Your squad will cover an obstacle course laced with barbed wire. You will wear your flak jacket because live ammunition will be fired overhead. This exercise will test your abilities to work as a team and to make it through battle conditions. Any questions?"

Live ammunition? No wonder they would be wearing their flak jackets and helmets. Carly couldn't think of a thing to ask. Evidently no one else could either.

"All right, break into your squads. Squad one, you will be headed up by Private Rains, and you will begin as soon as the machine guns begin firing."

Machine guns? Francie as the leader? Francie was the one who always needed help. Carly had, of course, along with her battle buddy, Alex, landed in squad one. Carly waited tense and silent, holding her weapon in front of her. Sweat poured down her face. Nearby a machine gun fired, spitting out shells that exploded the darkness with flashes of light.

"Go!" the DI shouted at squad one.

Carly and the rest of the ten dropped to their stomachs and began crawling toward the first line of wire. Through their sleeves, rocks dug into their flesh and bit their elbows. Francie reached the wire first and lifted it with the barrel of her weapon as she slid on her back under it.

Digging her elbows into the dirt, Carly stayed right behind Francie. Around them, the other members made it through the first obstacle. A simulated explosion like fireworks burst right beside them. Carly jerked in shock. Dust filled her mouth.

In rapid succession, explosions threw up dirt, flashing light and releasing smoke. Carly heard bullets thudding in the field beyond them. As she crawled through the second obstacle, the barbed wire tangled in her collar. She halted. "Caught," she gasped.

"Alex, take care of it," Francie ordered, looking over her shoulder, her foot by Carly's nose. Then Francie moved on.

Carly did not want Alex touching her. She slid forward, trying to let the barbed wire rip through the cloth and free her. But the front of her collar caught and held at her throat.

"Don't move!" Alex yelled. "It's about to rip into the skin on your back."

Carly froze. She felt Alex slide on her back beside her, lifting the wire away from her skin with the barrel of her weapon.

"I need help!" Alex called. "I can only hold the wire up. I can't cut it out."

Another squad member slid up on Carly's other side. The girl's cheek lay against the dirt. She pulled out a pocketknife. Carly closed her eyes and held perfectly still. She heard the cloth rip and felt the tug against her collar.

"You're free," Alex gasped. "I'll hold it. Get moving."

Carly surged forward as flat as she could, heading for the next obstacle, a gentle rise. Soon she was surrounded by other squad members, all grunting with exertion. She had no time to worry, she had time only to move. The whirlwind of sound pounded through her until she felt nauseated and her ears roared from the constantly firing machine guns.

"Last obstacle!" Francie yelled. And then she screamed—a real scream.

Carly dug in her elbows and slithered forward. Alex was

right beside her. "I'll hold up the barbed wire," Alex shouted. "You get to her first."

Carly increased her speed. Alex slid forward as if making home base and suspended the wire above Carly. Carly reached Francie. "What's wrong?"

"I think I'm hit," Francie gasped, "really hit!"

Carly wanted to deny the possibility, but the machine guns were still firing and bullets had to be landing somewhere. Then she saw the blood. "It's your arm." Carly raised her voice. "Soldier down!"

Bent over, the sergeant jogged to the sideline near their obstacle. "Move out. The next squad is going to be right on top of you."

"Francie's been hit, stray bullet!" Carly shouted.

"Get her out of there then!"

With Alex's help, Carly dragged Francie beyond the infiltration course finish line. Then the sergeant joined them but sat back on her haunches. "Go on," she said, "you know what to do."

Carly sat up beside Francie and, using her pocket knife, she ripped open Francie's sleeve. "It's just a flesh wound."

"It burns," Francie said in a tight little voice.

Carly nodded as she ripped away Francie's sleeve and used it as a field bandage around the wound. She wrapped it twice tightly and tied it, and the blood stopped.

"Right," the sergeant said. "Help your squad leader to the first-aid station and have the medic see if it is serious enough for her to go to the infirmary."

With Carly on one side and Alex on the other, they helped Francie move away from the finish line. Conscious of the live ammunition still flying overhead nearby, all of the squad jogged parallel to the ground, hurrying behind Francie. Beyond the course, they located an ambulance they hadn't realized was there. A medic leaped down. "What is it?"

Carly let Alex explain. With Alex's help, the medic assisted Francie into the ambulance and onto a gurney. Carly climbed in and Alex waited nearby. Carly watched as the medic took off her battle dressing. The medic swabbed the wound with antiseptic and bandaged it professionally. "That will do for now," the woman said. "But before I leave tonight, I'll give you some pain medication for later, Private Rains."

"Shouldn't she go to the infirmary?" Alex asked. "She was really bleeding."

"No, the flesh wound will heal on its own." The medic turned to Francie. "Just stop in the infirmary every day for the next couple of days for your antibiotic. You'll be fine." Then the medic handed Francie a tall bottle of spring water and two antibiotic pills to swallow. "Help her down and outside. Sit there and wait for your sergeant. She will check on you when the exercise is done."

The ten of them sat in a semicircle around Francie, who leaned back against the wheel of the ambulance. She took the pills and a swallow of the water, then handed Carly the bottle. "Have some. If I drink any more, I'll be sick." Francie closed her eyes.

Suddenly aware of being hot and sweaty, Carly took the bottle. The thirst to taste ice-cold water overcame her hesitance. She leaned back and squirted the water into her mouth, the best she'd ever tasted. Then she handed the bottle to

Alex, who imitated her. The sixteen-ounce bottle lasted all the way around the semicircle. They all sat, still covered with dirt, still winded, still hot and miserable. But each grinned as the cool water hit the inside of her mouth. One of them started to giggle. And then all of them were giggling.

Francie opened her eyes and gave a half-smile. "We made it."

Carly rested, with arms propped behind her. She realized that Alex was watching her. Twice during the obstacle course, her adversary had helped her. Was Alex changing? Or was she just putting on a good act?

CHAPTER SIX

A week later

In front of the shoulder-high mirror in the barracks' industrial gray lavatory, Carly twisted from one side to the other. Feeling like a bright new copper penny, she was trying to see as much as possible of the first dress uniform she'd just been issued. Though she had been slender when she'd arrived at camp, she'd lost a whole size in basic. That hadn't surprised her, after all the physical activity they'd done.

"Why don't they have a full-length mirror in here?" tiny Francie fussed, standing on her tiptoes trying and failing to see more than the collar of her uniform.

"I guess you can put women in the army, but you can't change the fact that men run the army. And," Carly teased, "we all know men *never* look into mirrors."

"Yeah, right." Alex stood in the doorway. "Francie, the DI wants to talk to you."

With a worried glance at Carly, Francie left quickly, the

short heels on her pumps clicking on the polished wooden floor.

Ready to leave, Carly walked toward Alex. She wondered if Alex would simply let her be or if her adversary would have something cutting to say. Alex had mellowed over the past month. Carly hoped that this was the result of the counseling; still, she prepared to defend herself if necessary.

Without a word, Alex stepped back and let Carly walk past her. Carly looked around and realized that she and Alex were alone in the barracks. Everyone else had already changed and left for chow. Had the DI really summoned Francie? Or had Alex set Carly up again? She felt her muscles tense, ready to strike back.

"My counselor said that it was time that you and me had a talk," Alex muttered without making eye contact with Carly. She moved sideways to stand by her gray metal locker.

Wary, Carly went to her locker and began unbuttoning her dress uniform jacket. *I don't want to have a talk with you.* "We don't have much time," Carly hedged.

"What I have to say won't take long," Alex snapped. She stopped and took a long, deep breath. Still avoiding Carly's eyes, she focused on hanging her jacket on a hanger in her locker. "I'm supposed to tell you"—her voice was low and level—"why I had it in for you. And . . . I'm supposed to apologize."

Carly didn't know what to say in response to this level of honesty. "Oh?"

"I don't want to get into it too much." Alex turned slightly away from Carly and began unbuttoning her dress blouse. "It's this way. My mom remarried last year."

Working the buttons of her dress blouse also, Carly waited to hear Alex's explanation. *It had better be good.*

"The guy is a real creep, all right?" Alex blustered. "I tried to talk my mom out of marrying him. But she did it anyway."

Carly felt sorry for Alex—just a little bit—and also she felt a little guilty. The best thing her mother had ever done for her had been marrying her stepfather. And now Nate was her adoptive father, since he had finished the legal procedure just before Carly left home. Still, what did Alex's having a creep for a stepfather have to do with picking on her?

"He started making moves on me right after they came back from their honeymoon." Alex's voice dropped lower, taking on a quality of shame and then pain. "I told my mom, but she wouldn't believe me."

Carly didn't like hearing that. She didn't really want to be part of this conversation. She slipped off her blouse, hung it on the hanger, and carefully smoothed it as she put it away. The wall of caution between her and Alex was showing stress fractures.

"To get to the point—I decided I had to get out. I ran away a couple times. And I had a couple of big fights with the creep. Mom got real angry with me. Said I was trying to ruin her 'chance at happiness.'" Alex's voice flowed with sarcasm. "Yeah, right—"

"What does this have to with me?" Carly interrupted, trying to shore up her defenses against the girl who'd tormented her so unjustly. *I'm sorry for you, but this doesn't involve me, Alex.*

"I didn't want to enlist." Her back to Carly, Alex swallowed something that sounded like a sob. "She made me quit high school and take my GED. And then she took me to the recruiter and made me sign up for the army."

Carly paused and looked at Alex's back, sympathy flickering to life. What must being sent away by a mother feel like? At least her own mother's objections to Carly's enlisting had been expected, and she'd wanted to keep her daughter nearby.

"It was okay." Alex shrugged and turned back. "Because then I could get away from him." Alex's chin quivered. "But I didn't want to leave my mother and my little brothers. Those little guys . . ." Alex's mouth twisted into an attempt at the smile. "I love those little guys."

Carly's love for her own little brother blazed through her. Carly gazed at her adversary, seeing the suffering Alex was trying to hide.

For a split second, Alex returned the gaze. Then her eyes shifted away. "Anyway I was just really mad when I got here. And then I saw you in front of me at the reception hall with all your designer clothes and diamond earrings. I think my mom married this jerk because he works a good job and we were so poor—I mean after my real dad left. And I thought if we'd had money like you, she wouldn't have had to marry the creep."

It came clear. "So you took it out on me?" Carly asked softly.

Alex nodded, looking dejected and guilty. "That was wrong. And stupid. And immature." She looked Carly directly in the eye at last. "But I'm feeling better now that I have talked things over with the counselor. And I talked to the priest here on base. They're helping me figure things out and get everything straight. I don't want to go home—boy, I really don't want that. I want to do my term of duty and then go to school and have a good life."

"That's what I want, too," Carly said gently, gripping the sharp edge of her locker door.

"Can I ask you a question then?" Alex's eyes again slid away.

"Okay," Carly said hesitantly.

"Why did you enlist? It's obvious you have money or your family does. So why?"

Why indeed? "Haven't you ever heard 'Money isn't everything'?"

Glancing up, Alex looked hurt and irritated, as if Carly were brushing her off.

Carly grimaced. Alex had opened up and Carly knew Alex needed to know that she could be real with some people. More than that she needed to know—money or not—Carly didn't have the perfect life. Carly leaned closer to Alex. "This is in confidence, okay? I never tell people this."

Alex stared at her, and then nodded slowly.

"You know your father, right? Your birth father?" Carly said, preparing to lay herself open, make herself vulnerable, too. It was painful, like pulling stitches out of a half-healed wound.

"Yeah, but he left us."

"Well, you're still ahead of me." Carly drew even nearer Alex. "I've never known my father. I'm illegitimate. And my mother won't tell me who my father is."

Wide-eyed, Alex gazed at her, evidently digesting this. "Heavy."

Should she, could she tell this woman about her father's coming to graduation? *No.*

Then, as if to lighten the load she carried, Carly reached up, stretching. She looked into Alex's deep brown eyes. "My great-great-aunt Kitty, who is almost ninety-three, once told me when I was very angry at my mother . . ." Carly paused, wondering if she was saying too much.

"Yeah?"

"Aunt Kitty said no one gets through this life without problems. So never look at someone and think, *She has it easy, no problems.* It's always a lie."

Solemnly Alex nodded and slipped out of her skirt. She hung it up on the skirt hanger and then turned back to Carly. "I'm real sorry about ragging on you." She reached into her locker and took out a twisted paper napkin. "Here." She handed it to Carly. "You'll want to wear these to graduation."

Carly took the paper and untwisted it. Her diamond earrings dropped out into her palm. Words failed her at first. "I thought I'd lost them. They were a gift from Aunt Kitty."

"I was watching you that night, and I saw you stash something. I didn't have a chance to look until a week later." Alex's face flamed. "I was out of line. Forgive me?" She offered Carly her hand. Her expression said that she wasn't sure of Carly's response.

Carly stared at Alex's hand. Was she adult enough to accept a fellow soldier's apology? Yes, she was. Carly squeezed Alex's hand once. She didn't want to say what Nate and Kitty would have said in this situation, but she couldn't remain silent. "No hard feelings."

Alex flushed bright red. She gave Carly a quick nod and

shy smile. "Thanks. Really. Thanks." Then she turned away, obviously very embarrassed.

Carly didn't blame her. Then the two of them finished undressing in silence, a peaceful one. Carly felt a deep sense of relief and satisfaction. She had her earrings back and could wear them at graduation. She now knew why Alex had behaved the way she had. And that made it easier to forgive and to put it all behind them.

When and if she recognized her father at graduation, would meeting him, seeing him, make her feel the same way about her mother?

July 15, 1990

Excitement tingled through Carly's whole body. At the sweltering outdoor graduation ceremony, the base's brass band had just finished playing the majestic national anthem. Carly stood in the ranks of the two hundred women of her company. She realized suddenly that she had a deeper pride in this accomplishment than in completing four years of high school in three. Eight weeks of boot camp had demanded more of her, pushed her to her limits. And she had survived.

One by one, each woman in her company marched forward to receive her next rank, E-2. After receiving her new insignia, Carly gazed out over the audience of family members that stretched as far back as she could see. At the last second, she located her stepfather's wavy auburn hair. Her family sat halfway back on the left side. A spontaneous smile lifted her face as she looked toward them, hoping that they realized she recognized them.

Then for one second, her lungs contracted with disappointment. The chance of pinpointing her natural father in this mass of people appeared impossible. Besides, how would she know what to look for? She and her father might not look anything alike. *I just don't know.* And that hurt.

Blinking back tears, she returned to her seat. The post commander stood and gave a speech about the dedication of the young women who had just completed basic training. At the end of her speech, she announced the name of the company's distinguished honor graduate: "Carlyle Sinclair Gallagher."

Carly sat petrified in her chair. Hands around her pushed her to her feet and guided her to the end of her row, where she straightened herself and marched forward onto the platform to receive her special commendation, based on her top scores and accomplishments. She was shaking so hard that she could barely say "Thank you" to the commander. But she managed to salute and grasp the hand that was offered to her. Then she marched back to her seat and sat down, her heart pounding.

And then it was over. Francie was hugging her. Other soldiers from her platoon were slapping her back. Alex stood back but gave Carly a thumbs-up. Then Carly saw Nate, wearing a lightweight tan suit, wending his way through the crowd toward her. Wishing everyone well, she turned and began pushing her way to him. The crowd of the surging bodies parted and there were her mother, her grandmother, and her great-grandmother.

Carly kissed both of Nate's cheeks and hugged him. Then she was the one who received kisses and hugs. Finally, she was able to step back. One she loved was missing. "Where's Aunt Kitty?"

Chloe put a frail arm around her. "Kitty's heart is bothering her more and more. Thompson and his family are seeing after her, along with Rose, back at Ivy Manor. And little Michael is with her to keep her spirits up."

Carly had a hard time believing that her indomitable great-great-aunt was slowing down, ailing enough to miss a family event. And Carly didn't like the way this afternoon's heat seemed to be affecting Chloe, who looked drawn and was pressing a vintage handkerchief to her perspiring forehead.

"Kitty has moved back full-time now to Ivy Manor to keep me company," Chloe said.

"And she can be closer to Thompson," Leigh added.

"We're so proud of you," Nate said, pulling Carly into a one-armed hug. "Distinguished honor grad!"

"Well, what would you expect?" Leigh asked archly.

Carly's mother was wearing a blue outfit that shrieked *designer original*, something she rarely did outside of New York. Was it a conscious or subconscious effort to show that she was a cut above the other parents there? Carly bristled with the injustice of her mother's very evident and very low opinion of Carly's peers. She wouldn't let her mother get away with it. "What about Lorelle? Is she chopped liver?"

Leigh had the decency to look embarrassed.

At that moment, Frank and Cherise appeared with Lorelle, her younger brother and sister, and her great-grandmother Minnie. In the crush of greetings and hugs, Carly saw her mother stiffen and stare into the distance. Carly felt the hair on her nape prickle as if she felt someone staring at her. Had her mother glimpsed Carly's birth father?

Swiftly Carly turned and followed her mother's line of sight. She strained to scan all the male faces in the direction her mother was looking. But the dazzling sunlight and the forest of heads defeated Carly. She turned to find her mother staring into her face. As if caught in a lie, Carly flushed warmly and then turned hastily toward Lorelle.

Later, at the best hotel in town, Chloe had reserved a room for Carly, a suite for Nate and Leigh, and a suite for Bette and herself at one end of the second floor. Now they all sat in Chloe's suite, which was decorated in soothing shades of wintergreen. They sipped lemon iced tea and gloried in the air conditioning.

"I don't know how you survived in unair-conditioned barracks," Leigh said as she pressed her wet iced tea glass against her forehead. Her pale face was still flushed from the heat.

"We got used to it." Carly was not going to give her mother the chance to criticize basic training, what Carly had chosen, had even succeeded in. But more pressing, the urge to question her mother about her birth father kept bobbing up inside her like a leaf upon a relentless tide.

"Well," Bette said, "have you found out what you will be doing next, and where?" Stylish in a lavender and blue dress, her grandmother looked lovely as usual with her hair swept up to stay cool.

"My highest score was in mechanical ability," Carly said. "I'm going to a transportation unit in the Midwest."

"Transportation? Mechanical ability?" Leigh sat up. "The army wants you to be an auto mechanic?"

"It's a lot more than being a mechanic. There are so many different and unique types of vehicles in the army. I'm looking forward to it," Carly replied, lifting her chin. She'd known just how her mother would react. "I think it will be interesting."

"If that's all you wanted, you could have simply gone to auto mechanic's school." Leigh set her tumbler down on the glass-topped coffee table with a snap of glass on glass. "And not had to go through boot camp."

Carly gripped her cool, moist glass. "I'm very proud of what I have accomplished. And if the army thinks I will make a good mechanic, I am willing to try it."

"Said well by the distinguished honor graduate." Nate smiled at her.

"We're all proud of you," Bette agreed quickly.

"I know what you're all trying to do," Carly said. "You're trying to keep peace between me and my mother again. Please don't. If she wants to start a fight, fine. I'm not a child anymore."

"We know that, dear," Chloe said soothingly.

"And I know my mother is still unhappy with me for enlisting. But I am also still unhappy with her." Carly locked eyes with Leigh.

"Your mother is coming around," Nate said softly.

Leigh's eyes threatened fireworks but she merely pursed her lips.

Evidently Leigh was trying not to cause a scene. But Carly felt a reckless desire to go too far, to push her mother. "Is she coming around to the point where she can tell me who my father is?"

"I am your father," Nate said without rancor.

"You know what I mean." Instantly contrite, Carly stood and then knelt by her stepfather, her adoptive father, and put her arms around his shoulders and her head upon his strong, comforting chest. "And you know I have always loved you and I always will."

Nate kissed her forehead and stroked her hair.

Carly kissed his cheek as she rose. She turned to face her mother. The time had come. "I have received four letters from my birth father."

The color drained from Leigh's pale ivory face until she looked as white and transparent as the petal of an Easter lily. "So he *was* here?"

To Carly, it sounded as if even speaking about her birth father caused her mother physical pain. Guilt nipped her. "I thought . . . I wondered if you recognized him in the crowd today. Who is he?"

"Why ask me? Don't you know now?" Leigh sat forward on her chair, her voice accusing, strident. "Didn't you see him today?"

"He's only given me his initials. Not a photo. Not his address." Carly felt herself shrink with each negative. "Not his name." The last twisted thorns around Carly's heart once more. Her father hadn't given her his name or more to the point, perhaps her mother hadn't let him. This last hope prompted her to tell more. "But he said he would come to see me graduate today."

"What has he told you?" Her mother's voice was taut and fearful and angry.

"Just that he wants to meet me sometime—soon." Said aloud, it sounded so very little. But wouldn't it be enough?

Leigh jumped up and walked to the window, turning her back to her daughter.

Leigh's characteristic shutting her out goaded Carly. "I know that you don't like this." Carly's hands fisted at her sides. "But I want to meet him. And if he ever offers to let me do that, I will go to him."

"Of course you will," Chloe said, "because when all is said and done, he is your blood. And blood is the strong, almost unbreakable tie that binds a family together. Carly, I am glad that your father has written to you."

Leigh swung around to face Chloe. "You're glad?"

"Yes," Chloe said, "Carly needs to know who her father is. His writing to her, but not revealing who he is as yet, shows wisdom and discretion."

Leigh made a sound of derision.

"Daughter," Bette said in reproof, "this isn't about you and the past anymore. This is about Carly and her future."

"None of you have ever met Carly's father." Leigh took a step forward. "You don't know the kind of man he is."

"What kind of man is he?" Carly asked, her heart hopping in her breast.

"He is not to be trusted." Leigh crossed her arms, glaring.

"Because he didn't marry you when you got pregnant with me?" Carly challenged Leigh.

"No," Leigh nearly shouted, "because when I got pregnant with you, he *couldn't* marry me! He was already married!"

Carly stared at her mother. She gasped. "You slept with a married man?"

Her face flaming, Leigh stalked from the room and slammed the door behind her.

In the shocked and horrified silence, Carly sank back onto her chair. Her knees would no longer hold her. "I can't believe my mother would do something like that."

"Your mother didn't know he was married." Nate reached over and took Carly's hand. "He didn't mention it to her until it was too late."

Bette turned to Carly. "You must understand, all this happened right after your mother's fiancé and your grandfather Ted had been killed—"

"And just months after she lost her grandfather Roarke, who adored her," Chloe added.

"She was very vulnerable," Bette continued. "I had a hard time understanding what Leigh had done. I know now that my lack of understanding made it harder for her to tell me the truth, just as it's harder for her now to tell you the truth."

"I disagree," Chloe said. "You were distraught over losing your father and then Ted, and you were also heartbroken for your daughter. You were entitled to your own grief and weaknesses at the time."

"And Bette, no one is harder on Leigh than Leigh is," Nate added, looking forlorn.

Carly clutched Nate's hand. She'd just learned something about her father and something about her mother. For so long she had wanted to know about her father, to know how she had been conceived. But she'd never imagined that she was a result of an adulterous love affair. Knowing this gave her a sick feeling in the pit of her stomach. What kind of man cheated on his wife? Why had he done it?

Was her father still married to another woman? Did she have a stepmother? Did this nameless woman know she existed? Did she have brothers and sisters? Why had her father lied to her mother? And in his letters, had he withheld his name and address from her so that he wouldn't have to answer these questions? Carly felt herself sinking into quicksand. Why couldn't life ever be easy?

A few minutes later, Nate left Carly with the two grandmothers and went to his and Leigh's room. He closed the door quietly behind him. Leigh lay on the king-size bed curled in a fetal position. Nate hung his tie and sport jacket over a doorknob and kicked off his shoes. He went to the bed and lay down behind Leigh, pulling her back against him. He smoothed her hair away from her face and held her close. He could feel her trembling.

"I didn't mean to tell her," Leigh whispered. "And not like that."

"I know."

"How will I ever face her again? Will she ever forgive me?"

"That's up to her. Have you ever forgiven yourself?"

"I can't. I tried. When you came into my life, I tried to accept that God had forgiven me, but it just didn't feel real. And it doesn't change anything."

"Why do you think you have to feel something to be forgiven? Why do you think you must be perfect? No one, no human is perfect."

"I don't want to be perfect. I just wish there was some way to blot it out."

"Leigh, you can never blot out what happened. This conflict with Carly has got to stop. You've got to let go of the past. You've got to make peace with yourself—and your daughter. If you had told her *all* the truth seven years ago, as you told me you were going to, all this conflict might not have happened. How long are you willing to let this grind on?"

Leigh turned in his arms to face him—nose to nose, lips to lips. "Let's not talk anymore. Make love to me." And then she kissed him, obviously trying to distract him from the truth.

Bowing to this, Nate gathered her closer against him and began a long, thorough kiss. He felt as if he was wooing his wife all over again. Maybe they had moved too fast seven years ago and married too quickly. Maybe they should have settled more issues before they began their life together. But he knew he'd do the same thing again. He'd never felt for another what he felt for this woman. "I love you, Leigh," he murmured against her soft lips. "I always will—no matter what."

"I know you do. I just don't know why."

July 23, 1990

In her dress uniform, Carly got off the van that had picked her and the other privates up in the small-town bus station. The three of them, headed for the same post, would begin training in their MOS, military occupational specialty. As she gazed out at her new post, Carly felt her stomach doing jumping jacks. Within a short time, she and one of the other privates had been dropped off at the huge warehouse-type garage where she'd been told to report to her direct supervisor, a Sergeant Haskell.

Carly walked inside and looked around the large metal building filled with vehicles—some on hoists, some on jacks. The aromas of motor oil and gasoline filled the air.

She and the other private, Bowie Jenkin, a tall blond guy with a heavy Southern accent, paused inside and looked around for someone to report to. "Do ya think the sergeant has an office here?" Bowie asked.

Carly shrugged.

A few soldiers who were working on a camouflage-painted truck had noticed them. One of them shouted, "Hey, Sergeant, we got a couple of visitors!"

Within minutes, a short man with white-blond hair and a sunburned face marched out.

Carly and Bowie began walking toward him. They handed the man their papers and waited for him to peruse them.

Haskell glanced up at Carly. "What are you doing here?" he growled.

"I'm reporting for duty, just as my orders say," Carly replied.

"What's your name?"

"Carlyle Sinclair Gallagher."

"Is this a joke?" he snapped.

Carly looked at him, dumbfounded. "I beg your pardon."

"Your name really is Carlyle Sinclair Gallagher?" he asked with dripping disbelief.

"Yes, I'm Carly Gallagher."

He swore.

She blinked. What could she have done wrong already? And what didn't he like about her name, of all things?

CHAPTER SEVEN

J don't want any women in my platoon. What were they thinking of? Women don't know diddly-squat about engines."

Carly stared at her new sergeant's red face. The words he'd just said were unbelievable. Could he get away with saying sexist stuff like that? The temptation to snap back swept through her, but she repressed it. What would Grandma Chloe or Aunt Kitty say? She decided a polite but succinct reply would do best. Breaking the vibrating silence that followed his tirade, she said calmly, now the center of attention, "Well, the army thinks I can. And I'm willing to try."

The man exuded waves of hostility that Carly felt break over her. But her reply had left him without anything to say. If he replied with anything negative, he would be speaking against the army, not her. He continued to glare at her but held his tongue.

Reprieve trickled through her, cool and welcome. Carly tried not to take a deep breath. She didn't want him to sense any sign of relief or weakness from her. The staring contest continued. Carly kept her face impassive and respectful, but unyielding.

"Head over to your barracks!" he barked. "Women's quarters are down two blocks, turn left, and then four more. You'll report to class tomorrow morning after PT—that's physical training." Then he smirked and turned away.

"What about me?" Bowie asked.

"Hang around here and the guys will fill you in."

Carly turned and started for the wide open doorway. She was left to ponder why he'd smirked at her. In short order, she found the entrance hall to the women's quarters: a single two-story barracks. She put down her duffel and waited. Within a few minutes, a female private first class, a young African-American woman with dark hair and eyes and wearing camouflage BDUs, showed up. "You the new soldier?"

"Yes, Gallagher, Carlyle—Carly."

"I'm Greene, Marla. Come with me. I'll show you your room."

"Room?"

Marla grinned at her. "Yeah, not too many women score high on mechanical ability. That means there aren't too many of us here, so we all have private rooms. But there are only two bathrooms on each floor, so it's not exactly the Hilton."

Marla's friendly manner did a lot to settle Carly's nerves. But her mind still buzzed with her new sergeant's un-welcome welcome.

Up the flight of concrete steps to the second floor, Marla ushered her into a simple room painted stark white with a bed, a desk with chair, and a closet. It reminded Carly of the many college dorm rooms she'd seen on campus tours with her mother the year before. But a room all to herself—heavenly. Carly heaved her duffel onto the single bed against the wall and beige vinyl bolster. "Looks like the Hilton to me."

Marla sat down in the chair. "You got Haskell for your sergeant."

The young woman's confiding and sympathetic tone let Carly know that she wouldn't stand on rank with her. Carly still didn't want to blurt out what she was thinking. After all, Aunt Kitty had always taught her not to say anything about someone unless it was something she wanted the person discussed to hear. Carly opened her window, letting in the warm breeze and the sound of distant voices. She dropped onto the bed, suddenly feeling very tired.

"He's a tough old bird," Marla confided, glancing at the closed door. "He sees no place in the army for women except as nurses or as secretaries to generals."

Carly nodded, remembering what Bette had told her about her war work as one of the few women on Bermuda. And Haskell had white hair. Was he close to her grandmother in age? "Still fighting World War II?"

"More like Vietnam. Don't let the white hair fool you."

"Any advice?"

"No, a warning. So far he's managed to get rid of every woman assigned to him."

Carly's stomach clenched. "How?"

Marla shrugged. "I think he made life so miserable for them that they all finally gave up and asked for reassignment." Marla rose. "Get settled in here and change into your BDUs, then come down to room 105. I'll walk you around the base, and then we'll head to mess."

Carly nodded. "Thanks."

The door closed behind Marla. Carly rose and unzipped her duffel and began unpacking her BDUs, underwear, and toiletries. As she put things away, her mind played back the scene in the garage. She went over and over what Haskell had said to her. Could she have handled it any better? After several minutes of thought, she decided that she'd probably done the best she could.

Still, Marla's saying that no woman lasted long with Haskell began tolling in her mind like a mocking death knell. She'd been told that she would spend two years there learning to maintain and drive all types of military vehicles, and then she would be transferred to a base where she'd put her training into use. What would happen to her if she didn't last there? If she couldn't make the grade, would it be a mark against her—not Haskell?

July 24, 1990

The next morning, at the first glimmer of a hot, muggy dawn, Carly rose and dressed in her lightweight gray knit top and shorts. Reporting for physical training at six o'clock sharp, she found out what Haskell's parting smirk the day before had meant. Evidently, he'd decided to start his campaign against her during daily physical training. She didn't think his plan would work. Though everyone knew that most women couldn't do as many push-ups, say, in a single session as most men, Carly knew that she was able to do more than the average female.

So Haskell poured on the push-ups in vain. Carly kept her face impassive, but she was still doing measured, rhythmic push-ups after two of her fellow soldiers, both males, had dropped facedown into the dirt. A visibly disgruntled Haskell ordered them to run laps around their physical training area.

Carly settled into the easy lope she'd learned in high-school track, which she could keep up for miles. She let the men pass her, sensing that Haskell would go for distance over speed. Both men and women could achieve speed, but Haskell probably hoped to wear her out with laps. Pretty soon, it was very obvious that the other soldiers were unhappy about the added distance they were being forced to run. They kept glancing at her and over at Haskell and frowning. A few grumbled to each other as they jogged, sweat starting to pour down their faces, their shirts sticking to their backs.

Carly felt perspiration springing out all over her and she swiped her forehead with the back of her forearm. Two more laps and the other soldiers were glaring not at her, but at Haskell. Still, she loped around the training area. She felt her muscles heating but she knew she could run much farther before they began to burn. The breeze created by running evaporated her perspiration, cooling her body pleasantly. Still, she made sure she kept her expression neutral and her gaze away from anyone's eye.

As three of his men slowed and fell to the rear of the platoon, Haskell brusquely called the run to a halt and released them for showers and breakfast. Carly didn't even break stride. She jogged away toward her barracks.

Bowie, the other new private, caught up and ran alongside her. "Hey, you can really run." He sounded impressed.

She gave him a grin. "I lettered in track in high school. I used to run marathons." Then she sped up. She had farther to go to her shower and didn't want to be late.

Bowie called after her, "See you at breakfast."

She waved in response. In replying to Bowie's admiring comment, she'd purposefully raised her voice just enough so that Haskell could hear her if he were listening. It might do him or at least her fellow soldiers some good, cut them a break. Personally, she loved a good early morning run.

After breakfast, she and Bowie, along with ten other privates, took seats behind well-worn desks in a classroom on base where an instructor began to teach them the rudimentary anatomy of a spontaneous combustion engine and a guide to the different types of military vehicles. Carly was temporarily appalled by the number of them and the fact that she'd be expected to know the engine parts of each one and how to maintain said parts for all of them.

She recalled her mother's scathing remark about if she'd only wanted to be an auto mechanic, she could have just gone to mechanics' school. It was immediately clear to Carly that at the end of her training, she'd be much more than an auto mechanic. She felt like sending her mother a copy of her syllabus. But it would be a waste of time.

Carly liked the theory instructor right off for his businesslike manner and obviously excellent grasp of how to convey his subject and even make it interesting. She decided to be sure she ranked at the top of these classes to offset whatever

Haskell did. Then she got caught up in the instructor's fascinating lecture on the history of military vehicles.

After lunch the next day, she and Bowie headed over to the huge garage. Carly had no expectations of the hot, breezeless afternoon going well, not after she'd foiled Haskell's efforts for the past two days to exhaust and/or humiliate her in PT. *He'll have something unpleasant planned for me today.*

Unfortunately, Haskell didn't disappoint her. He was waiting for the privates just inside the wide doorway. "You two better figure out that being on time in the military means being early. I don't want you two making any side trips. Your schedule for the next eight weeks will be physical training"—he gave Carly a disgusted look—"breakfast, classes, lunch, and then the rest of the day here in the garage. Today, you two are going to watch what's going on. And you'd better be on your toes. At any time I'll expect you to be able to tell me what anyone is working on and how the task should be done."

Bowie openly gaped at the sergeant. Haskell turned his gaze to Carly as if waiting for her to speak.

Carly gave nothing away. Being forced to say, "I don't know" wouldn't bother her. Or at least, that's what she told herself. She refused to let Haskell intimidate her. On the other hand, the sheer, overwhelming size of the vehicles she was supposed to become expert at was beyond anything she'd ever been close to. They made civilian vehicles look like toys.

At Haskell's gesture, Bowie and she edged close to two privates, one white and one black, in BDUs smudged with black grease. A nearby transistor radio softly played "La Bamba." Haskell hovered behind Carly as if waiting for a chance to hit her with a question. She tried to figure out what the two soldiers were doing. But she'd never even looked under a hood before. Haskell finally walked away.

"You changin' spark plugs?" Bowie asked after another few moments of silent watching.

The men ignored Bowie. Carly wasn't so lucky. "Sweetheart," the white mechanic said under his breath, his eyes on Haskell's receding back, "I'd like to check your spark plugs." Then he gave her a sly once-over. "Anytime."

The other private just grinned.

Carly froze. She'd been prepared for Haskell's hostility. After all, when he'd enlisted probably back in the dark ages of the sixties, women hadn't yet been integrated into the services. But these two guys were nearer her own age. Had Haskell poisoned their attitudes or were they naturally just like him?

She leaned closer as if studying what the private, whom she now thought of as Mr. Smarty Sparkplug, was doing. He leered at her, and she leaned a little closer.

Abruptly, she lost her balance and bumped against him. He tripped on a red metal toolbox just sitting on the concrete floor. He smothered a yelp as his shin and the unforgiving toolbox collided. And then he was on his seat looking up at her.

"Oh, sorry," Carly murmured. "I'm not usually so clumsy." She gave him an innocent smile.

Mr. Smarty Sparkplug got to his feet again. His blistering expression could have stripped the paint off the nearby

Humvee. He swore at Carly under his breath, and then he leaned closer to deliver his next insult. "So, sweetheart," he jeered, "do you know anything about spark plugs?"

Carly was ready for him. "Yes," she deadpanned, "I don't have any." *And I wouldn't show you mine if I did.*

A grumpy silence followed, which Carly didn't mind at all. Did they think she didn't know how some men hated women competing with them? In her last year of high school, she'd tried out for coed soccer and had to put up with the stupid masculine pride thing. But she'd showed those soccer jocks a thing or two by the end of the season. And if in basic she'd taken what Alex and her DI had dished out, she could handle this garbage. She just didn't look forward to it.

Matters settled down for the rest of the muggy afternoon. Carly watched and tried to take in as much as she could without asking questions. Fortunately, Bowie asked enough questions for both of them, and she memorized everything he said and was told, and thought of questions she'd ask him later. He seemed to know quite a bit about engines already. But then she recalled that Bowie had told her his ambition was to start his own garage in his little hometown in Alabama. That's why he had enlisted.

"Private Gallagher, get over here!" Sergeant Haskell shouted very near to the end of the day.

Carly marched swiftly over to him where he stood next to a huge truck. It was, according to Bowie a HEMTT—or a heavy expanded mobility tactical truck specifically, if her memory was serving her—a M977 cargo truck with a material handling crane that towered over her. "Yes?"

"Get up in the cab and drive this truck outside."

With a sinking feeling, Carly stared at the sergeant. No sense in trying to bluff her way through that. She lifted her chin. "I don't know how to drive," she announced loud and clear.

Haskell gawked at her. And then he swore for a full sixty seconds. Then he said, "You came here, and you don't even drive?"

"I grew up in New York City," she replied calmly, not in the least perturbed by his rudeness. "I took buses, subways, and taxis. Cars are a nuisance in the city."

"Well, isn't that just ducky? I suppose you expect somebody to teach you how to drive?"

"I'll teach her," Bowie offered, coming up behind her.

Haskell glared at him. Carly knew that Bowie had put himself in the line of fire for her. In boot camp, they'd all learned never to volunteer for anything. Coming to her aid would not win him points.

Haskell ordered them both up into the cab. "All right—you want to teach her, Jenkin, get started."

This was easier said than done for Carly as she looked up. She had to climb way up into the cab. When she got a good look at the dashboard, she sucked in breath. She saw immediately that driving a car looked like child's play compared to driving the monster truck.

Haskell stomped away into his office.

"Here's the ignition," Bowie pointed out.

Carly got up onto her knees so she could see clearly everything that Bowie was showing her.

"She won't even be able to reach the pedals," Mr. Smarty Sparkplug sneered, his comment floating into the cab. "Doesn't even know how to drive. And she gets paid just as much as we do."

"Yeah," another unseen soldier replied, "and we'll have to do all the heavy work for her." These comments were followed by a general grumbling of agreement.

Beside her, Bowie tried to give Carly a grin. He started up the engine, had her put her hand over his, and shifted to drive.

By then, Carly had endured a full day of innuendo and mocking. All through basic, she'd weathered a storm called Alex and now the army expected her to go through one to two years of *this* abuse? She remembered Marla's comment that Haskell always got rid of his female soldiers. Boot camp had taught her not to react to superiors' abuse even if pushed to the wall. She only hoped that Haskell would have enough sense not to do that. She never wanted to lose control the way she had that Sunday in the laundry room. And right then she made her decision.

August 1, 1990

Carly waited about a week for the opportunity she'd been waiting for. Once more, she was in the large garage in the middle of yet another hot and humid summer afternoon. The platoon was spread out over the garage, overhauling engines on more huge vehicles: three cargo and troop carriers. From classes and Bowie Jenkin, who'd proved to be an encyclopedia on military vehicles, Carly knew that the troop carrier used a Ford low-profile F-600 body. It had a Ford-model 165 diesel engine and an Allison AT545 five-speed transmission.

Haskell was standing with the group nearest Carly. "Gallagher," he yelled, "get over here!"

Carly walked quickly to him.

"Here." He motioned to her. "Get up under that hood and take out the air filter."

Carly wondered if this elementary order was designed to show how inept he thought she was. Did he hope she wouldn't be able to find something that simple? Or what? Who knew? Haskell hadn't let up a bit. But by this time, Carly was used to climbing up the sides of the vehicles. So she scrambled up the running board and on top of the wheel well, then leaned inside.

With her head under the hood, she felt it.

One of the nearby soldiers had touched her inappropriately and it was clear to her from the sudden, complete silence that everyone nearby had witnessed it. Shock and outrage pulsed through Carly. She didn't hesitate. She'd made her decision, prepared herself for that moment.

She swung around, leaped down from the vehicle, and attacked the soldier nearest her, Mr. Smarty Sparkplug. His eyes flew open with shock. He didn't have a chance. With all the skill of seven years of martial arts training, Carly flattened him. Then she stepped back, poised and ready to continue.

Silence reeked in the large warehouse. No one moved. It was as if everyone was holding his breath. Haskell stood to one side, his hands on his hips, looking simultaneously murderous and shocked.

Carly finally broke the silence. "Is that enough for you?" she asked in a bored, "I couldn't care less" tone.

Mr. Smarty on the ground slowly got up, dusting off his seat. Carly moved back and prepared to defend herself again.

He shook his head and mumbled, "Sorry."

Slowly Carly let down her guard. She looked to Haskell then, waiting to hear his punishment for fighting. She didn't really care what it would be. She wasn't going to take it, and he and everyone else in the garage might as well know it.

Carly had decided it would be better *not* to let things progress to the point where she totally lost control, as she had with Alex in the laundry. She'd chosen to make her point at a time when Haskell was present so he would know that she would not tolerate sexual harassment from him or anyone. She stared him straight in the eye.

He stared at her. The silence between them grew and grew. Finally he barked, "Get back to work, Gallagher!"

A moment passed. Then Carly clambered back up onto the vehicle. Relief whistled like a cool breeze inside her. But had she achieved her purpose? Had she made her point that she would not be harassed or belittled? Would it stick? Only time would tell.

Ivy Manor, August 2, 1990

Chloe and Kitty sat together watching *Jeopardy* on TV in the cottage where the window air conditioner hummed. As usual, they both kept score of their correct and incorrect answers and were eagerly waiting for Alex Trebek to give the final question to see who on-screen, and which of the two of them, would win that day's game.

Suddenly "NBC Special Report" flashed on the screen, and Tom Brokaw spoke from his desk, "Iraqi dictator Saddam Hussein has invaded neighboring Kuwait, penetrating deep into Kuwait's capital city. Casualties are called 'heavy.' The emir's palace has been besieged as explosions jolt the city. Hussein announced he intends to annex sovereign Kuwait as Iraq's nineteenth province." A map of the border between Kuwait and Iraq and the nearby Persian Gulf flashed onto the screen, and then video showed Iraqi soldiers running through city streets, shooting at fleeing Kuwaiti civilians and what must have been Kuwaiti troops.

Without saying a word, Chloe and Kitty joined hands. In Chloe's memory, black-and-white newsreels of goose-stepping German soldiers invading the Sudetenland, Austria, Poland, the Netherlands, Belgium, and France zipped past as if on fast-forward. *Not again.*

"Do you think President Bush will let him get away with that?" Kitty asked.

"A World War II veteran?" Chloe shook her head. "No, we learned what winking at aggression leads to. I need to call Bette and find out if she can get more information about what's really going on from her friends at the CIA. What if they take our embassy employees hostage like Iran did in the seventies?" She rose and headed for the phone in the kitchen.

"President Bush will address the nation this evening on the state of affairs in the Middle East," Tom Brokaw finished, and a commercial for Taster's Choice Instant Coffee came on.

New York City, August 2, 1990

In Leigh's office at *Women Today*, her desk phone rang. She picked it up.

Before she could speak, Nate's voice demanded, "Have you been listening to the radio?"

"What's wrong?" She turned to look around the office and realized that people were gathering near the TV that sat in the corner of the nest of cubicles.

"Hussein just invaded Kuwait!" Nate yelled.

"He did?" Leigh's memory immediately brought up scenes of the U.S. Embassy in Iran during the Carter administration. "Has he taken the embassy?"

"So far, no. But I'm worried, Leigh."

Leigh frowned. Her journalist's mind had begun coming up with questions on the invasion and angles to pursue. "Why is that worrying you?"

"Because we have a daughter in the army, remember?"

This stopped her. "But we won't go to war just because—"

"Leigh, we import oil from Kuwait. And Hussein is a dangerous nutcase. He's gassed his own people and is trying to gather the ingredients for nuclear weapons."

Leigh's stomach went cold. "Surely they wouldn't be sending Carly anywhere. She's barely out of boot camp. And they don't allow women in combat zones."

"Maybe the UN can pressure Hussein to pull out."

Leigh rubbed the back of her neck. She recognized that Nate had no faith in what he'd just said.

"Come home early tonight, okay? The president is going

to address the nation, and I'd like us to be together to reassure Michael that everything will work out."

Leigh thought of all the work stacked on her desk and her daughter who'd looked so young and innocent at her recent graduation. *Why did I fight with her?* "Okay, I'll be home early."

"Promise?" His one-word request jabbed her as if an accusation of her breaking promises before.

She stifled the urge to argue. She didn't want to fight with him or anyone now. "Promise."

In the faded utilitarian rec room at the women's barracks that evening, August 2, 1990, no one gathered around the ping-pong table. All the women in khaki tank tops and shorts clustered around the small TV in the corner of the room. Carly sat on the cool, speckled linoleum floor beside the long, well-worn avocado sofa. President Bush sat in the Oval Office with the American flag behind him, saying "Saddam Hussein's naked aggression will not stand." He went on to list in detail all the international laws the Iraqi dictator had broken that day and talked about the barricaded U.S. Embassy in Kuwait.

Finally, the president finished his address and the talking heads came on to discuss their reactions. More film showed Iraqi tanks rolling over the desert into Kuwait, a video shot by a foreign businessman staying in a downtown hotel in Kuwait City, and footage of the American Embassy, locked up tight against assault.

The women sat as if in a trance, all silently watching. Finally, the late night news show came on. The local anchor was talking to their own base commander about the chances of the deployment of local troops. Still, not a word was spoken until an "I like the Sprite in you" commercial came on.

War had never been declared in her lifetime. Carly looked from face to face around the room. Did they feel the same sense of disorientation she did?

Marla cleared her throat. "Well, this could develop into something interesting."

"Not for us," Carly said, each word sanding her nerves. "They don't allow women in combat zones."

"That doesn't mean some of us might not end up there," another private said. "Some of us could be sent there in transportation units in a support role."

"Bush will have to do something," Marla said. "We get too much oil from Kuwait to let it fall into the hands of Iraq."

Carly looked back at the screen where now some girl was washing her hair in a misty tropical shower. The idea of combat seemed too impossible to imagine. It overshadowed all the anxiety she'd expended over how to handle Haskell's intention to rid himself of her. For some reason, her mind brought up the fact that her grandmother Bette's first wedding day had been the same day as the attack on Pearl Harbor. Now Carly had some idea of how Grandma Bette had felt that day almost fifty years before.

With the fall of the Berlin Wall just a few years before, the Cold War had ended. Now the U.S. Congress was busily downsizing the military, a hot topic of conversation on base at mess and off-duty. Would this invasion mean war? If so, would this war spark something like Vietnam? Or would war be averted if the UN persuaded this ruthless dictator to leave Kuwait and its oil? Would Hussein back down, or would the U.S.?

CHAPTER EIGHT

*T*he next day, during another steamy afternoon, Carly climbed into the cab of an older version of the camouflaged cargo truck she'd been working on the day before. Bowie already sat in the passenger's seat. Both of them wore khaki tank tops with cotton slacks that matched the truck. After Carly's admission that she couldn't drive, Haskell had ordered Bowie to spend the rest of the afternoon finishing Carly's driving lessons. Through the open windows, she could hear the voices of the other members of the platoon who were still overhauling engines and the scrape of tools on metal.

"Okay," Bowie said, "this truck has a stick shift. Most newer military vehicles have automatic transmissions."

"But our sergeant thinks I need to know how to drive a stick. And he thinks learning to drive a stick shift will be harder on me." Carly gave Bowie a wry smile. Her eyes felt sandy from lack of sleep. The nightmares had begun again the night before.

"Yeah, you're probably right. There's always somebody

around like him." Bowie looked at her, as if checking for understanding. "You know, somebody who wants to make everythin' harder than it needs to be."

"You mean like Saddam Hussein?" The heat of the day was pressing in on them, and she wished she could wear her physical training shorts and tank set all day. But no, the tank top instead of the sleeved shirt was the only concession allowed them in the heat.

Bowie made a sound of disgust. "Yeah. Now this is the gearshift, and there is the clutch pedal. Put your foot on it and get the feel of it. You just have to remember to always push down the clutch when you shift gears. Try that." He watched her. "What do you think about all that happenin' in Kuwait?"

Carly had thought of little else since the president's address to the nation the night before. The speech must have been what triggered her nightmares. The threat of war could give anyone nightmares, right? "I don't like it." Perspiration trickled between her shoulder blades.

"The Kuwaiti people must sure agree with you." He slid toward her, almost sticking to the black vinyl bench seat. "Now press down the clutch pedal a few more times." He watched her perform this and said, "The question is, will Bush send U.S. troops in?"

"I don't think he has any choice if the UN can't persuade Hussein to withdraw, do you?" Carly pushed down the clutch pedal and then lifted up and pushed it down again.

"Okay. Start the truck," Bowie said. "Well, I don't think Hussein will go along with the UN."

"Why do you say that?" Carly started the vehicle. It roared to life.

"Because Hussein just marched in and took over his neighbor, didn't he?" Bowie paused, gave a pronounced shrug, and then wordlessly showed her how to shift into first. "Hussein wants what he wants, and only force stops that kind of bubba—not right or wrong."

"Sounds like you know a lot about Hussein." As the vehicle inched forward, her dog tags jiggled and Carly felt distinctly uneasy. It was such a big truck and it made her feel so small in comparison. What if she lost control and rammed something? Wouldn't Haskell love that?

"Naw, just my opinion." Bowie raised his voice over the grumbling engine. "He kind of reminds me of an uncle of mine I didn't cotton to. He run every pastor out of the local Baptist church for over twenty years until he finally had a coronary and died."

Carly grinned at the peculiar comparison while following Bowie's wordless instructions to press the clutch down and shift from first into second. The vehicle shimmied as it moved forward.

"You think I'm jokin'," Bowie said. "I'm not. Haven't you known a body that has to run everythin' and who's always right even when they're wrong? If you don't, believe me, you're lucky."

Carly thought of her mother then. Not a pleasant thought. And not a completely honest judgment. Her mother didn't want to control everything, just Carly and Carly's contact with her birth father. Thinking of the latest argument with her mother was like probing a raw wound. Learning that her father had cheated on a wife had ripped deep. Carly pushed away her raw, visceral response to this. At Bowie's nod, she shifted into third. Soon, she was traveling fifteen miles per hour down the deserted street.

Why couldn't Leigh see that keeping Carly from meeting her birth father was wrong, hurtful? Momentarily, Carly let herself feel the deep, lingering ache of not knowing her father and the emptiness of wondering why he'd done what he had. "What causes people to act like that?" she whispered.

Bowie hovered close to her, evidently ready to stomp the brake if he needed to. "I don't know what causes it. But it's like they think they're God. And they're not."

Glad Bowie didn't know what she really meant, Carly eased the vehicle down the empty base road. "You think this will turn into a war then?"

"It's already a war. Those Iraqi soldiers we watched on TV last night weren't shootin' water guns. When people start killin' each other, it's a war." In contrast to his words, he gave her an encouraging nod and said to give it more gas.

Carly drew in a shaky breath and obeyed him. She couldn't argue with Bowie's assessment. As they sat there on a summer day, safe and sound, innocent civilians were dying in Kuwait. It just didn't seem real, seem right.

"Do you think—" She braced herself to ask the question that had been nibbling at the back of her mind since the day before. "Do you think we'll go . . . over there?"

"Naw, don't think we'll get that lucky." He nodded with approval. "You're doing great. Just drive to the end of the street and then I'll have you stop and downshift. Anyway, everything in Kuwait will probably be all over but the shouting before we get half-trained."

She sincerely hoped Bowie was right. But was that what

she should hope? After weathering basic and taking action against harassment, Carly had thought she'd conquered the fear and uncertainty that were always with her. The nightmares and panic attacks had seemed to end. But Saddam Hussein had invaded Kuwait, and thousands of miles away, Carly felt it shake her to her depths. She was back at square one, nightmares and all.

August 24, 1990

In her fatigues, Carly stood at the black pay phone just outside the rec room in her barracks. After the latest startling news on Operation Desert Shield that evening, everyone seemed to want to call home or friends and that included Carly. It was nearly ten o'clock and time to turn in before Carly got near the phone. The local nightly news was about to begin. She plunked in her coins and then dialed the numbers included in a letter she'd received that day. The line connected and a stranger answered.

"I'm calling for Lorelle Dawson," Carly told the stranger. "Can she come to the phone?"

Since the reply was yes, Carly waited on the line for Lorelle to be located. No one in Carly's family would understand the complex morass of emotions that the president's recent announcement had triggered. But Lorelle would.

Just after Carly had been asked to slip more coins in, a breathless Lorelle came on. "Who's this?"

"It's me, Carly."

"Carly? Hey. Great. Did you get my letter? How are you?"

Carly had intended to write Lorelle, too, but hadn't found the time. "Yes, I got your letter. Thanks. I'm getting settled in. Oh, I have a sergeant who doesn't like women."

"Too bad," Lorelle said cheerfully. "My sergeant's a woman."

"You get all the breaks."

"Just call me Lucky. So what's up?"

"I just wanted to hear your voice." Carly suddenly wished that Lorelle were standing beside her. "This thing with the president calling up the reserves," Carly put her reason for calling into words, "the first time since Vietnam has got me—"

"Worried? I don't think you should be. My dad called me this morning and said not to worry. We're still in training, Carly. They'll want seasoned troops in a combat zone and we're women, remember? We won't be called up."

Carly tried to feel reassured. If Lorelle's dad at the Pentagon didn't think they'd have to go, they probably wouldn't, right? Still, she felt afraid and ashamed of herself for being unenthusiastic about going to a combat zone. Hadn't she signed up with the army, knowing that war was always possible? But after the invasion of Kuwait, the recurring nightmares wouldn't stop, leaving her tired out every morning.

Carly turned her thoughts back to the phone call. "Do you like training to be an MP?"

"Yeah, I think I'm going to like law enforcement and I might go into that when I get out. That will thrill my parents. They wanted me to study law, not enforce it. So how's the military vehicle thing coming along?"

Carly tried to think of something that would make

Lorelle grin. "A tall blond hunk is teaching me how to drive each of the military vehicles."

Lorelle laughed. "In that case, we'll call *you* Lucky."

"He's just a friend." Still, Carly had come to value the tall blond Alabaman. He was solid, steady, and possessed an easy grin.

"Have you heard anything from your father?" Lorelle lowered her voice, "I mean, your birth father?"

Carly gripped the receiver tighter and looked around to see if anyone was close enough to hear her. "He came to our graduation."

"How'd you know that?"

"My mother saw him." Carly pictured in her mind's eye her mother's unhappy expression as she had scanned the crowd at graduation.

"She did? Wow. What did she say? Did you see him, too?"

Carly didn't want to tell even Lorelle what her mother had revealed about her father. Surely there were extenuating circumstances to explain why her father had . . . why he would . . . How did one explain being unfaithful? "Nothing new," Carly fibbed miserably.

No matter how angry she was at her mother, she didn't want Lorelle to know what Carly's mother had done. Or maybe Lorelle's parents already knew . . .

Ivy Manor, November 8, 1990

Wearing her dress uniform, Carly got out of a red pickup and looked down the long lane, littered with burnished fall leaves, leading to Ivy Manor. She glanced back at the driver, a grandson of Rose's. "Hey, thanks for the lift from the airport."

"No problem. We're all hopin' your great-great-aunt comes through okay. Have a nice visit with your family." He waved and drove away.

Carly nodded but couldn't bring words to her lips. She'd gotten a four-day family leave to visit Aunt Kitty, who was "failing fast"—her great-grandma Chloe's words. An unseen hand gripped Carly's lungs and for a moment, she couldn't breathe. Then she forced in a draught of cool autumn air and started up the drive with her duffel on one shoulder, feeling a million years old.

The last time she'd been at Ivy Manor had been on the occasion of her high-school graduation party. Basic training and three months of MOS training stood between her and that untried girl. Her mind called up the echoes and tremors of that battle in the flat over whether she'd be allowed to enlist at seventeen. And then she added the conflict with her mother over Leigh's continued refusal to tell Carly who her birth father was. But this trip wasn't about her. What did "failing fast" mean? Did it mean that Kitty was dying? *I can't lose Aunt Kitty. I can't.*

The brisk wind gusted. Gold and red maple leaves cascaded, showering over Carly as she trudged around to the back door. Without knocking, she stepped inside and called, "Grandma! Rose! It's Carly. I made it."

Only Rose, the longtime housekeeper at Ivy Manor and an older cousin of Lorelle's, came to greet her. "Honey, you look good! A little thin, but good." White-haired Rose wore a flowered apron over a blue dress. "The army must agree with you. Take that duffel up to your bedroom." Rose began rapid-fire instructions. "We've moved your aunt into the den here on the first floor so we can take turns caring for her. Miss Bette and Miss Chloe are in with her now. Get your stuff put away. Wash your hands, and by then I'll have a snack whipped up for you."

Carly grinned. Hearing Rose's orders brought a rush of remembrance of all the long, happy summers she'd spent at Ivy Manor, usually with Lorelle. A scene popped into mind. Lorelle and she were barefoot, dancing in the cool, green grass with bottles of soapy water and red plastic wands in hand, blowing bubbles.

"You need anything?" Rose asked, a hand on her hip.

Carly leaned over and kissed Rose's milk chocolate cheek. "Whatever you're cooking sure smells good."

"You better believe it. Now hurry up. Your Aunt Kitty wants to see you."

Obediently Carly ran upstairs to her room and put her things in the armoire and dresser. Everything was just as she left it, but she was different. Each memento from childhood tugged at her, many reminding her of Chloe and Kitty and the fun they'd had together. Carly stroked the sterling silver brush and comb set that had belonged to her great-grandmother Chloe's mother. It had been Carly's graduation present when she'd finished eighth grade.

For the first time in months, Carly slipped out of uniform and pulled on comfortable worn jeans and, for Kitty, a New York Mets T-shirt. Aunty was a Mets fan. Carly felt a catch in her throat. How could she meet Kitty with the crushing fear that it might be the last time?

Stalling for time, for wisdom, Carly turned her back to the freestanding mirror and gazed around at the room. This room had been Great-Grandma Chloe's, then Grandma Bette's, Leigh's, and now hers. It was a room of priceless antiques that could easily have been moved to the county museum. But Chloe insisted they were family pieces and they would be happier being used by the family that had chosen and cherished them over the centuries than gathering dust in a museum.

All the women of Ivy Manor that had gone before, even the ones Carly knew only from family portraits, crowded around her. Here she was never alone. Here, away from New York City where she'd been kidnapped, was the only place she had ever felt truly wanted and truly safe. But she couldn't hide in her room for the next four days. She had to break through her reluctance to face the fact that she might lose Kitty.

Disheartened, she went to the door, and there, paused again. She pressed her hand against the solid plastered wall beside the doorjamb as if drawing strength from the centuries of women who'd passed through this same door.

When Aunt Kitty and Great-Grandma Chloe were girls, Kitty slept in the trundle bed in this room. Grandma Bette and Aunt Gretel shared this room. Her mother, Leigh, and Aunt Dory had, too. Would she be a mother someday, and would her daughter love this room as she did? Carly drew up her strength, the strength that came from that house. *I am a woman of Ivy Manor.*

Taking a deep breath, she willed herself down the steps to the den. She pushed open the pocket doors and faced the maple-paneled room, now dominated by an incongruous hospital bed. At first, Carly didn't look directly at the occupant of that bed. Instead, she scanned the others in the room. On one side, Bette, in gray slacks and a lighter gray blouse, was reading aloud with Minnie, Lorelle's great-grandmother, near her. Wearing a pale green dress, Chloe sat on the other side, holding Kitty's hand. Where was her mother?

"Carly," Chloe said, her eyes widening. "Carly." She rose and opened her arms.

Carly hurried into them. She hugged Chloe, feeling the fragility of her age. It frightened her. In contrast, her great-grandmother's arms tightened around her. "We've missed you so." Then she released Carly to Bette's arms.

Carly let herself rest her head on her grandmother's reassuringly firm shoulder. "We're so glad you could get leave," Bette murmured, kissing Carly's forehead. Minnie, dressed fashionably as always, patted her shoulder.

Finally, Bette released Carly, and she turned to go to Kitty's outstretched arms. Carly tried to hide her shock. But Kitty looked too frail to still be breathing. Her cheeks were sunken, and her skin was sickly sallow.

"I look like the wreck of the *Hesperus*, don't I?" Kitty teased in a thread of a voice. "No, don't answer that, *please*."

Carly leaned over and kissed the lined cheek and let Kitty kiss her back and then stroke her face.

"Seeing you is good medicine," Kitty murmured. "I'm terribly sorry I missed your graduation from boot camp. I was so proud of you—distinguished honor graduate. I still have the photos right here beside me."

Carly sat down on the bed, thigh-to-thigh with her great-

great-aunt. "You were missed, too, but I understood why you couldn't come."

Kitty nodded and then stroked Carly's face again. "They cut your hair."

"I was lucky. I got a barber who liked long hair." Carly turned her head and touched the tight braid at the back of her neck. Her aunt's body looked like bones in a sack under the thin cover. It shook Carly. "I like it like this. It's off my neck and easy to care for." Then she burst into tears.

"Oh, my sweet, my precious girl," Kitty crooned. And then Carly was alone with her aunt. Bette, Minnie, and Chloe left quietly, closing the door behind them.

"I'm sorry," Carly said, taking a tissue from the bedside table crowded with medicine bottles and other sickroom paraphernalia. "I didn't mean to cry."

"I've cried a few times myself over the past few weeks. It's hard to die. It's hard to let go."

Kitty's calm words iced Carly's insides. "Can't they do anything for you?"

"Well, they could start replacing all my body parts or hook me up and electrify me like Frankenstein's monster. I'm ninety-three, Carly, and it's a miracle that I'm still alive. I nearly killed myself with bad liquor in the twenties."

Carly looked at her.

"Yes, you're a grown-up now, and I don't have to act as if I've lived a perfect life. I was pretty wild when I was young. I didn't have your common sense and steady temperament. I nearly destroyed my liver when I drank some doctored wood alcohol during Prohibition. And you know that I was never married to Thompson's father. I haven't lived the life of a saint."

"You've been good to me."

"That was easy. I loved you the moment I knew you were on the way. I probably wouldn't have lived as long as I have if Leigh hadn't given me my second chance to be a true aunt and almost your second grandmother. Helping raise you has been the joy of my life." Kitty folded one of Carly's hands in her thin, age-spotted hand.

The frailty of the hand made Carly speak. "I love you, Aunty."

"I know, dearest. And now I'm going to ask you to do something for me." Kitty raised her hand to stop Carly from speaking. "This request is going to be very hard for you, the hardest thing you may be asked to do in this life."

Carly stared at her aunt, fearing she would ask something Carly couldn't do. "What is it, Aunty?"

"I want you to start forgiving your mother for not telling you who your father is and keeping the two of you apart."

Flushed, Carly looked away. "No fair."

"It may seem that way," Kitty conceded. "But I'm going to give your mother the same treatment."

"Where is she?" Carly faced Kitty again. "I thought she would be here by now."

"I think my dying is frightening your mother even more than you, more than she can face. You see, I know about her first love. Or should I say second love? The year before you were born, your mother suffered three terrible losses."

Carly didn't know what Kitty meant and didn't want to

ask for more to complicate everything now. "Is Mother coming, and Nate?"

"Yes. But Leigh does not want to face me. She does not want me to press her once again to tell you the truth. She knows that it is very hard to refuse a dying request."

Carly shook her head. *Don't talk about dying, Aunty.*

Kitty touched her arm. "But the truth needs to come out, and if I have to die in order to make it happen, fine."

"No," Carly objected and gently gripped both of Kitty's hands, now fragile as parchment.

"Yes, my death should have something good come of it."

Carly bent her head to Kitty's hands and wept.

Leigh and Nate arrived just before dawn. When she saw that Ivy Manor was lit up like morning already, Leigh knew she'd waited too long. She hurried inside the back door, calling for her mother and grandmother. She found Minnie, Bette, Chloe, and Carly in the den on the first floor. And Kitty was asleep, but they were all sitting around her. Then she realized that it only looked as if Kitty were sleeping. She was not breathing. Leigh felt a moan trying to work its way up in her throat. She clamped her lips together tightly and forced the moan back down.

"You delayed long enough, Mother," Carly accused. "She left us about an hour ago. She'd been waiting for you."

"Yes," Minnie added, "she told us to tell you she couldn't wait any longer."

The words blasted inside Leigh. She sank to her knees beside the hospital bed, closing her hand over Kitty's cool one. "I'm so sorry, so sorry," she whimpered.

Two days later, venerable St. John's Episcopal Church was filled and overflowing as most of the county folk, dressed in their best, gathered to say farewell to Kitty McCaslin. At the front of the packed church, Rose and her daughter were singing a duet of the hymn Kitty had requested. "Thy strength indeed is small. Child of weakness, watch and pray; find in Me thine all in all."

In her dress uniform, Carly sat between her parents with little Michael on her lap, listening. She wrestled with grief and anger as her fretful little brother squirmed. She was incensed at her mother for not coming in time. Had her mother really delayed because she didn't want to face Kitty's dying plea?

"Sin had left a crimson stain," Rose and her daughter harmonized, "He washed it white as snow." They walked down the steps and back to their seats.

The priest stepped to the high pulpit and began reading from Scripture. Beside Carly, Leigh gave a gasp or a sob. She'd not stopped crying since she had collapsed next to Kitty's bed upon arrival.

Carly tried to hold in her anger. She knew that Kitty wouldn't want her to argue with her mother, especially in public at her funeral. But her mother's hypocritical tears made that difficult. She could have gotten there earlier. She should have. How could tears change facts?

The funeral was over before Carly knew it. Everyone made the solemn trek to the family plot in the church cemetery. Thompson, with his wife, stood at his mother's graveside weeping without a sound. Massive two-hundred-year-old oaks and maples shaded the mourners. The stubborn bronzed oak leaves, still clinging to branches, whispered condolences on the wind. As the pallbearers lowered Kitty's casket into the grave, Carly closed her gritty eyes. She hadn't slept for nights now. Fear and nightmares kept her awake.

Her father tugged her along as they walked to the car and then drove back to Ivy Manor. There, all the rooms on the first floor were open and ready for the funeral luncheon. The ladies of the nearby Baptist church had insisted upon preparing and serving the buffet in the dining room. Mourners milled in the den and the parlor, overflowing into the front hall out onto the front porch, even out into the backyard and into the gazebo. Fortunately, the day was bright and temperate.

Carly encouraged her little brother to go outside and play with the other children who lived nearby. And then she tried as well as she could to avoid her mother.

In the crush of people, Nate watched Minnie's grandson in his dress uniform working his way through the crowd to reach him. "Frank," Nate said, offering his hand, "glad you could come."

Frank shook his hand. "It's really hard to see someone like Kitty McCaslin pass."

"Did you know her well?" Nate asked, wondering why Frank had approached him alone. Their wives were close, but he and Frank had only a nodding acquaintance. He'd assumed that Frank and Cherise had come because Minnie had come. But was there something more?

"No, but Kitty McCaslin is an important symbol to me. She was one of the first women lawyers in New York City and one of the first to represent black actors and actresses. She was a trailblazer in her own way."

"She was quite a woman," Nate agreed. "I'm glad Carly was able to get leave to be here with her . . . at the end."

"Yes, the timing was right. I'm pretty sure that with what's going on over in Saudi Arabia, the brass won't be giving many more leaves."

Nate caught the change in Frank's tone. This wasn't just idle conversation.

"You've heard that the president is going to double the U.S. troop strength to over four hundred thousand in Saudi?" Frank asked, looking into Nate's eyes. "You know what that means, right?"

On the other side of the room, Cherise appeared beside Carly and touched her shoulder. She said a brief prayer for wisdom. "Lorelle wished that she could have gotten away for the funeral," Cherise said, "but Kitty was a friend of the family, not close family."

Carly nodded. "I talked to Lorelle. She seems to be enjoying her MOS."

Carly's attempt to sound normal touched Cherise. "Yes, my daughter the cop," she replied wryly.

Cherise watched Leigh stand very close to her great-grandmother Chloe just feet away. "Losing your Aunt Kitty is going to be very hard on your mom."

"Yeah." Carly's tone was flat, unforgiving.

Cherise looked into Carly's troubled, very beautiful gray eyes. Why tiptoe around? "We've all urged your mother to tell you about your birth father, especially now that you're an adult."

Carly look surprised.

"I was really glad that you and Lorelle got to know each other as kids and that you were close to each other during basic training. Your mother and I coordinated your vacations when you were kids, so you two would be close to each other. I have never had a friend more honest, more faithful, more loving than your mother."

"Then why didn't she get here in time before Aunt Kitty died?" Carly snapped.

Nate didn't mistake Frank's meaning. "Surely that wouldn't affect our girls."

"The president has called up the reserves for the first time since Vietnam. In the first time in U.S. history, a president has called nearly five hundred people out of retirement. Iraq has assembled another seventy thousand troops into Kuwait on the Saudi border."

"But we have allies joining us," Nate objected.

Cherise decided to do what she could to help Carly understand Leigh. "Carly, have you ever heard about your mother's engagement?"

"What engagement?"

"She was engaged to be married to a good friend of your Grandfather Ted in March of 1972. His name was Dane. He was killed in the same explosion that killed your grandfather."

"Why are you telling me this?" Carly's lower lip drew down.

"Because you are mourning the loss of a very dear aunt. How would you feel if you were mourning the loss of Grandma Bette, Nate, and the man you were to marry in a week's time?"

Carly's eyes widened. "Are you telling me that that was why my mother . . . ?"

"I'm trying to show you that it isn't just about you and the man who is your birth father. There is so much grief wrapped around the year 1972 in your mother's heart that she has trouble looking back."

"Well, it's been taken out of her hands." Carly's tone had stiffened. "My father has written to me and I'm sure I will meet him soon, with or without my mother's permission."

"We have allies, yes, thirty-two to be exact," Frank replied. "But America is now the world's leader, the only superpower left. And our president wants to make sure that we win this war."

"But war hasn't been declared yet."

"It's just a matter of time. And I'm almost positive that both our girls will be heading to the Middle East soon."

Nate stared at Frank, then looked across the room and met Carly's eyes, a deep uncertainty growling to life inside him.

CHAPTER NINE

November 29, 1990

Carly stood with her platoon gathered in silence around the radio in the garage. The announcer was summarizing that day's UN ultimatum to Saddam Hussein. The Iraqi dictator had been ordered to withdraw before January 15, 1991, or face retaliation. Chilled inside, Carly listened stone-faced as the male members of her platoon jeered Hussein.

"It won't be long till we show him what's what!" whooped Mr. Smarty Sparkplug, who was really Joe from Indianapolis.

"We leave in six days," Sergeant Haskell announced unexpectedly, looking the happiest Carly had ever seen him.

There was a stunned silence, and then all the males broke into large grins. Carly wondered if her own very different state, one of numbness, was just plain fear or if it was the result of sleepless nights and her loss of Aunt Kitty just weeks before. Was their contrasting eagerness for battle just a male thing?

She forced a slight smile, trying to act as if she shared her male counterparts' enthusiasm for deployment. *So we've got our orders. We're going to Saudi.* The words filled her with nauseating dread.

"You guys, get back to work, get all your assignments done, and start cleaning up. We need our vehicles in top shape to leave the training area ready for another platoon."

Hiding her true feelings, Carly followed Bowie back to the engine they were just about finished overhauling. Though she still had much to master, she was amazed at how much she'd learned in just four months of training. By now she could drive every vehicle they'd worked on and had been thoroughly trained in the basics of auto maintenance. Much of her success was due to Bowie's knowledge and help.

"Hey," Sam, an African-American from Kansas City called, "Carly, can you help us a minute?"

She nodded to Bowie and then jogged over to Sam. "What do you need?"

"Can you reconnect this to the wires and secure it in the dash?" Sam handed her a shortwave radio.

"Sure." Carly climbed up into the mammoth boxy truck, an HEMMT, and crawled up under the dash. On her back, she pulled out the dash wires and connected them to the radio's. Then, with a screwdriver from her pocket, she secured the radio and its metal harness back into place. She slid out of the vehicle. "Done."

Sam nodded his thanks.

By now, the platoon had discovered that Carly's thinner,

lithesome body could do jobs in tight places easier and her smaller hands and slender fingers worked better for some of the more intricate tasks. Carly looked down at her hands, covered in grease and her nails clipped as far down as possible except for the thumb and index finger of her right hand. Sometimes her fingernails could grasp tiny things in a way no pliers could.

Usually she and Bowie worked on their own as a team, with supervision since they were still in training. But the other members of the platoon regularly called on Carly for her specialized skills. For a moment, she felt satisfaction over this progress. Haskell still wasn't thrilled to have her, but he'd ceased dogging her more than anyone else. *But now we're going to be deployed to a combat area.*

Carly rejoined Bowie, and the two of them worked side by side doing last-minute chores before putting the engine back together. She concentrated on what her hands were doing, letting the therapy of the routine job lull her fears. The end of the day came, and Bowie and Carly had not gotten as far as they needed to. The two stopped at Haskell's door. "We're going to come back after mess and finish," Bowie said.

Haskell nodded.

After mess, Bowie walked beside Carly back to the garage in the chill twilight. It felt as cold as Alabama in January to him, but it wasn't even Christmas yet. He pulled up the collar of his jacket and glanced at the pretty woman beside him. Something was wrong. Carly had barely lifted her eyes all through mess and now she was looking down as they walked. He knew he wasn't all that good around women. Just ask his three sisters. But it had become obvious even to him that Carly wasn't recovering from her trip home, or maybe something else had upset her. Was she worried about Saudi Arabia? But should he risk asking her or just let it ride?

Inside the garage, the engine block had been lifted back into place. Bowie and Carly started working silently together, reconnecting everything and then checking the electrical wiring with an ohmmeter to make sure the connections were unobstructed. It was tedious and time-consuming labor. The evening chill came on stronger and Bowie closed the massive doors. They were alone in the low light of the vast warehouse of a garage, crowded with vehicles and parts. He glanced over at Carly. Tears were dripping down her face.

He couldn't ignore tears even if acknowledging them might take him into dangerous territory. "Carly, hey, what's wrong?"

She swiped at her face with the back of her hand, smearing a little grease on her cheek. "Sorry."

"What's wrong?" He tightened a connection, put down the pliers, and wiped his hands on a nearby rag. He pulled out a clean handkerchief and dabbed the grease from her cheek.

When he was done, Carly turned away from him. "Nothing."

He hated when women did that. Something was obviously very wrong. "You've been upset since you got back from your family. Are you still grievin'?" He could tell she was still crying from the way her shoulders kind of shook. He reached out and took them in his big grimy paws. She was so delicate and yet so strong. All he wanted to do was steady her, let her know he was concerned—though in all honesty, he'd wanted to touch her since the first time he saw her.

Without warning, she rotated within his loose grasp, drawing nearer. She looked up at him.

Close contact with her jolted him. She was just as sleek and soft as he'd imagined. *But we're just friends.* Holding her loosely, cautiously, he waited. When she didn't speak, he asked, "Do you want to talk about it?" He'd overheard his sisters use this line more than once when a distraught girl-friend had come by.

Instead of speaking, Carly leaned forward and rested her head on his chest.

This launched a response inside him as big as Desert Shield. From the very first, he'd thought Carly one of the most dainty and attractive girls he'd ever met. But they were soldiers in the army together. And he'd known from the little she'd told him about her family that she was way out of his league. After all, her stepfather was a police detective and her mom wrote articles for magazines and her family had a house with a name, Ivy Manor. He'd known a down-home boy like him didn't have a chance with someone like Carly.

But none of that mattered now as she pressed her face against him. His arms went around her but gently, so he wasn't putting her under any pressure. After all, she could just be using his chest as a place to cry, to let out whatever her sadness was about. The desire to stroke her glossy blue-black hair taunted him.

"I'm frightened, Bowie," she murmured.

"Of what?" He couldn't resist now: he stroked her hair, shining in the low light.

"I've been frightened all my life."

This sounded serious and baffling at the same time. Carly was in his platoon and his friend. He didn't want to cross any line with her, but the temptation to lean down and find her lips with his nearly overcame his good sense. "What are you afraid of?" he forced himself to ask.

She gave a little shudder that was somehow sexy. "It's hard to put into words. I . . . keep having these . . . nightmares."

"What kind of nightmares?"

She shook her head. "They don't make sense. There are just some things I can never forget. I just know that none of them will make any sense until I have all the pieces."

This made no sense to Bowie at all. But that wasn't unusual. He never understood his sisters. Still, holding Carly like this made him want to comfort her, to help her through this sadness. "You can trust me, Carly. I'd never tell anyone a word you told me not to."

"I know that."

He stroked her head again and the roughness of his calluses caught in her hair. He felt so clumsy and big around her. But when she moved her head as if asking him to stroke her hair again, he obliged. *So soft, like silk.* "Go ahead and tell me then."

She shook her head against his chest. "It's too long a story."

Then, before he knew what was happening, she had turned up her face and was looking at his lips. He was mesmerized by the way she ran her dainty tongue over her bottom lip. And then she was on tiptoe just inches from his mouth, poised in a silent appeal.

Where this request had come from he didn't have a clue.

But he couldn't say no to save his life. He lifted her off her tiptoes and pressed his mouth to hers. She reached up, wrapped her arms around his neck, and returned his kiss. A groan of satisfaction sounded deep in his throat.

"Nice," Sergeant Haskell said. "Very nice."

Bowie released Carly and stumbled back from her. "It's not what you think," he stammered.

Haskell barked a laugh. "That's funny. I thought you two were kissing. If you weren't, what were you doing?"

December 1, 1990

Leigh didn't believe her eyes. She read the brief note from her daughter again. "Mom, by the time you get this, I'll be leaving for Saudi. Our orders are to be airlifted in three days. Our battalion will be supplying troops and repairing vehicles. Don't worry. I'll be fine." Then Carly gave Leigh her APO address. Only a few times in her life had Leigh felt this magnitude of shock. She recalled a time years earlier, when she had to identify a friend of a friend at a morgue. Now that same horror drove jagged shards through her.

Without stopping to think, Leigh dialed Frank Dawson's work number. She tapped the phone as she waited for Frank to answer. He came on line with a brisk greeting.

"Frank, it's me, Leigh," she said abruptly. "Carly leaves for Saudi tomorrow. I don't want her to go."

There was a pause at the other end of the line.

"Frank," Leigh repeated, "I don't want her to go."

"I know what you mean. Lorelle should be arriving in Saudi today."

Leigh gasped. "Frank, no."

"I thought Cherise had written to tell you."

"Her letter came today." Leigh slid down to sit beside the table. The mail was scattered there. Cherise's distinctive lavender stationary peeked out from underneath the electric bill. Leigh picked it up. "I hadn't opened it. I opened Carly's first."

"Cherise has taken it pretty hard. It reminds her all too much of my tours in Vietnam."

Leigh's mind churned with images from the past: hippies burning draft cards, Chicago policemen clubbing yuppies—and her. "I can't believe," she whispered, "this is happening."

"I don't think either of us thought our girls would enlist just in time for the next war." Frank's voice was harsh with emotion, too.

"My daughter must not go to Saudi." Shaking with resolution, Leigh spoke low in her throat, rasping almost. "I won't have it."

"There isn't much you or I can do about it. The U.S. is going to have over four hundred thousand troops in Saudi in time for the January fifteenth deadline."

"There must be something you can do. You can't want Lorelle over in that awful place. They still make the women cover themselves from head to foot. They cut off thieves' hands!" Leigh felt her voice thinning, spiraling out of control. "They behead murderers!"

"Leigh, we didn't choose the site for this war. Saddam Hussein did. The Saudis have allowed us, whom they view as infidels, to set up posts in their country."

"That's what I mean," Leigh declared. "I don't want my

daughter in such an awful place. It was bad enough that she enlisted, but this. . . ." She closed her eyes.

"There's nothing we can do but pray for their safety." Frank's voice blended understanding with uncompromising determination.

"I can't accept that," Leigh snapped. "There must be something you can do."

"Even if I could do something, which I can't, I wouldn't try. Part of growing up is taking the consequences of one's actions. Carly and Lorelle enlisted and now war has come, and they must face it. Just like we faced 'Nam in the 1960s."

"I don't want my daughter in the middle of a war," Leigh said, desperately searching for a way out, any way.

"I don't either, but what choice do we have?" Frank's tone was dismissive.

At last she understood the heart-stopping truth. *He isn't going to help me.* She drew up what was left of her self-control and said a polite good-bye. She hung up the phone. And sat. She couldn't move, breathe. She stared at Carly's brief note on the kitchen table. It was as if someone had settled a heavy boulder over her lungs. She strained for each breath. Was it all going to happen again?

Her mind drifted back to 1972, to her grandfather's funeral at Ivy Manor and then to the joint funeral for Dane and Ted that same spring. Now this November, Kitty had passed away and had been buried near her brother, Leigh's grandfather. Long ago, at her stepfather and fiancé's funeral, people had said over and over, "Deaths come in threes." She didn't believe in superstition, but unbidden fear blossomed cold and dark inside her. Kitty was gone. Would Carly and Lorelle follow her in death just as Dane and Ted had followed her grand-father? "Oh, Kitty, I need you now."

Her fingers trembling, Leigh reached again for the phone and dialed Nate's work number. His answering machine picked up. Barely able to speak, Leigh stammered, "Nate, Carly is being sent to Saudi. Please . . . please come home. I need you."

Five days later

Carly knew she should have said no, but when Bowie had asked her to meet him after mess, she'd only nodded. Now in the early darkness of winter, they sat side by side on the pic-nic bench in a small, deserted park on base. Leafless branches flickered, rustling drily in the wind, and Carly thought about the desert ahead of them. When would they return to trees?

But most of all, she was very aware of the man sitting close beside her. She remembered the touch of his lips on hers and the feel of his arms, his strong arms around her. Had it been his embrace that had helped her sleep the night they'd heard about their deployment?

"You never told me what you were frightened of," Bowie said. "Is it because we're being shipped to Saudi tomorrow morning?"

Carly wanted just to say yes, leave out all but the simplest truth, and put an end to the conversation. But Bowie deserved better from her. "That's part of it."

"If it makes you feel any better, heading to Saudi bothers me, too."

Carly nodded, but she felt compelled to reveal something

else that had been bothering her. "I keep waiting for Haskell to say or do something."

"You mean because he saw us kissin'?"

She nodded again, feeling a warm blush on her face.

"He just told me to make sure I didn't touch you unless it was after hours. And to keep a low profile."

Carly tried to sort out what these cryptic words indicated and failed. "What do you think that meant?"

"You know, after you took care of Joe that day." He looked as if to see if she understood what he was saying.

"You mean the day he . . . touched me?"

"Yeah," Bowie went on quickly, "that kind of told everyone, 'Hands off.' And the sergeant doesn't want that to change."

"What does one have to do with the other?" Carly asked, still baffled. Why would Haskell give her a pass on this? Was he softening toward her?

"Well, maybe he thinks if the other guys see me kissing you, they might try it, too. And then there might be fights." Bowie looked chagrined and slightly embarrassed.

Carly exhaled loudly. What a ridiculous idea. She couldn't help but grin. Men fighting over her? "So Haskell thinks I'm going to go luring his men to disaster?" she asked, momentarily diverted. "Kind of like a *femme fatale?*" *Men*, Carly thought.

They sat in silence for a few moments. Then Bowie spoke up, "So what upset you? I mean, besides heading to Saudi?"

Carly sighed. How she wanted to lay her burden down.

Bowie tentatively touched her cheek. "You don't have to tell me."

His accepting words released her. She turned her face in to his shoulder. "I have nightmares. I've had them for a very long time."

"What kind of nightmares?"

She rubbed her face against his cotton camouflage jacket, feeling the hard muscles of his arm and chest. "When I was ten years old, I was kidnapped."

Bowie gasped and folded her in his arms. "What . . . what happened to you?"

"I wasn't molested. They just grabbed me and taped my eyes and mouth shut, put a sack over my head, and kept me tied up. Then two days later they dropped me off at a hospital."

"Did your parents have to pay a ransom or something?"

"No, that's what made it all so weird. I think my mom knew why I was taken and that it had something to do with my father. But she would never tell me everything—or anything, really."

"Was this a kind of custody battle?"

Carly rested her head against his unyielding chest. He was so strong. "No, I was born out of wedlock, and I don't know who my birth father is. I keep thinking he might have had me kidnapped so he could be with me. But if he did, he never let me know it was him. And I can't think he was one of the men who scared me, was so rough with me, and made me cry."

"So your nightmares are about your kidnapping?"

"I think so. In the dreams I'm just so very frightened and cold, and I can't open my eyes or my mouth. I feel as if I'm being smothered. And shadows are moving toward me and I think they're going to hurt me. And I scream but no sound comes out."

"Scary." Bowie stroked her back.

She shuddered at his gentle touch, breathing in his soap-clean scent. "They stopped while I was in basic. I got over them. It was great. I think I was too tired to have dreams or to remember them, and then at graduation, I felt as if I had made it, as if I didn't need to be frightened anymore. You know what I mean?"

"Yeah, I know. It's a real high to graduate from basic. When did the nightmares start again?" He stroked her cheek.

His fingers ignited magic sparks that danced through the nerves of her face and down her neck. "When Saddam Hussein invaded Kuwait. I must have known that we would end up going there."

"Well, you know we won't be on the front lines."

"Yeah, I know." And then there didn't seem to be anything more to be said. Bowie had no control over the U.S. army or Iraq's. Carly remembered how Bowie's kisses had made her feel. She had slept better that night. She leaned forward, tempting him to make the first move.

"Can I kiss you again?" Bowie asked, sounding as if it would be too good to be true.

He's so sweet. Just like Nate. She nodded, not taking her eyes off his.

Looking as if he'd just opened a birthday gift he'd really wanted, he leaned down and pressed his lips to hers.

Her arms naturally circled his neck and she prolonged the kiss. She knew that she hadn't sorted out her feelings about Bowie as a friend or possible boyfriend. But his kisses made her feel she could do anything, even sleep through the night.

*　　*　　*

On Pearl Harbor Day, Carly arrived in a foggy and unexpectedly chilly Saudi Arabia. It had taken her company two days by airplane, with a stopover in Germany, to reach the Mideast. After a tense eight-hour flight from Germany, they'd been warned that the army didn't have time for jet lag and Haskell had ordered them not to have any. With her duffel on her shoulder, Carly climbed down a narrow ladder from the upper deck of the C-5 onto the tarmac at the air base near where their battalion would be stationed. She felt fuzzy, as if she had left her brain somewhere over Italy.

Bowie caught up with her and steadied her with a touch on her elbow. "You okay?"

Carly had no answer for him. She hadn't flown internationally since the summer she'd visited Paris with Chloe and Kitty. And when they'd arrived in France, they'd been whisked away in a limousine to a four-star hotel. She doubted those types of accommodations awaited her. Wishing a hot shower awaited her somewhere soon, Carly walked side by side with Bowie to where their platoon was meeting up.

Having Bowie near gave her strength. She glanced up at him and found him smiling at her. She tried to smile back. Facing a war, even in a support role, had hit her as though she were starting basic all over again. The universe had once again been turned upside down.

Haskell motioned for them to gather around. "It'll be morning in a couple hours. Just bunk down anywhere here in this area." He motioned to the concrete floor of the hangar. "After morning mess, we'll be processed in and then head out to get our camp set up. While you're here, you'll keep your chemical warfare gear with you at all times. If you hear a siren, put it on immediately." He gave them all a stiff glare. "No exceptions, got it?"

Only solemn silence answered him.

"And everyone will be briefed on how to get along with Arabs," the sergeant continued. "Not only will you be meeting Saudi citizens while you're here, but other Muslims are here as part of the coalition. Oh, Gallagher, women get a special training session after the men's. The Saudis evidently don't like the idea of women in uniform." He gave a wisecrack grin.

Carly just nodded. She was so tired, even the floor looked inviting. And if the Arabs weren't thrilled to have her, she knew how they felt. She wasn't thrilled to be there.

CHAPTER TEN

Saudi Arabia, December 15, 1990

*O*utside the desert-camouflaged tent she shared with several other women in the battalion, Carly waved to
Bowie and he hurried toward her. They'd survived their first
cool, foggy week in Saudi. She'd never been so homesick in
her life, not even during basic. Every day she'd felt like running away but had nowhere to run. Only Bowie and the good
humor of her other platoon members had made it bearable.

That day, she and Bowie were embarking on another ven-
ture, a few hours spent in Riyadh. This filled her with a sharp
sense of anticipation—and danger. Did she really want to go
where she must hide her face?

"I can't believe we got a whole day off." Bowie greeted
her with a big smile. He wore the same desert camouflage
they all wore, which was a dappled mix of beige, tan, white,
and gray. "And just in time for Christmas shopping."

Carly saw in his large blue eyes that he wanted to kiss her in the worst way. They'd been so busy they hadn't had a moment alone all week. They were officially off duty now. And frankly, touching Bowie would provide a needed boost to her nerves for the mission into the risky unknown. After glancing around to make sure no one was paying them any attention, Carly herded Bowie back to where the tent flap was fastened. Then, in its partial cover, she stood on tiptoe and kissed him briefly but thoroughly on the mouth. Touching his lips slipped a knot free inside her, and she let him take over the kiss.

"Hey, hey!" Joe called out, jogging toward them. "None of that! The Sheiks of Araby will have your head."

Stepping away hurriedly, Carly blushed and she noticed that Bowie was red, too. "Where did you two come from?" she demanded.

Joe hustled up to them with Sam bringing up the rear. "We're Bowie's backup," Joe said. "If he can't protect you from the locals, we will."

His words made her stomach do a yo-yo swing. But she gave him a satirical glance. After all, it had been Joe she'd flattened. "Like I need protection," she mock-boasted. "You should know better, Joe."

His hands covered his heart. "Oh, she got me . . . again." Then he laughed at his own joke. "I'm hoping you'll help me pick out something to send to my girls back home."

"You have *girls* back home?" she teased in a mystified tone. "Are they blind, deaf, and dumb?" Secretly, she was glad to have Joe and Sam's company.

Joe punched her arm. "Hey, what about you? We saw you kissing this jerk."

Looking wide-eyed and innocent, Carly shook her head. "I don't know what you're talking about. I was just wiping a bit of dirt off his cheek."

Both Sam and Joe hooted as the four of them began ambling toward the waiting bus. "Is that what you've got to wear in town?" Sam asked, pointing at the long black *abayah* and black veil slung over Carly's arm.

"Yes," she answered. "I can only say that I'm glad I was born in the USA." She dreaded the moment she'd have to put on the humiliating garb. Why had the U.S. brass bowed to this degradation of American women soldiers? Easy: they were all men.

"Hey, Carly!" a familiar voice hailed from behind.

Carly turned and squealed with delight, "Lorelle!"

In her MP uniform, Lorelle jogged over to Carly and hugged her.

Carly hugged back, and then they were both giggling.

"Women," Joe commented.

Lorelle turned her head. "Watch it, soldier. I can arrest you, you know."

"Hey, you can arrest me anytime," Sam piped up and then looked abashed.

Lorelle chuckled. "You say that now, but . . ."

Carly quickly introduced Lorelle as a lifelong friend. She caught Sam studying Lorelle's face and hid a grin. Lorelle did look very good in her MP uniform. "We're catching the special bus into town."

"Hey, me, too." Lorelle fell into step with them and

Carly noticed that Sam managed to drift to Lorelle's side. "Otherwise, I wouldn't be dragging this along." She waved the veil and *abayah*.

They reached the bus. "Better put that stuff on," the driver said, lounging beside the vehicle.

Carly grimaced, then both she and Lorelle dropped their *abayahs* over their heads like ponchos and pulled the drawstrings around their necks. The black clothing covered them completely, from their necks to their toes.

"And the veils," the driver persisted. "We don't have blinds on this vehicle, and your faces must not be seen through the windows."

With exasperated groans, Carly and Lorelle both settled veils onto their heads and adjusted them so they could see through the small rectangular spaces left for their eyes. How did the Saudi women stand that costume in the heat of summer? Carly felt almost smothered, and the winter day was cool. "How the women here put up with this garbage I'll never know," Carly complained. "I think I'll start a revolution."

"Well, that's why you're wearing this gear, aren't you?" Joe said. "They don't want their women getting ideas."

Carly didn't bother to reply. Bowie helped her into the crowded bus and sat beside her in the far back. Joe and Sam sat just ahead of them with Lorelle between them.

"Get ready for a bumpy ride!" the driver said as he climbed in. He started the bus and drove forward slowly, the engine laboring over the barely improved road toward the highway to the big city.

In spite of her depressing garb, Carly felt her spirits lift as they departed the military base and were out in the open. Adjusting to desert life in a militarized zone had taken its toll on her, on all of them. The guys she worked with had coped by joking more, swearing more. Somehow the others had guessed about the budding romance between Bowie and her. They had all begun giving her weird advice about men and teasing good-natured Bowie.

The bus driver merged onto the modern highway. Datsun pickups zipped around the big army bus. In the back of one, a young camel was lying in the bed, its long neck high above the cab. Carly stared at this odd mixture of a modern vehicle and an ancient beast of burden that had made up caravans for thousands of years. Another Datsun zipped past with goats crammed in the bed along with a woman. Carly gaped at the sight.

Under cover of her *abayah*, she took Bowie's hand, drawing strength from his nearness, his honest affection for her. He smiled and overwhelmed her slender hand with his larger one. Suddenly it felt good to be alive.

As they approached the city, traffic increased. The road branched into many lanes of small, darting cars. Lorelle turned and asked Carly where they were going in the city.

"I hear that they have some lovely jewelry shops," Carly answered.

"Hey," Joe muttered, "we're not made of money, you know."

Carly gave him a seraphic smile that she realized he couldn't see and said, "Any girl who dates you deserves twenty-four-carat gold."

"Everybody, get ready for the Saudi Sweep!" The driver

took a sudden turn and skated over four lanes of traffic. The maneuver swept Carly almost onto Bowie's lap. "Hey!" all the passengers exclaimed.

The driver laughed. "Hey, I'm just blending in. They drive like maniacs over here."

So do you! Carly surveyed the broad boulevard before them. Riyadh certainly looked like a modern desert city: stucco buildings with arches, courtyard walls, many cars, and tall palm trees. Still the strange sight of women all dressed in the outmoded, cumbersome garb, which Carly had been forced to adopt, made her uneasy.

If all the men had been attired in the traditional white flowing robes and Arabian headdresses, it would have struck her as fair. But many men sported Western dress. It was definitely unfair and a bit intimidating. Carly moved closer to Bowie's comfortingly large form. And as always, nearness to him ignited an inner glow. Carly smiled secretly behind her veil.

The bus driver jerked to a stop and parked. He gave out maps of the nearby shopping district of Riyadh and warned the soldiers to return by five o'clock for their ride back to base. Lorelle and Sam took over navigation and led them to a narrow street of gold and jewelry shops. They strolled down the alley to get the lay of the land.

Carly made sure that she didn't touch Bowie. She'd been instructed that no public physical contact was to occur between males and females in Muslim areas. Smiling shopkeepers stood in the doorways of their shops, motioning them to stop in, speaking some pidgin English. Carly still felt like a freak, wearing the *abayah* and veil. It was like attending a sick masquerade. A glance at Lorelle's dour eyes told her she felt the same way.

They trooped to the end of the street and then paused. The three guys looked to her for guidance. She and Lorelle compared impressions of the shops and led them back to one that had caught their interest. Carly stepped inside and everyone paraded in after her. The proprietor beamed at them, greeting them warmly in Arabic. Carly walked to the glass-covered display case. "Joe, here are some lovely gold chains. The quality looks good."

The proprietor lifted one out and laid it on a black velvet cloth. He motioned for Carly to pick it up. She recalled the instructions about haggling being important in this culture. "How much?"

The proprietor responded and Carly did a quick mental calculation between the two currencies. "Too much." She shook her head. Then she turned to Joe. "He wants more than I'd pay in New—"

The proprietor said something and pulled out another chain. He quoted another price, a lower one. Carly examined it and turned to Joe. "This is a good deal. It's twenty-four carat. See the mark?"

Joe looked at the proprietor and quoted a few drachmas lower price. The man beamed. "Yes. Deal."

"Do you like chains, Carly?" Bowie asked as the proprietor was wrapping up the purchase.

She grinned up at him and then realized with chagrin that her expression was completely hidden from him. This made her cross, but she didn't let it tinge her voice. "They're okay, Bowie." She wanted to say, "Bowie, you don't have to buy me anything." But of course, they were . . . well, they couldn't exactly date. But they were a couple. The thought made her blush warmly, and this time she was glad Bowie couldn't see her face. In high school, she'd dated only a couple of times for big occasions such as homecoming and prom. She'd never had a boyfriend, just guy friends—as Bowie had been at first.

They stopped at a few more stores. Carly was beginning to feel more comfortable. Shopping in the quaint foreign shops was not much different from shopping in some areas of Greenwich Village. Along with the guys, she purchased jewelry for her female relatives and then Bowie said, "Carly, just step outside the door a minute, okay? Lorelle, you stay?"

Carly blushed again. It was obvious that Bowie wanted to buy something for her and ask for Lorelle's approval. She stepped outside, joy bubbling inside her.

Without warning, she felt herself lifted off the ground from behind. She yelped. Shock lasted mere seconds. Then she launched herself into a rigid backward arc. Her heels kicked muscle and her assailant cursed. She jabbed her elbow back into his breastbone and he groaned, his grip loosening.

Then Bowie descended. Over her head, he slammed his fist into the Arab. The man went down like a sack of wet sand. Released, Carly sprawled onto the dusty street, her *abayah* tangling around her legs. She struggled to breathe, the wind partially knocked out of her.

Bowie leaned over and helped her up. Her pulse raced. Her veil had shifted and she righted it. Joe and Sam were circling the downed Arab, cursing him and taunting him. "Stop that, you two," Carly gasped. "We need to move on. We don't want an international incident."

"He can't manhandle one of our women and get away with it," Joe objected. Then he shoved the Arab again and challenged him by taking up a boxing stance.

"Stop that!" Lorelle ordered. "You'll have the police on us. Come on. They warned us in training that Arab men have some really weird ideas about Western women, especially American women. They all think . . . well, you can guess what they think."

Suddenly there was the sound of boots running toward them. Two armed Arab policemen shoved their way through the crowd that had gathered around Carly and the rest of them. The first cop barked something in Arabic at them.

"We only speak English," Lorelle said respectfully.

Bowie moved closer to Carly.

Carly felt her heart thumping. How could they explain that she was the one who'd been attacked? Were they all going to end up in a Saudi jail?

Greenwich Village, the same day

After dusk, Leigh paced the kitchen waiting for Nate to come home. She wanted to tell him her news. She dreaded telling him her news. But putting it off would only increase her stress level.

To have time alone with Nate to explain everything to him, she'd already fed Michael his supper and put him to bed. She'd read him *How the Grinch Stole Christmas!* three times, but he was finally asleep. He wouldn't be awake to hear the argument she was sure would come. She rubbed her taut forehead. She could have easily lain down next to Michael and fallen asleep herself. Fatigue dragged at her spirits.

Over the past week, since Carly had been airlifted to Saudi Arabia, Leigh's nights had been sleepless and before that, they hadn't been that good since Kitty's funeral. Leigh glanced up at the clock for the thousandth time. Nate had said he'd be home at 8:30. It was now 8:36 p.m. She rubbed her arms, resisting the urge to rake them with her long fingernails.

Ever since earlier that year, when Kitty had moved back to Ivy Manor, the silence from the downstairs apartment had depressed Leigh. The phrase "as silent as the grave" now haunted her. Kitty would never be coming home, and Carly was in harm's way in a war zone thousands of miles away. Tears spilled from Leigh's eyes. Angrily, she wiped them off her face and stiffened her spine. "Deaths don't come in threes," she insisted to the empty room, the universe at large. "That's just nonsense. I won't give in to morbid sentimentality."

But her heart longed for Kitty, yearned for the woman who'd twenty years before known Dane so well, who had stood by Leigh through her pregnancy when her mother had practically disowned her. *I love you, Kitty. I always will. I just wish I'd done better. I should have left New York and come to you as soon as Grandma Chloe called, but I was a coward. I couldn't face losing you and so I delayed. I'm so sorry for that. Please forgive me.*

She heard the door open downstairs and braced herself for Nate's arrival. At the kitchen sink, she splashed cold water on her warm face and wiped it dry with a paper towel.

"Hi, honey," Nate said as he strode in. He glanced at the

wall clock. "Just a few minutes late. I don't have to go in till later tomorrow so I'll take care of getting Michael off to school in the morning." He kissed her cheek.

His kiss warmed her as always in a way nothing else could. But she felt as if she didn't deserve his kiss. He was going to be so angry with her. "Good," she murmured. "I'll put your plate in the microwave." She moved, but his arms stopped her as they wrapped around her from behind.

"I'm sorry," he whispered, "I miss them both, too."

She didn't mistake his meaning. He missed Kitty and Carly. She drew a shaky breath, dreading the impending conflict. She forced herself to nod and proceed to the refrigerator and microwave. Within minutes, she was sitting with him at the table while he ate. She bided her time, knowing it would be poor strategy to broach anything while he was hungry and thirsty.

"You've got that look in your eye," Nate said between bites.

"What look?"

"The look that comes right before you tell me something I don't want to hear. It's as if you've girded yourself for battle and we're facing off for round one."

She stared at him, nonplussed.

"Leigh, I know you." He wiped his mouth and fingers with his paper napkin. "You're the only woman I've ever loved. You're my wife of seven years and the mother of my children. When will you learn that I'm not some Joe Schmoe who doesn't get it—who doesn't get you?"

"Do you know what I'm going to say?" she challenged.

"I know it probably has something to do with Carly. So what is it?"

His astute surmise shook her confidence. But it gave her the opening she needed. "I'm flying to Saudi January thirteenth so I'll be there for the deadline of January fifteenth."

A shadow crossed his face, and then Nate stared at her. "No discussion? Just 'I'm going'?"

"My editor wants me to do an in-depth analysis of the modern woman in the army in a combat zone."

"You mean you convinced your editor you should do an in-depth analysis." He shoved his half-eaten food away. "You don't fool me, Leigh."

Chagrined, she flushed. She had indeed convinced Dorcas to send her. It was expensive for the magazine and difficult to get accommodations in Saudi Arabia, especially for a woman reporter alone.

"And what are Michael and I," his voice sharpened, "supposed to do while you and Carly are in Saudi Arabia, getting bombed with Scuds and perhaps *engulfed* in chemical warfare?"

"I'll get a nanny to come and stay with Michael. Or maybe Grandma Chloe will come up—"

"Chloe is ninety years old," Nate snapped. "She can't take care of Michael. He's high energy."

"Well, what about your mother?"

Nate stared at her. "What if I tell you I don't want you to go? Why do you think that you can just make life-altering decisions and never check with me? Are we married or not? More and more you act as if I am a nuisance, not the man who should be at the center of your life." He leaned forward, pinning her with his intense gaze. "What is going on, Leigh?"

She buried her face in her hands. His words stabbed her right in the soft spot of her hurt. "Why is everything so out of control?" she whimpered.

"What are you talking about—the Iraqi invasion?"

"Why can't life ever be easy?" Leigh felt her panic rising. "Why couldn't Carly just go to college? Why did she have to put herself into harm's way?" She began rocking on her straight chair.

Nate took over and began asking questions. "And why didn't your fiancé live, and why did you have a one-night stand with Carly's father, and why couldn't Kitty live forever?" He reached out and snatched her hands with his and gripped them. "Life is never going to follow your orders."

The strength in his hands didn't frighten her. He'd never do anything to hurt her. And everything he'd said was true, but she couldn't stop herself from keeping her assignment to the Gulf. "I have to go." She wouldn't meet his eyes.

"Do you think that your presence in the Gulf will protect your daughter?" He squeezed her hands as if wringing a confession out of her.

"Of course not." Still, she wouldn't meet his eyes.

He leaned close as if to kiss her. "What would you say"— his warm breath wafted against her face—"if I said I will divorce you if you go?"

The Saudi policemen yelled more Arabic at Carly and her friends. Then the proprietor of the shop they'd just left pushed his way forward. He began speaking rapid-fire to the policemen, gesturing toward Carly, her companions, and the man who'd accosted her, who also contributed a few sullen words to the exchange.

In a lull, Lorelle spoke up in her MP voice, "I'm a police officer. Does anyone here speak English? Please?"

A woman draped in black moved forward. "I speak English."

"Great," Lorelle replied with relief. "Will you tell us what's being said about us?"

"The policemen want to know why you have attacked this Saudi citizen. And the shop owner is explaining that this young woman was attacked first."

"Thanks," Lorelle said. "We don't want any trouble. We just want to shop, and then we'll head back to our base at five today."

The police asked the Saudi woman a few questions, which she answered. Then she turned to them. "The police say, 'Don't cause trouble. Go on with your business.'"

"Well, duh," Sam said. "That's what we were doing."

Bowie took Carly's elbow.

"Don't do that," the Saudi woman said sharply, "people will get the wrong idea about her."

Though he dropped his hand, Bowie looked as if he was about to say something rude.

"He's just trying to protect me," Carly said. She gave Bowie a pleading glance. He looked stubborn but nodded.

"Let's get our packages from the shop and go find someplace to eat," Sam suggested.

"There is a good café just around the corner," the Saudi

woman said. "I'll take you there if you like. It's on my way home."

"Thanks," Lorelle said. They all accepted their brown paper and twine packages from the bowing shop owner and then followed the Saudi woman down the narrow lane. Other Saudi bystanders gawked as if the circus had come to town. Or that's how it felt to Carly.

"I know it's hard to understand our ways," the Saudi woman said as they followed her down the lane. "But I remember how exposed I felt the first time when I was at school in London and I went out on the street without my *abayah* and veil."

"Why would you come back here?" Carly couldn't stop herself from asking.

The woman shrugged. "This is my home. This is where my family is. I liked London, but I didn't like everything there either. Here is the café. The men and women have separate entrances"—she pointed these out—"but after you go inside, the men can come over to the family side and join you women there."

"So we have to walk in separate doors but we can sit down together?" Joe asked, sounding as if he had plenty to say about this.

"Thank you so much," Carly said and offered her hand to the woman.

They shook hands and then with a quick farewell, the woman left them. "See you guys inside," Carly said and walked into the café. "Boy, do I need a cup of coffee."

Lorelle chuckled as she trailed in after Carly. "Remember, they make their coffee strong and sweet here."

"Fine." Carly drew a deep breath and, at the motion of the waiter who met them inside, made her way toward a table.

Soon she saw Bowie's blond head towering over everyone. Then he was beside her. "You okay?"

She grinned at him. "I'm fine," she said with sincerity. As long as Bowie and Lorelle were with her, she was fine. "Let's order."

Virginia, December 15, 1990

Feeling like a teenager again, Bette stood at the phone in her kitchen, speaking to Chloe. "Mother, I'm thinking of bringing a friend for Christmas dinner."

"Wonderful. There's always room for more at my table."

Bette smiled. Yes, there had always been room for more around the table at Ivy Manor. For a moment, she was transported back to 1936, and Gretel and her great-uncle Ira were sitting around the dining table at Ivy Manor. Rory and Thompson were just little boys again, champing at the bit to be excused to listen to *Jack Armstrong, All-American Boy*. Her stepfather was sitting at the head of the table, laughing. Telling herself not to be maudlin, Bette pulled herself back to the present. "Do you think Leigh will mind? Will think it's an intrusion on our family day?"

"Bette, I'm the hostess. Bring your friend. I want to meet him."

CHAPTER ELEVEN

Ivy Manor, Christmas Day 1990

*I*n the kitchen fragrant with sage and butter, Bette hovered uneasily, ready to help Leigh who was in charge of the day's feast. Rose had the day off, though for the past two days she'd done the Christmas baking. Bette was uneasy because she needed an opening to prepare her daughter for her Christmas surprise, one that had nothing to do with food or gifts. But she sensed that her daughter was troubled already. And why not? *It's Christmas and Carly's in a war zone. And Leigh is still trying to cope with Kitty's death. Just like the rest of us.* But Bette detected an underlying current of deeper stress in Leigh.

"Mom, I think I'm just going to put potatoes in to bake instead of making mashed potatoes. Baked potatoes are less work and fewer calories." Leigh sounded distracted.

Bette nodded. "Fine." How many times had she longed

to take Leigh aside and help her find a way to peace? *Look who's talking. I'm stressed out as well. Maybe I shouldn't have . . .*

Bette pushed away her own uncertainty. One thing didn't have anything to do with the other. She didn't have to depend on imagination to know what her daughter was going through that day. Hadn't she spent the Christmases of 1942 through 1945 worrying about Leigh's father, who'd been fighting in World War II? *Curt, our little girl grew up beautiful, accomplished, and . . . unhappy.* But Leigh seemed more tightly wound today than usual. Was she still at odds with Nate? How Bette wished Ted were there. He'd always known how to make Leigh laugh.

"Leigh, I know this holiday is hard for you—"

"Mom," Leigh answered, "we've got the turkey and stuffing well on their way. And I'll just get the potatoes ready to pop into the oven. Why don't you just go and sit with Grandmother?"

Bette looked into Leigh's eyes and saw that her daughter didn't want her comfort. That hurt. Made mute, Bette tried to smile, failed, and left the room. Well, the chips would have to fall where they would.

Saudi Arabia, Christmas Day 1990

In the long evening shadows cast by an empty tent, Carly sat with her arms wrapped around her knees beside Bowie on the cool desert sand. Because of the holiday, they'd had light duty and a big Christmas dinner in the mess tent. In the distance, someone was playing a CD of country Christmas music.

Some guy was singing "There's No Place Like Home for the Holidays" to a weeping electric guitar.

"I wish they'd turn that stuff off," Bowie said, looking over his shoulder toward the source of the music.

Though in full agreement, Carly didn't answer. She just closed the distance between them and rested her head on his shoulder. Fortunately Bowie didn't seem to mind that she'd barely said a word all day. Homesickness had a choke hold on her throat. Her first letter from her birth father since her deployment was tucked into her pocket. The note had been brief but had promised that if she wanted to see him, he would arrange it in the new year. The thought was both thrilling and terrifying.

"It's time." Bowie helped her up.

She again said nothing but let him lead her to the USO tent and the line of people waiting for their turns at the telephones to call home. She and Bowie had signed up and been given an hour time frame in which to report. So they waited patiently, silently.

She appreciated that Bowie was never uneasy over her silences. She took his hand and squeezed. He squeezed back. The line moved slowly, and the heart-wrenching Christmas song "I'll Be Home for Christmas" floated over them. Finally, Carly arrived at the head of the line. She dialed Ivy Manor's phone number from memory. Her pulse quickened as the phone rang and rang.

"Hello." Nate's rushed voice came over the line.

"Dad, it's me, Carly." And her throat closed up again as tears trickled down her cheeks. She kept her back to the soldiers behind her. Only Bowie stood at her side, a comforting arm around her shoulders.

"Carly!" Nate exclaimed and then called, "It's Carly! Pick up the extensions!" Then he spoke to her again. "Sweetheart, we've missed you so today. How are you? We saw some footage of the army's Christmas meal. Have you eaten—"

"Carly," Chloe and Bette said simultaneously, "how are you?"

Carly sucked in her tears and tried to speak normally. "I'm fine. Just miss all of you."

"We miss you," her mother said, coming on the line. "What are you doing today?"

"The usual stuff." Carly forced the words over the lump in her throat. "Ate turkey and dressing, pumpkin pie. There's lots of Christmas music, and thanks for the care package. I really needed everything you sent."

"I thought you needed the chocolates the most," Nate said.

Carly laughed in spite of her tears. "Yes, and tell Rose her sugar cookies vanished in record time."

"What do they have you doing?" Chloe asked.

"Oh, the usual. We're fixing vehicles. Windblown sand here is constant and we have to keep cleaning and double-filtering fuel and oil lines."

"Do you need anything more?" Bette asked in an anxious voice.

"I could use some more foot powder. I really use it up fast. Since the Saudi water supply is being strained by the sheer number of all the troops, we have to use water sparingly. The foot powder and talc really help keep me comfortable."

"I'll send you a case," Nate said.

"I have a surprise for you, Carly," Leigh said. "I'll be seeing you soon. I'm going to be on assignment in Saudi in January."

Carly stood frozen in place—part of her happy, part of her shocked and suddenly very angry. Couldn't her mother stick to her own life? "I want you to meet someone," Carly retaliated instantly, her voice becoming stronger. "This is my very good friend, Bowie Jenkin."

Bowie's eyes widened, but he accepted the phone. "Uh, Merry Christmas, everybody." He pulled Carly close to his ear so they could listen together.

"Merry Christmas," the voices from Ivy Manor chorused in return and then there was a pregnant silence.

"Where are you from, Bowie?" Bette asked. "Did I get your name right?"

"Yes, ma'am, I'm Bowie from Red Bay, Alabama."

"I bet you're missing your family, too," Bette said.

"Yes, ma'am. I got to call them right before Carly called you. Well, here's your girl." He handed her the phone.

The USO volunteer waved her wristwatch at Carly, the signal that Carly was to finish up her call. "My time's almost up. Where's Michael?"

"I'm here, sis," her little brother spoke loudly into the phone. "I'm with Dad in the front hall. I miss you."

"I miss you, too, munchkin." How Carly wanted to hold her little brother on her lap again. "Was Santa good to you?"

"Yeah." Michael sounded sad. "When can you come home?"

"I don't know, kid." Suddenly the bond of family, the ties of blood, hit Carly like a Scud. And in that moment, she forgave her mother for butting into her life once more. The letter in her pocket tugged at her, too. Why were family ties never easy for her?

The USO volunteer tapped her watch.

"My time's up. I love you all." Carly's love was echoed back at her and then with a final "Merry Christmas," she hung up. She turned to Bowie, who took her hand and led her away. Tears blurred her vision, and his arm came around her shoulders again. "Let's go somewhere where we can be alone," she whispered.

Bette had been on the den phone while Chloe, Nate, and Michael had been in the front hall. Leigh had come from the kitchen and they all met in the parlor where Nate bent to light a fire.

Still reeling from Leigh's unexpected announcement about going to Saudi Arabia, Bette crossed to the sofa. Opposite her, Leigh setttled on the love seat and Michael knelt on the floor, playing with his newest Matchbox cars.

"Carly sounded well," Chloe said. She wavered a little on her feet, and Nate sprung up from putting the fire screen in place and helped her into the wing chair.

"Thank you, Nate. I feel a little shaky today. Maybe I should get out my cane again."

"Good idea. I'll get it for you before you get up again," Nate said.

"I wonder if Bowie is just a friend or if Carly's dating him," Chloe said, obviously steering the conversation away from Leigh's bombshell.

Bette studied Nate, who stood by the hearth, not moving to his wife's side. He looked stiff and unhappy. What did he think of Leigh going to a war?

"But this Bowie's from Alabama," Leigh blurted out.

Nate chuckled. "Alabama notwithstanding, I would guess she's at least *interested* in him. Otherwise I doubt she'd have put him on the phone."

The doorbell rang and everyone looked up. Bette leaped to her feet, her heart suddenly hammering. "I'll get it." She hurried to the front door and there he stood—silver-haired, fit-looking, handsome in a gray trench coat and carrying a beribboned box of candy.

"Merry Christmas, Bette." Dan leaned over and kissed her lips. "You look lovely."

She wanted to warn him that she'd been a coward and hadn't told anybody but her mother about inviting him to Christmas dinner. But his kiss muddled her mind. And she couldn't hold back a smile. "And you look very dashing."

Hanging his coat on the hall tree, he chuckled and then took her elbow. "Let me guess. I'm your Christmas surprise?"

She blushed and opened her mouth.

But with a finger pressed against her lips, he prevented her from speaking. "Let's go in then."

Stomach fluttering, she led him to the parlor door. "Everyone, I'd like you to meet my friend Dan Greenfield."

Chloe stood and held out her hand. "Dan, Merry Christmas."

Dan hurried forward and clasped her hand while urging her to sit back down. He set the box of chocolates on Chloe's lap.

Bette made the introductions, not once meeting her daughter's eyes. Bette and Dan sat down on the sofa side by side.

"Dan," Chloe said, "we're trying to decide something. We just spoke with Carly—"

"Bette's granddaughter who's in the Gulf?"

Chloe nodded. "Carly surprised us by introducing a young man. I'm thinking that must mean he's important to her. What do you think?"

"I agree. Otherwise, she wouldn't have put him on the line. Inviting someone to a family holiday is a statement." Dan's audacious words hung over the parlor.

Blushing, Bette hazarded a glance at her daughter. Leigh's face was flushed, and she'd crossed her arms tightly. Bette's heart sank. There was no peace on earth this Christmas, not even at Ivy Manor.

Troubled, Bowie led Carly away from the lights of the USO center back to where they'd been before. Quiet corners were hard to come by in a camp of over four hundred thousand soldiers. The tent she shared with the other women of the company was still quiet, so Bowie led her behind its shelter.

He eased down and then pulled her so she was sitting between his thighs. He nudged her head onto his chest; she curled up like a kitten against him. He liked that image. He took off her hat and stroked her hair. He couldn't keep silent. "Why'd you introduce me to your parents? You know they wouldn't want you involved with someone like me."

"What's wrong with you?" She lifted her eyes to his and the moonlight illuminated her face.

"I'm a redneck from Nowhere, Alabama."

She sighed and cuddled closer to him. "I haven't chosen to live my life, or I guess I should say *start* my life, like my mom wanted me to."

"She wanted you to go to college, right?"

"Yes."

"Just yes?" He let his fingers trail over the soft skin of her cheek. Carly was so strong and yet so feminine. It awed him that she could care for him.

"What do you want me to say, Bowie?"

"I'm just tryin' to say you shouldn't have introduced me to your family. I know I won't fit into your life away from the army."

"Don't say that."

"It's the truth, honey, and you know it."

She sat up straight, pulling away from him. "I don't know where you get this!"

"I'm from a family that lives out in the sticks." He missed her warmth immediately. "My mama sews quilts for craft fairs. My daddy works construction and farms a few acres. My sisters all got married right out of high school and started producing grandkids—"

"Bowie," Carly interrupted, "what is happening between you and me has nothing to do with where we were raised and who we're related to. If you think you wouldn't be welcome at Ivy Manor, you don't know anything."

He liked the starch that had come bristling into her tone. "Carly," he whispered, leaning forward, "I think I'm fallin' in love with you."

"Good," she replied and kissed him.

This kiss was nothing like the quick stolen kisses they'd shared before. This was a full-blown kiss. He put his arms around her and pulled her against him. "Oh, Carly, you're so special," he murmured against her soft mouth.

She responded by parting her lips and deepening their kiss.

Rational thought left him and all he could process was the glorious feeling of holding Carly and kissing her.

Saudi Arabia, December 26, 1990

At 7:30 in the morning, Carly and her platoon were busy as usual cleaning out the sand-clogged fuel and oil filters of Humvees. In spite of improvising extra coverings for each of the critical openings in the engines, the blowing sand always got through. The constant desert wind, called *Shammal*, had picked up in the days heading into January. At the end of every day, Carly looked into a mirror and saw her eyebrows and hair white with the insidious sand. The rushing wind also provided a constant white noise behind every voice, every sound they made as they worked. It dulled Carly's hearing.

When Haskell walked up to the vehicle Carly, Bowie, Joe,

and Sam were working on, she saw his lips move but didn't hear his words at first. She moved closer and then she heard him. "You guys got lucky. A Marine observation post needs to be resupplied. It will give you some practice for what we'll be doing soon. Our company will be moving farther forward in a few days to get in place and set up to supply our ground troops when the real war begins."

The words "the real war begins" caught Carly unexpectedly. She realized that she'd gotten accustomed to the daily routine and hadn't thought very far ahead.

"Here's the map. Your squad will head out as soon as your vehicle is loaded with supplies. Gallagher, you did the best of the platoon on map reading, so you'll be the navigator. Get the trucks there and back before nightfall."

Carly looked at the map he'd handed her. "What about GPS?"

Haskell snorted. "Combat troops get GPS. Support gets maps."

Carly watched him walk away, a chill running through her. The Marine OPs were charged with keeping an eye out for any Iraqi movement, so they'd be far forward. A scary thought. Her instant apprehension was a stark contrast to the guys' reaction—they all were grinning. Again, she felt the odd man out. Was her fellow crew really thrilled to be going so far forward, or was it just a male thing? Since she wasn't going to ask them, she'd probably never know.

Bowie, Sam, and Joe stepped up the pace and she had to hustle to keep up with them. Before Carly could deal with the throbbing fear inside her, she was sitting beside Bowie in the front seat of the first truck, the map and a compass on her lap.

Joe and Sam were in a smaller truck behind them. The rest of the squad rode inside the back of both trucks. Carly studied the topographic map and then gazed out at the rough desert terrain far ahead of them. A distant memory came to her. She was back in basic, trying not to fall asleep during a lecture on map reading.

All too soon, Bowie had driven them through the troop concentration areas, over the good highways and then the unimproved roads and finally beyond, into the desert proper. They saw a herd of camels loping across the uneven ground, an eerie sight. It made Carly feel as if she'd drifted into an earlier time or a Barbara Cartland romance.

"You okay?" Bowie asked.

"Fine," she lied. The topographic map she'd been given didn't inspire confidence. It was stamped: "Not Suitable for Ground Use." "I'm just worried that I might miss a landmark or something." In fact, there didn't appear to be any landmarks in this vast open county. The terrain ahead was beautiful in a stark way, with low red sand dunes and outcroppings of rock.

"You'll do fine. You've got a sharp eye."

Carly gave him a grateful smile. During their workdays, they tried very hard to keep their personal feelings hidden. So even though she thought a kiss now might help her feel better, she turned back to focusing on their course. If the map failed her, she'd been taught how to navigate by dead reckoning using a lensatic compass and the truck's odometer. She noted down the reading from the latter. The wind whipped up a bit more, and gusts buffeted the side of their high vehicle.

"This is the kind of day where at home, they'd be taking trailers and RVs off the highways," Bowie commented.

Carly only nodded. Saudi Arabia wasn't like the Sahara with its classic white sand dunes. Its desert was flatter with boulders, lots of rocks, and scrub vegetation. Her mind drifted momentarily back to summer and Ivy Manor's lush green garden. Then she snapped herself back to the present. It wouldn't do for her to let Bowie drive them into something like a *sabkhas*, a salt marsh.

At that time of year, just before the January rain, Carly had learned that *sabkhas* could be concealed by a fragile crust. And she'd also been warned that the desert landscape changed with the wind. There was plenty of wind that day. She had to keep the platoon on track. Haskell would never let her forget it if she got them all lost. Feeling disoriented, she prayed for the first time in a long time. *Dear God, don't let me screw up.*

Ivy Manor, December 26, 1990

Bette came in from the cottage for morning coffee. She had recalled that long-ago childhood day in 1929, soon after her mother had come back to stay, when they had gone to clean up the cottage for her mother to live in. Since then, the cottage had rarely been empty. That day, light snow was falling, and the summerhouse looked forlorn and out of place presiding over the dormant garden. Bette walked into the kitchen and Leigh was sitting at the table alone. Bette had hoped to have the first cup of coffee by herself, but she couldn't retreat now. "Good morning, Leigh."

"Hi, Mom." Leigh sipped her coffee.

Bette poured her coffee and sat down across from her daughter.

"Your friend went home then?" Leigh lifted an eyebrow.

"You know he drove back to Washington last night."

"How long have you been dating him?"

"We met at a World War II War Department reunion a few months ago."

"I thought you worked for the CIA."

"The CIA didn't start until after the war. I started out working at the War Department while your father went to school at Georgetown."

"I don't believe it. You mentioned my father."

Bette ignored Leigh's tone. "There isn't much to tell about those days. Curt went to school. We married. He went to war. He came home and died when you were a baby." Protecting her secret, Bette kept all emotion from her voice.

"Why do I always get the feeling that there is something you haven't told me?"

Bette carefully controlled her expression. She'd promised Curt that she would never tell their daughter the truth. "You will just have to accept the facts as they are."

Leigh looked unhappy.

Bette waited to see how her daughter would try to find out more about her growing friendship with Dan.

Instead, Leigh brought up a different topic. "I might as well tell you: Nate and I are at odds again."

The cold way her daughter said the words stirred Bette's worry and caution. She'd been right then. The unspoken conflict between Nate and Leigh was over Leigh's upcoming trip to Saudi Arabia. But Bette said nothing, merely sipped her coffee. Whatever she said would be the wrong thing. That much the years had taught her.

"Don't be a coward," Leigh said, sounding as if she were taunting her. "Ask me."

"It's not my place to ask you. You and Nate are adults, and you don't need me to stick my nose into your marriage."

"You think Nate can do no wrong."

Bette closed her eyes, summoning up her forbearance. "Leigh, I wish that someday the war between us could end. I've admitted I was wrong about the way I treated you when you got pregnant with Carly. I sincerely regret the hurtful words I said and the way I pushed you away. I cannot unsay or undo any of it. Will you never forgive me? Why can't there ever be peace between us?"

Leigh wouldn't meet her gaze.

"We're about to start a new year. Can't we bury the hatchet and start out fresh?"

Leigh burst into tears.

Bette didn't know whether to comfort her or just let her weep. Her beautiful daughter had become as prickly as a porcupine. *Lord, help my daughter. I can't. I'm at the end of my rope with her.*

In the truck, Carly watched the sun lowering on the western horizon. The daylight dimmed, along with her hope of getting back to base before dark. They should have reached the Marine outpost by now. Night came fast in the desert, and it was on its way. And they had been expected back before nightfall.

"How much farther?" Bowie asked her.

Carly bit her lower lip. "We should be there."

"Where?"

"At the Marine PO."

"I don't see anything," Bowie said.

"Let's stop. Maybe if I get out and look around, I'll catch a glimpse of it."

Bowie slowed to a stop. The truck behind did the same.

Carly climbed out and scrambled up onto the broad flat top of the truck. She lifted her binoculars to her eyes and slowly pivoted in a complete circle. Nothing moved. No glint off glass or a Humvee mirror. When the circle was complete, she stopped and stared at the wasteland in front of her. A stray thought occurred to her. Why were they there anyway? Who would want this barren stretch of desert enough to kill for it?

"Any luck, Carly?"

"I don't see a thing." She felt the sick ache of failure, spiced with sheer panic. She controlled her voice. "Come up and try yourself."

Bowie climbed up beside her. He went through the same procedure she had. "No, don't see a thing." He leaned close and asked in an undertone, "Are we lost?"

She had felt they were lost the moment they left the main troop area. But she couldn't say that. She shrugged. "I'll check our location with dead reckoning again."

They both climbed down. The guys crowded around her as she checked the odometer reading and her compass. "From this, it looks like we're right where we're supposed to be."

"Then why aren't we there?" Joe, the squad leader, asked, sounding edgy.

Joe's words sparked a breakout of grumbling, and Carly held up a hand to halt murmurs. Her mind zipped through all her options and found the remaining one. "I'll check it one more way. The map Haskell gave me isn't for ground use. See?" She pointed to the map. "It's marked as made by the British Airways. The distances could just be wrong. And the topography might have just been roughed in." She looked to Bowie. "I need something like a stick, about this long." She held her hands about two feet apart.

"You goin' to try the shadow-tip method of reckoning to check your compass?" he asked.

She nodded.

"Okay." He ran back to the truck and popped the hood. He came up with the oil dipstick. As he ran toward her, he wiped the oil from the stick on a rag and then handed it to her.

She smiled her thanks and stepped over to a flat area blown clean by the wind. Bowie's quiet confidence was keeping the rest of the squad from voicing doubt. Trying to look sure of herself, she stuck the dipstick into the ground. Then she picked up a rock and marked where the shadow of the tip fell on the ground. "We wait about fifteen minutes and we'll mark it again."

"I don't have a clue what you're doing," Sam said.

"I'm finding due north so I can check the accuracy of my compass. If my compass and the shadow tip coincide, I'll know if we're on course. And if not, I can fix it."

The guys looked to her and then at Bowie, who began doing some stretching exercises, looking completely unconcerned about whether they were lost or not. "Feels good to be out of the truck," he said in an unconcerned voice.

Carly took a cautious deep breath. *Dear Lord, let me be on course.*

The fifteen minutes crawled by. Finally, Carly set another rock at the new shadow tip and drew a straight line in the dirt connecting the two. Then she placed the toe of her left boot at the first mark and the toe of the right foot on the second. "I'm facing due north now." She pulled the compass from her pocket. "And my compass is right on. Gentlemen, we are on course. We just need to go a little farther. The map deceived us about the distance. And I think we've been going a bit slower because I've cautioned Bowie about *sabhkas.*"

"What?"

"Salt marshes," Bowie answered. "Kind of like a dry swamp if we get into them."

"Yeah, we get into one of those and with a little drizzle, we're stuck till they get the big tow truck out here for us," Carly added.

"And wouldn't Haskell just love that?" Joe added. "Okay," said he said to the platoon, "you heard Carly. We've just got a ways to go."

They all hustled back into their vehicles and Bowie set off again. The topography changed over the next few miles. It had more contour than the open expanse behind them. Berms of sand and rock made it impossible to drive in a straight line as they had been. The wind had died down as night was falling. As Bowie drove on the leeside of one of the tall berms, Carly heard something odd. A clicking noise. "What's that?"

Bowie shifted into neutral and put his head out the window. The truck behind them halted, too. Over the idling hum of their motors, that same clicking noise came again.

"Sounds like something out of an old war movie," Bowie muttered.

The innocent comment sparked a dreadful thought. "Shut off your motor and radio Joe to do the same, and tell everyone to be quiet," Carly said, urgency and caution icing her nerves. "I'm going to go to the top of the berm and take a look." She grabbed her binoculars. She let herself out of the truck, careful not to make any noise. Heart pounding, she ran lightly over the sand, mounted the side of the berm, making sure of her footing at each step. Near the top, she lay on her belly. She lifted her binoculars.

CHAPTER TWELVE

Like a white-hot blade, sheer terror seared through Carly. Two enemy tanks were rolling over sand and around berms, rattling with the tinny sound she and Bowie had heard. Choking down nausea she closed her eyes, praying that when she opened them the tanks would have disappeared. Fighting hysteria, she bit down so hard on her tongue that she tasted blood. Could this be some odd desert phenomenon, like a mirage? But mirages didn't rattle with the scrape of metal against metal, and she wasn't half-dead of thirst and susceptible to hallucinations. She opened her eyes. The tanks were still headed straight for them.

She threw herself down the berm, skidding and sliding on the sand and rubble. She raced to the HEMTT, straight to Bowie, and leaped inside. "Tanks," she gasped. "Tell Joe."

Bowie grabbed the shortwave radio and then cursed. "It's dead." He jumped out of the truck and ran back to Joe. Carly followed at his heels. She swallowed the shriek at the back of her her throat and said in a low voice, conscious of how sound could travel in the dry air, "Joe, two Iraqi tanks headed this way."

Joe switched off his truck. He jumped out and dashed up the hill near where Carly had been and peered over the top. Within seconds, he was back with them. "Everyone, get your weapons ready. There's a chance they might pass us by. It'll be black in a few minutes, and they're moving slow. Now!" Bowie sprinted back to the HEMTT and silenced the motor. Joe grabbed Carly's shoulder. "Did we cross the border?"

Her pulse raced and her mouth was dry. "No, even if our map is skewed, we're miles from it. They must be lost."

"Or Iraq is starting something." Joe swore. "I can't raise anyone on the shortwave. That means the Iraqis could be jamming it, or the desert wind might be mucking up stuff." He swore again. "Get back up on that ridge and give us warning if they head this way. They shouldn't try to go over that berm. It's a high one. It will be easier for them to go another way. Then they could miss us in the dark." Joe gave her a gentle but urgent shove. "Now."

Panting, Carly scurried up the berm again and just below its lip, flattened herself on her belly and lifted the binoculars. Daylight was just a glimmer on the barren horizon of shifting sand. Would the berm and the night be enough to hide their two trucks?

Suddenly the tanks stopped. A soldier popped out of the hatch of one and scrambled over to the other. She heard scraps of Arabic words on the night wind. The voices sounded worried. Were they lost? Were their radios acting up, too? Or were they talking about the Americans, deciding whether to attack them?

The weapons Carly's squad had brought along were no match for a tank, even if they used the M203 grenade launcher in the back of Joe's truck. Her whole squad could end up being killed or taken prisoner. Naked terror made Carly's insides shake. She felt nauseated. The memory of the Arab grabbing her in Riyadh swooped to mind. Arabs had no respect for women like her, women who did a man's job and didn't wear *abayahs* and veils. She gasped silently, pushing down a consuming panic.

Through the haze, the Sundays she'd gone to church with Chloe and Nate flooded back clear in her mind. These memories eased her pounding heart, let her draw breath. Chloe had taught her that God was equal to any challenge. And Carly needed help, help no human could give her. *Now.*

Dear God, don't let them see us. Hide us from their sight. I'm the navigator. I don't think I read the map wrong, but I might have. Don't let my friends suffer because I didn't get them where we were supposed to go. Dear God, don't let the Iraqis see or hear us. Dear God, I'm only seventeen. I don't want to die out here in this desert.

Ivy Manor, December 27, 1990

Sitting on their colonial four-poster, Nate watched his wife pack to leave. She had to go back to New York for a few days, but he'd gotten the week off and was staying at Ivy Manor. They'd decided Chloe shouldn't be alone after the first Christmas without Kitty. And Michael would enjoy special time alone with his great-grandmother.

But all this was secondary in Nate's mind. *I have to find*

a way to get through to you, Leigh. If he didn't, soon the gap between them might widen so far, their marriage could be damaged beyond repair. *I can't let that happen.* "Why did your mother go back to Arlington yesterday?"

Leigh was folding her clothing neatly into the dark bag lying open on the Wedding Ring quilt. She didn't meet his eyes. "I don't know. Perhaps she had social engagements."

He never became inured to his wife's fair beauty, a beauty she never used to manipulate him. His Leigh always came right at him, honest and outspoken. He loved that about her, yet it sometimes drove him crazy. "You mean you think she had a date with Dan?"

Leigh shrugged.

"What's wrong with your mother dating someone?" he pressed her, watching emotions flit over her expressive face, her large blue eyes troubled. "I've been surprised she hasn't dated before this," he continued. "Your stepfather's been gone almost twenty years."

"If Mom wants to date," Leigh snapped, "it's none of my business."

"You're exactly right, but you know and I know you don't mean that. You were icily polite to Dan all day yesterday." He took a chance. "Did you do that just to get back at your mother for siding with Carly over enlisting?"

Leigh turned away and went to the armoire. She glanced inside as if making sure she hadn't left anything there. Ignoring his question, she said, "I'll be back before New Year's Eve."

"That's good of you," Nate murmured, letting irritation slip into his tone. He couldn't let her get away with running this conversation. He had something to say, and he was going to say it his way.

"I have to get shots," she retorted, "and the magazine is still working on my visa application."

"What happens if it doesn't come through in time?" He hoped that would happen. So much easier and not his fault.

"It will," Leigh said with evident confidence and unconcern.

"I've been thinking," he said, ready to broach his real concern. "I want to find a counselor and get some help for us, for our marriage."

Leigh halted where she stood and turned to gawk at him. "Counseling? I can't believe you want to go to a counselor. Don't you want *me* just to go to one and get fixed?"

"Why do you have so little faith in me?" Nate asked, his patience holding. She looked so exquisite, so proud standing there in the winter light. His hand itched to brush her soft ivory cheek. "Why do you distrust my every word?"

Looking abashed, Leigh went over and sat down on the bed beside him, making the soft mattress dip. "Is that how you see me?"

He let the back of his hand sample the velvet of her cheek then. "Do you think I'm being disingenuous? I'm talking about us. I'm not going to bring up you and your mother or you and Carly. This is about us, just us."

"How do you think a counselor could help us?" She glanced out the window, chin down. She looked like a lost little girl.

He ran his index finger around her delicate earlobe. "I think we need to come to terms about boundaries. Both of us have demanding careers. That's good, but it's not good if they cut into our time together too often."

"You're just saying the same old thing." She looked into his eyes, defiant. "You think my career means more to me than my family."

"I think that sometimes your actions make it appear that way," he said very careful to keep his tone even. "But I am very sure that, however much you irritate me, you love me, Michael, and Carly." He lifted the side of her shoulder-length hair. He ran his fingers through its silk. He never tired of touching it. "It's just that you get distracted. A part of you is still driven to achieve. Again, that's good, but it can take over a life and squeeze everything else out."

She turned away from him, her head bent. "I do love you, Nate. But my career is at that stage where I'm getting to do things that I only dreamed of twenty, even ten years ago. It's not that I want to be away from you."

He put a tender hand on her shoulder and she fell silent. "Leigh, we need to do some work on our marriage. We're a team and team members don't make decisions—like this trip to Saudi—without discussing it first with the other team member."

She turned back to him. "I want to do this assignment. And I don't think you're going to divorce me over it, are you?" She nailed him with her eyes, but guilt colored her face.

"No, but I think that you're making a big mistake and that you should have discussed it with me first." He bent close enough to smell her floral shampoo.

Looking away, Leigh stared at the portrait of Lily Leigh Carlyle, her great-grandmother, dressed as a Gibson girl in the 1890s. Had Lily ever had problems like these? "Why do you have to make so much good sense? It's irritating."

He half-grinned. "We've gotten in the bad habit of being angry and snapping at each other. I want to break it and do better." He ran his hand up her arm, trying to remind her of the bonds between them, both physical and emotional. "What about it?"

She sat very still. "Okay. Shall I find a counselor or shall you?" She hazarded a glance at him.

Relief like warm honey flooded him, filling all the jagged cracks etched by their discord. "Why don't we both look into it and come up with a few to try out? We may not find the one we want to work with right off the bat, and I don't want to just pick a name out of the phone book."

"Okay. When I get back from Saudi, we'll set up some appointments."

He nodded and braced himself to bring up one more point, one that could blow the lid off everything. "Now, one thing more. Have you thought of how your trip is going to affect Michael?"

"What do you mean?" She stood up, looking perplexed.

"He's already really scared about his sister being in a war."

She frowned. "How do you know that?"

"I was home when his teacher called last week. She says that he's been acting out in school."

"How?"

"Fighting. Since picking fights wasn't usual behavior for Michael, she had the school counselor talk to him. The counselor dug out the fact that Michael is very worried about his older sister's being killed or hurt in this war."

"Why didn't you tell me?" Leigh reached out to him.

Nate took her cold, slender hand. "I was hoping for a moment alone together and the holiday ate up all our time. But the counselor suggested you and I not discuss your going to Saudi in front of Michael. That's why I've kept quiet. I didn't want Michael to overhear any angry words or sense any more conflict between us."

Sitting, Leigh said, "I didn't realize."

"He loves his sister and his mom, and he doesn't want anything to happen to them." Nate stroked her gleaming hair back from her face. "I love his mom."

Leigh leaned forward and pressed her soft, urgent lips to his. "I love his dad."

Nate drew out the kiss, feeling their long attraction flare to life again and wanting to prolong it, cherish it.

There came a sharp tap on the door. Rose didn't wait for them to answer. She pushed the door open. "I'm sorry to bother you two, but you got to come. Miss Chloe is bad. I think she needs to go to the hospital."

"What?" Parting, Nate and Leigh jumped up and followed Rose down the hall.

In the next bedroom, Chloe sat up in bed. Her face was very white. "I'm sorry," she said and then coughed into a white tissue. "I think I may . . . be coming down with something."

Leigh hurried to her side. "Did you have your flu shot this fall?"

"Yes, but I feel so weak and my chest hurts."

"I think she may be getting pneumonia," Rose inter-jected. "I've seen it start this way. I was coming along the hall and I heard that rattle deep in her throat. I heard that rattle before, and it always means pneumonia."

Leigh pressed her hand to Chloe's forehead. "She feels feverish. Let's call the doctor and see if he can stop by."

"I'll do it." Nate picked up the bedside phone. He watched Leigh stroke her grandmother's cheek and speak soft words of love. His Leigh did have a full heart of love. She just didn't always show it.

Saudi Arabia, December 27, 1990

It had been the longest night of Carly's life—the most miser-able, the coldest, the most frightening. She'd never felt more vulnerable. The fear that the tanks would return and find them had woven her stomach into an intricate rosary of knots. Breathing had become difficult. Now she gazed at the first pink of dawn glowing on the horizon and praised God with her whole heart.

The tanks had passed them by in the night. The berm and darkness had hidden them—or maybe it had been the hand of God. This feeling of connecting with God was so new. Maybe only such overwhelming fear drove a person this close to God. The scene of Kitty's deathbed came up in her mind. Chloe, Minnie, and Kitty had held hands and prayed for God's forgiveness, thanking him for his grace. Carly swal-lowed a sob and tried to clear her mind. *Thank you, Father. You saved us. Thank you.*

"Well, we made it through the night." Joe voiced her sentiments. He sat beside her on the top of the berm, his knees bent and his elbows resting on them. "Now if we could just figure out where the heck we are, we could get this all over with and head back."

"I'm sure we are on course," Carly insisted. The tightness around her heart was still loosening. "If we just go ahead, we should be okay."

"You're sure, Carly?" Joe asked.

She nodded. "I'm sorry, Joe. I've done the best I can with this lousy map." She waved it at him. "I'm wondering if the Marines moved, or maybe the right coordinates weren't given in the first place."

Joe shrugged. "I believe you. You're sharp and usually right on. We'll go on a few more miles and hope that the shortwave will start working again. What a Godforsaken place."

"Yeah, it really makes me want to go home and see green grass and blue rivers again."

Bowie joined them, standing tall behind Carly. "I know what you mean. I been thinking about fields of ripe corn and the smell of red earth after a hard rain."

Joe snorted. "Let's not all start up. I don't want us all humming 'The Green, Green Grass of Home.' Come on. We'll eat some MREs and head out. Those Marines have to be somewhere around here."

All ten gathered around the two trucks, swatting flies away from their "meals ready to eat," MREs, and drinking lukewarm bottled water. Then they headed out. Carly sat quietly beside Bowie, feeling dirty and wrung out. "I keep wondering if the Marines' OP moved or something." If only they could find the Marines this morning, Carly could relax.

And then she saw it—a Humvee draped with netting. "That's one of ours." She pointed toward the windshield. "Honk or flash your lights."

The Humvee headed right for them. Joe stopped his truck and Bowie followed suit. With weapons, everyone climbed out, keeping the trucks between them and the strangers.

The Humvee stopped about ten feet away. "Hey! You the bunch that was supposed to bring us supplies?" Two Marines climbed out and came forward, also armed.

Joe identified their squad and the Marines did the same. Then all of them lowered their weapons.

"What took you guys so long?" one Marine asked.

"This lousy map," Carly replied and offered it to him. "Look at this and tell me how wrong it is."

"Hey," the Marine said, opening his eyes wide, "you got a woman with you."

Carly chuckled, near weeping over their deliverance. "Glad your faculties are still working." She waved the map in front of him, blinking away tears. "Where is your OP on here?"

They spread it out on the hood of the Humvee. "Well, from this, I'd say they got you close. But it's good we came out looking for you. We're about four miles south of where they told you we were."

"Did you see any Iraqi tanks last night?" Joe asked.

"Tanks?" The Marine stared at him.

"Yeah," Carly agreed, "we saw two Iraqi tanks back

there." She pointed to the spot on the map. "Last night just at dark. We think they might have been lost."

"Did you radio it in?" the Marine asked.

"We tried," Joe said. "Our shortwaves haven't worked since yesterday afternoon."

"Well, come on. Follow us. You can unload our supplies and we'll try to raise our commander and alert him to tank activity in the area. It's probably good your radios didn't work. All messages need to be encoded."

In a few short miles, Carly's squad was unloading fresh water, food, and other supplies to the OP, which was occupied by five Marines. Their radio worked, and the Marines reported, in code, the tank sighting and the fact that the resupply trucks had arrived and would head back soon.

Watching the last of the supplies being set on the sand, Carly leaned against the side of the truck, still hollow with relief. She hadn't led her squad astray.

"Hey, you're a sight for sore eyes," one of the Marines said, walking up to her. "We haven't seen a woman in a few weeks."

"Oh?" Carly grinned at him cautiously, hoping he wasn't going to be a jerk.

"Yeah, have you been off base at all?"

"Once. I didn't really care for it. I had to wear that black getup, and some Arab tried to pick me up and run off with me anyway. And their police came and told *us* not to cause trouble."

He shrugged. "They got weird ideas. Where you from?"

"New York City."

Bowie walked over. "Carly, Joe says come on. We're heading back now."

Carly moved to follow Bowie.

"Hey," the Marine said, stopping her with a hand on her sleeve, "you dating anybody?"

Carly started to reply, but Bowie stopped her. "Yeah, she's my girl—when we're off duty."

"The story of my life," the Marine said with a shake of his head.

Carly chuckled and waved as she headed for the truck. Bowie's possessive words had given her a thrill.

Joe and the other guys were waiting for her. "Well, it wasn't you. It was the map. And now we just have to get back before nightfall."

Carly suddenly felt lighter than air. "Right! And even Haskell will look good to me."

All the guys laughed as if she'd really said something witty.

Bowie got in as she slammed her door. "That Marine come on to you?"

She smiled. "No, he just wanted to talk to a female for a few minutes."

Bowie made a sound of disbelief. "Wanted to do more than talk to you."

"Yeah, but that doesn't mean anything, right? You told him the truth." A smile spread across her face.

Bowie nodded and turned the big truck around, heading them home, or at least to the post they called home. Carly looked out her window and smiled again. *Thanks, God. Just thanks.*

Hospital in Croftown

An hour later, Leigh worried and walked beside her grand-mother as Chloe's squeaky gurney was being pushed back to the unevenly lit ER. Chloe's doctor had told them to take her straight to the ER.

Chloe had just had a chest X-ray. Nate stood when he saw Leigh. The nurse pushed the gurney into the white-curtained area and told them the doctor would join them as soon as the X-ray had been developed and he'd had a chance to view it. Leigh let Nate make the polite responses while she took Chloe's cool frail hand in hers. "Grandma, don't worry. You're going to be fine."

"I love you, too, sweetheart." Chloe's voice was thin and quiet. "But I have been feeling rundown ever since Kitty's funeral. Losing her has taken its toll on me."

These words hit Leigh hard. The old saying about deaths coming in threes struck her again. She had not thought of the possibility of her grandmother dying. Chloe was indestructible.

"Even if it is pneumonia," Nate said reassuringly, "it's just started and they have good antibiotics now."

"I think I'll just rest for a few minutes." Chloe squeezed Leigh's hand. "I'm so very tired." She closed her eyes.

Nate went to Leigh's side and took her hands in his, silently giving her comfort.

Leigh needed that boost. *Michael is worried about my going to Saudi Arabia—is worried about his sister's safety. Why didn't that occur to me? Have I really become so self-absorbed?*

Right then Leigh was not sure of anything except that Chloe needed to get better, and that she wouldn't leave until Chloe was home, breathing easy. She looked into Nate's face. "I'm going to call Dorcas and tell her I won't be coming to

New York. I'll just have to get the shots I need here and do what I can long-distance."

"You should call your mother, too," Nate pointed out.

"I will, but I can take care of Grandma." *Nate, it's time I accepted responsibility for my family.* "I'll be right back."

Late that afternoon, back on the good highway, Carly saw the U.S. troop area ahead on the horizon. Within ten minutes, Bowie pulled the truck into the garage and Haskell was waiting for them. His hands were on his hips and he was trying to look disgruntled. But Carly could read the relief in the lines of his face.

"You sure took your sweet time," Haskell growled predictably. "That's what I get for putting the woman in charge of navigation."

Carly walked over to him and put her hands on her hips. "An accurate map might have helped me."

"I gave you the map I was given." He shrugged.

"That's what I thought you'd say."

"You could all use a shower," Haskell commented, wrinkling his nose. "Report for duty as usual tomorrow."

An impromptu cheer went up from the squad. And before Haskell could change his mind, they all jogged off toward their quarters.

"I'll come and walk you to mess for lunch," Bowie called to her.

She nodded and waved, already anticipating the feeling of being in a refreshing shower, shampooing her hair. As she neared her barracks, she wondered about the vast difference between the night of terror and this sunny, warm day back at what she called home. She was more exhausted by these widely divergent and heightened emotions than by the lack of sleep. And this was definitely one experience she wouldn't be writing home about.

A radio nearby was playing "I Want to Know What Love Is" as she walked inside her tent and saw three letters lying on her pillow. One was from Alex. One was from her great-grandmother. And one was from her birth father. She sat down and, forgetting about the shower, tore open her father's letter. Would he tell her his name this time?

After Chloe had been wheeled upstairs to her room, Leigh dialed her mother's phone number. She got the answering machine and left a message, telling Bette about Chloe's pneumonia and her room number at the hospital.

Outside, as Bette fumbled with her key at the back door, she heard the phone ring. She made it inside just as Leigh hung up. She'd caught the words "Chloe" and "pneumonia." *Pneumonia?* Bette quickly took off her coat, hat, and gloves and hung them up. She reached for the phone but before she could dial, it rang again. "Hello?"

It was her doctor.

After he ended their brief conversation, Bette stood holding the receiver. Her mind stuttered on his frightening words like an old-fashioned phonograph needle stuck in a groove of an old record.

CHAPTER THIRTEEN

Saudi Arabia, January 2, 1991

Perched on the fender of an HEMTT, Carly leaned over the side of the mammoth truck, her head under the raised hood. She was painstakingly taking out spark plugs, cleaning them and putting them back, sand-free. Her life seemed similarly clogged. The days since returning from the supply mission had been a tangle of emotions.

She had to find a way to sort everything out, put her uncertainties into perspective. Saddam Hussein's UN deadline was only thirteen days away—along with her mother's arrival. But as part of four hundred thousand soldiers, she might not see her mother. A hot war to deal with might even stop her mother's meddling. But Carly felt all of the turmoil would be easier to cope with if she could settle her nerves.

So far, she'd made no progress. After the night in the desert, she'd returned to those three letters on her cot. Chloe's letter had been the usual cheery, chatty note. But her father's letter had contained a promise, one both welcome and disturbing. He would come to meet her when she returned from Saudi—if she wanted him to. Her insides had buzzed at that promise and its qualifier. She wanted to meet her father, but how would that affect her already rocky relationship with her mother? Why was her life so complicated? Other people had mothers and fathers without all this craziness added on. She looked up and out of the small window nearby.

Outside, the desert daylight was muted by a sandstorm in progress. The soldiers had closed the doors and windows of the garage, but that didn't keep out the insidious, swirling sand. Carly breathed through her nose to filter out the sand ambient in the air. She could still taste its grit on her tongue.

And the third, Alex's letter, had asked for advice. Still stateside, Alex was attracted to a guy in her company who seemed nice. But Alex was still going to counseling. Should she tell him that? Carly wondered why Alex wanted her advice. What did she know?

Giving a soft grunt, Bowie called her back to the present. He was underneath the truck, changing oil and putting on another new filter. Having him near always gave her a good feeling. Joe's radio was softly playing "Lean on Me." She recalled Bowie's statement to the Marine that she was his girl. "Bowie's girl." It sounded good. But was she just leaning on him?

Carly felt that might be true in a sense, but she did care for him. She also sensed Bowie still held back just a bit of his heart from her. He was protecting himself. Did he really believe that they were too different to be a couple? The memory of his stolen kiss in the shadows the night before curled her toes inside her desert combat boots. The man did know how to kiss.

Haskell had told them a few days before that the brass had decided that the two Iraqi tanks had been lost since they'd been seen only by their supply squad, and the Iraqis hadn't fired on anyone. They'd just disappeared. And for some reason Carly's nightmares had slacked off since her terrifying experience. She would have thought that a night spent in the desert with deadly enemy tanks lurking nearby would have doubled, tripled her fear. Did the waning of the nightmares mean her fears were ebbing? Or was this just a brief time-out?

Suddenly a siren sounded, droning over the constant swishing sound of the sandstorm. Haskell shouted, "Get on your NBC gear!"

Carly pushed the spark plug into place and jumped down. Her nuclear biological chemical gear was on the ground nearby. She pulled the mask over her head and then tugged on the pants, jacket, boots, and gloves. All around her, the guys rushed to do the same. When she was finished, she looked around. They looked back at her through their masks like outer-space monsters from a 1950s film.

The rubberized outfit shut off any air to her skin, which was its job, but this immediately caused Carly to break into a sweat. It was January, but it still hit a sweaty eighty or ninety degrees every day though the nights could drop to freezing.

Suddenly, memories of the gas chamber test during basic training gagged Carly. Desperately, she tamped down the urge to rip her mask off. *I have to keep it on. This might not be a drill.* Hussein might have really launched a missile armed with toxic chemicals. She tried to slow her rapid breathing, control her throat.

If she didn't get a grip, she could easily hyperventilate and pass out. And wouldn't her sergeant love that? Carly would never hear the end of it. Relentless, the sensation of being strangled from inside was fighting its way to the top of her consciousness. If it took over, she didn't think she could keep it together.

Carly closed her eyes. *God, help me out again. If I take my mask off and this is for real, I'll die. Help me out just as you did on the desert that night, making the lost tanks miss us in the dark.*

Minutes passed. "Okay," Haskell ordered through his mask, "go on with your work until we get the all-clear."

The sergeant's order struck Carly as ridiculous. She looked down at the large, clumsy rubber gloves she wore. Work? How? She waved her hands at Haskell. "I can't pick up a spark plug with these on." Her voice came out muffled, and the effort to speak spiked her panic. "What should I do instead?" she gasped. The rest of the platoon nodded in agreement and also held up their hands. Haskell looked disgusted. His phone rang and he jogged to it.

Bowie came up beside her. She turned to him, his nearness welcome. Her pulse and breathing were still escalating. Her heart felt as if it were bouncing off her breastbone. She began hiccoughing inside the restrictive mask. How long would this go on? Would she have to wear the mask for the rest of the day? How long before the poison gases dissipated in the strong desert wind?

A second siren sounded. "All clear!" Haskell shouted, his

gas mask already under his arm. "It was just a test. Keep your gear with you at all times from now on. Intelligence suggests that we might have the real thing at any time."

Carly wrenched off her mask, gasping for air. Anytime? Did he have to add that?

A strong hand gripped her shoulder. "You okay?"

She turned to Bowie and tried to smile. "I didn't like the gas chamber in basic." *Make that: I freaked out.*

"Well, who did?" Bowie tugged off his gloves and bent to pull off his boots.

"I'll be fine." *As long as these are just drills.* Would she panic, completely lose control, if it were the real thing?

"You want to go to church on Sunday?" Bowie asked in a low voice as he pulled off the second boot.

Carly stared at him. Where had that come from?

"I haven't been since we got here, but I think it might be a good idea." He glanced up.

Carly slowly nodded. "Yeah, I'll go with you." Had this chemical warfare drill done the same number on Bowie? *God, I need you. This is all too scary and too real for me to handle alone.* And wasn't that what Chloe always told her? She heard her great-grandmother's voice saying, "We can't do this life without God, honey."

"Yes," Carly said. "Bowie, remind me. I'd like to go and take communion."

Ivy Manor, January 2, 1991

Leigh and Nate rode in the front seat and Grandma Chloe, pale and weak, in the back. She'd just been released from the hospital after her strenuous bout with pneumonia. She would be on antibiotics for another week and required careful nursing. Her own eyelids drooping, Leigh was exhausted from spending most nights sleeping in the chair beside her grandmother's bed. Chloe had begged her to go home, but Leigh hadn't felt right about it. Chloe had been dangerously ill, and Leigh wouldn't let her slip away without a family member there. A spasm of fear jerked through Leigh as she tried to appear unconcerned.

"Chloe, Michael is really looking forward to seeing you at home again," Nate said as he turned onto the road to Ivy Manor.

"I love that little boy."

Her grandmother's breathless voice tightened Leigh's nerves another notch. "Me, too."

Nate moved his right hand over until it covered Leigh's resting on the seat. She turned her palm up and gripped his comforting hand. She'd miss him so when she left for Saudi Arabia later that month. "Mother is supposed to meet us at home," she said.

"Bette has been looking tired," Chloe said.

Leigh nodded. Her mother had looked more than tired. Bette looked distressed and preoccupied. Could it be that man she'd brought to Christmas dinner? Was he pressuring her mother into a relationship she didn't feel ready for? Leigh smiled to herself. No matter how handsome Dan Greenfield was, he'd find out her mother was never easily persuaded.

Ivy Manor loomed ahead of Leigh. The January clouds parted and sunlight flowed over the old house. It needed a new coat of white paint. Why hadn't she noticed that before?

Someday the house would be her responsibility. It had stood for nearly three centuries and been owned that long by her family, something very few American families could say. Love for Ivy Manor and for the woman who was synonymous with it expanded inside her heart. *I love you, Grandma Chloe. And you're going to get better.*

Bette was waiting at the back door for them, along with Rose and Michael. "Mother," Bette said as Nate carried Chloe inside, "are you sure they should have released you from the hospital?"

Leigh noticed that her mother's hair wasn't styled as it usually was. It was a mess. What was that all about?

"I was sick of the food and dreary room," Chloe said in the breathless voice that spoke of lingering lung congestion.

"Well, that don't surprise me or anybody else," Rose replied. "I got a pot of homemade chicken dumpling soup on the stove for you."

"I feel better already." Chloe sniffed the air. "And I bet Michael would love those dumplings, too."

"Hi, Grandma Chloe, I'm glad you got to come home." Little Michael patted her forearm as he ran to keep up with his father as he carried her through the dining room.

Soon they were all upstairs in Chloe's faded bedroom, still the way it had been the day Roarke had died. Nate settled Chloe onto her bed. After switching on the multicolored Tiffany bedside lamp, Bette and Leigh lifted away her coat and scarf and helped her lie down. "I'm sorry, children. I think I'll need to rest a few minutes before I come down for lunch."

"I can bring it up on a tray," Rose offered.

"No, I'd like to see if I can come down and sit with the family for a meal."

"You ring that bell. I don't want you walking those steps without someone with you," Rose ordered.

Chloe replied with a nod.

"Can I lay down with Grandma Chloe?" Michael asked.

"Yes, please," Chloe said, touching his shoulder.

"Just for a moment," Leigh said. "When she tells you it's time to leave, you go to your room or come downstairs. Promise?" Michael nodded earnestly.

Rose smoothed Chloe's pillow and checked her forehead for fever, then followed the rest of them out of the room.

Downstairs they all gravitated to the kitchen, warm and fragrant with chicken soup. Nate and Leigh sat at the table. "Mother looks really weak," Bette said, wringing her hands. "I've never seen her this frail."

"I'm sorry I've got to go back to New York today," Nate said, "but I have to be on duty tonight."

"Me, too," Leigh added, watching her mother's hands with apprehension. "I've got to clear my desk before I go to Saudi on the thirteenth. And Michael starts school again in three days."

Bette stared at them, her hands frozen. "We can't leave Mother alone."

Leigh looked at Bette. "I thought you were staying," she balked. "I thought that's why you came today."

"I can't." Bette wrung her hands almost frantically. "I have to be back to Virginia today, this afternoon before three."

Leigh gawked at her. "You're leaving?"

"Yes, I have to." Bette paced in front of them. "I'm sorry."

"You can't leave," Leigh objected. "I've got to go. I was supposed to be in the office on the twenty-eighth."

"I can't stay," Bette repeated, drawing toward the back door.

"Well, I'll be here," Rose said, "but I'm not family, and Miss Chloe needs family now. Losing Miss Kitty has really taken the stuffin' out of her. She needs family."

"Mother, Nate and I are both working." Leigh stood up. "I stayed with Grandmother at the hospital practically night and day. You came for two short visits. Is Dan Greenfield keeping you so busy—"

"I can't explain. Something's come up."

Leigh gazed into her mother's pained but stubborn face.

"Leigh, I know you need to get back," Nate said, "but your schedule is more flexible than mine. I'll take Michael home with me—"

"No!" Michael yelled from the doorway from the dining room. "I don't want to go home without my mama!"

Nate rose and went to him. "It'll be okay."

Michael ran around his father, straight to his mother. "I don't want to go. I want to stay here with you and Grandma Chloe." He wrapped his arms tightly around Leigh's waist. "I don't want you to go!"

Leigh looked to Nate. He came over and put an arm around her shoulders and a hand on Michael's. "Calm down, son. Tell me: what's the matter?"

Michael clung harder to Leigh. "I don't want to be away from my mama. I don't want to."

"Mother," Leigh said to Bette, "Nate, Michael, and I need to go home together. You *have* to stay with Grandma."

Bette looked wildly at them and then hurried toward the back door, grabbing her gray wool coat as she went. "I can't. I just can't." A sob punctuated her words.

Dumbfounded, Leigh stared as the door closed after her mother. What was going on? Bette wasn't acting anything like her calm, self-possessed mother.

Nate put his reassuring arm around Leigh and murmured, "You're going to have to find out what's upsetting her."

"You got that right," Rose agreed.

Saudi Arabia, January 10, 1991

After taking communion for the first time since her visit to Ivy Manor, Carly sat beside Bowie in a tent church, the *shammal* blowing as usual, ruffling and billowing the canvas. Beside them sat Lorelle and Sam. Carly felt an ease she hadn't experienced since she arrived in Saudi. Taking communion had fed her spirit, made her feel a part of God's power and love in a fresh way. She noticed a few others from her platoon, whom she'd not thought religious, were present, too. Maybe being in a combat zone heightened everything, made every emotion—the good and the bad—sharper, deeper. Perhaps this drew many back to faith.

At the front of rows of soldiers on folding chairs, a uniformed chaplain was preaching on 2 Corinthians 4:6–9. He read:

For God, who commanded the light to shine out of the darkness, hath shined in our hearts, to give the light of knowledge of the glory of God in the face of Jesus Christ. But we have this treasure in earthen vessels, that the excellency of the power may be of God, and not of us. We are troubled on every side, yet not distressed; we are perplexed, but not in despair; persecuted, but not forsaken; cast down, but not destroyed.

Carly couldn't remember ever hearing this text preached on before. She had no trouble seeing herself as a plain, earthen, probably cracked, vessel. She'd never felt secure or whole. Never.

And after the kidnapping, these insecurities had grown. Not even taking tae kwan do and karate for seven years, or running marathons where she put herself to the test physically, had soothed those deep, nagging fears. Did this all go back to not knowing her father? Could that be what made her feel isolated, orphaned? She thought wryly of Alex's concern over telling the guy who liked her about going to counseling. *Maybe I'm the one who needs counseling.*

Bowie took her hand. She closed her eyes, letting the comfort of his strong, rough hand work its way through her. She saw clearly that Bowie had been a gift from God. His quiet strength and confidence in her had carried her over the first few terrifying weeks in a war zone. *Thanks for Bowie, Lord. And for Joe and Sam and Lorelle—all the friends you've blessed me with.*

The chaplain ended his message with verse 17: "For our

light affliction, which is but for a moment, worketh for us a far more exceeding and eternal weight of glory." Then he asked them to rise and open their hymnals.

The chaplain possessed a strong melodious baritone, and he led them in a hymn that sounded so familiar to Carly. As they sang the chorus, "Jesus paid it all, all to Him I owe," she remembered that Rose and her daughter had sung that hymn at Aunt Kitty's funeral. Carly stared down at the tattered hymnal that looked as if it had survived many wars and skirmishes. The first verse of the hymn hit her: "I hear the Savior say, Thy strength indeed is small; Child of weakness, watch and pray, Find in Me thine all in all."

Carly closed her eyes again. *I am weak, Lord. I don't have much strength. But how do I find my all in all in you? What does that mean? I need to know.*

Arlington, Virginia, January 10, 1991

In the lavender nightgown and matching velour robe she'd worn all day, Bette glanced at the blackness outside her kitchen window. She looked around imagining that Ted was just in the other room and that she was brewing tea for both of them—an exquisite torture. But she was glad that Ted wasn't there. He wouldn't have to deal with her problem.

Dan's face came to mind. He'd phoned repeatedly this week, but she hadn't returned his calls. She and Dan had just been getting to know each other. If she told him, he would only back off, so why make him feel guilty for nothing? *I'm going to die anyway.* She'd tried to rid herself of that thought but had failed.

The stainless steel kettle whistled and Bette took it off the burner, wondering why she'd wanted tea in the first place.

A knock came at the back door. And then before she could move, a key was turned in the lock and the door opened. Leigh stepped inside.

Bette stared at her. "What's wrong?" She moved to the counter for support. "It's not Mother. She's not—"

"Grandma is sound asleep and is doing better." Leigh took off her blue down jacket and hung it on the peg by the back door, the way she had as a girl. Walking through that door had always comforted Leigh, brought memories of her stepfather and her little sister, Dory, and the untroubled days of childhood. But one look at her mother swept that illusion aside. "What I want to know is"—Leigh stopped directly in front of Bette—"what's wrong with you?"

Her mother looked away. "You've got enough on your plate right now, Leigh. Don't ask for problems. Did you get your visa?"

"Yes. Nate's going to take leave for the days I'm away, and Minnie will drive down with him to keep Grandma's spirits up. But you are the one who's got me worried. Now what is it?"

Bette turned away. "I'm making tea. Would you like some?"

Leigh put her hands on her mother's shoulders and turned her so they were face-to-face again. "I'll be glad to drink a cup with you *after* you tell me what's got you so upset."

Bette's composure crumbled before Leigh's eyes. Tears flowed down her cheeks.

"Mother, I love you. I need to know." Leigh squeezed Bette's shoulders. "Tell me."

Bette leaned her head onto Leigh's shoulder. "I've been diagnosed. . . ." Sobs shook her.

Leigh's breath caught in her throat. "What? Diagnosed with what?"

"Cancer."

The grim word wrapped around Leigh like a suffocating shroud. "Where?"

"My left breast."

Leigh experienced a moment of pure shock, then tightened her hold on her mother. "Oh, Mom." Leigh kissed her cheek and hugged her close. "Why didn't you tell us—me?"

Bette wept on her daughter's shoulder and just shook her head.

"How bad is it? Has it spread?" Leigh lifted her mother's chin.

Bette nodded miserably and wept more silent tears. "I didn't want to tell you. You're already worried enough about Carly and Mother."

"How far has it spread?"

Bette didn't reply.

"How far?" Leigh almost shook her.

"They think it may be in my lungs. I'm scheduled for a mastectomy on the seventeenth, then radiation and chemotherapy."

Leigh closed her eyes against this onslaught of disaster. "Mom," she whispered. "Mom."

Leigh clung to Bette and pushed down the hysteria that threatened. No wonder her mother had been distant and unnatural. Cancer. Once again the "deaths come in threes" mantra repeated in her mind. *No, I'm not superstitious, and I'm not losing anyone this year. Not without a good fight.*

"Mom, I wish you'd told me."

"I didn't want—"

"I know you didn't want to worry me. But you have worried us all anyway."

"I don't want you to tell Mother. She's just recuperating—"

"I will be telling everyone," Leigh said flatly and led her mother to a kitchen chair. "This isn't the Dark Ages. You're going to need a lot of support to fight this, and your family and your friends will be hurt if you don't trust them."

"No, Leigh, I won't have my mother told. Do you understand me?"

Leigh turned as she heard another car pull into the drive. Who would be visiting at this hour? Swift footsteps sounded, and then a brisk knock.

Chapter Fourteen

I don't want to see anyone," Bette said listlessly, resting her head in one hand.

The back door swung open and in walked Dan Greenfield. He looked questioningly at Bette and then Leigh. "Okay, I'm through trying to get to you by phone, Bette. Once and for all, what's wrong?"

Bette stood and turned to leave the room. In two strides, Dan was beside her and jerked her into his arms. "I'm not going to leave until you tell me."

"Dan, she's been diagnosed with breast cancer and has surgery scheduled on the seventeenth," Leigh informed him. "I just wormed it out of her."

"My poor girl." Dan leaned down and kissed Bette, pulling her closer and holding her.

Leigh observed this, her heart tightening and then lifting a bit. She found that most of the antagonism she'd felt for Dan at Christmas suddenly evaporated.

After Dan had kissed Bette, he tugged her back to her

chair and urged her to sit. He turned to Leigh. "What's the plan?"

Leigh looked to him and then her mother. Both of them were looking at her for guidance. Her responsibilities seemed to have multiplied in a moment. "Grandma Chloe is recovering slowly, steadily, but she still needs TLC," Leigh said. "And Dan, I think it would be best to take my mother back to Ivy Manor until her surgery."

"But you won't be here for my surgery. You have to go to Saudi," her mother protested in a worn-out tone.

Grandma Chloe, Michael, Carly, my job, and now my mother has cancer. I was supposed to go to Saudi. I can't go. Hot regret came and went in an instant. Leigh knew she had no choice. "The U.S. forces will have to take care of themselves," Leigh said. One last lightning strike of disappointment flashed through her and vanished. *Mother, you're more important than any story. And so are Michael, Nate, and Grandma Chloe.*

"Leigh," Bette said insistently, "I forbid you to tell your grandmother about my cancer until after the surgery." Bette stood up. "And I'm not going to Ivy Manor. I'm perfectly capable of staying here alone. Chloe is not well and is still heartsick over losing Kitty. I won't add to her burdens."

"Let's not discuss that right now," Dan said, easing Bette back into a kitchen chair. "We have time to decide all these things later."

Leigh drew in a deep breath, grateful for Dan's help. The words *breast cancer*, however, still sent shivers of ice through her. Though she began to go through the motions of making tea, her hands shook and she had to fight tears. Her mother's plea on that morning after Christmas came back to her, something like: "Can't there ever be peace between us?" And should Leigh tell Grandma Chloe or not? Leigh suddenly felt weak and inadequate. How would she juggle everything? But with her younger sister out of the country—who else was there?

Saudi Arabia, January 15, 1991

Carly stared up at the night sky, feeling oddly empty and on the verge of tears. Saddam Hussein had ignored the UN deadline. War could detonate at any moment. What would that mean? Would Iraqi planes soon be dropping bombs or worse, poisonous chemicals, onto their tents? They'd been repeatedly reminded of the order to carry their NBC warfare pouches with them everywhere.

Bowie stood beside her. "It feels funny, knowing we're here and a war is about to start. I don't know how I'm supposed to feel."

She turned to him, needing him, but not wanting to give in to this weakness. "I know. We've been working, preparing, and maintaining our vehicles to supply troops, but when, where, how?"

Bowie just shook his head.

"Something funny's going on at home, too," Carly confided. Maybe this was the reason behind her empty feeling. "When I read the last few letters from my family, I don't know . . . I can't really put my finger on it, but they're not telling me something."

"Wasn't your mom supposed to come over here?"

Carly nodded. Only something really important, something devastating, could have caused Leigh's absence. "Yeah, my mom isn't the type to up and change her mind." Carly swallowed to moisten her dry mouth. "I just wish I knew what was going on."

"Maybe you should ask."

Carly gazed into Bowie's clear, honest eyes and realized that she couldn't handle any bad news from home. "Maybe." *I can't think about that right now.*

Ivy Manor, January 15, 1991

Leigh paced the floor in her bedroom. The UN deadline had come and gone. She pressed both hands to her face as if holding back her raucous fears and doubts. *I was supposed to be in Saudi now. And should I tell Grandma Chloe about my mother or not?*

Nate walked into the bedroom and closed the door behind him. "I got Michael to bed. How are you doing?" He came up behind and wrapped his strong arms around her.

"I feel weighed down, Nate." *Nearly flattened.* Would the news of Bette's cancer crush Chloe's spirits? "First Kitty's death, then my grandmother's pneumonia, now Mom's cancer. And Carly is in a real war." Each beloved name and worry dropped and slid down her spine, pellets of cold lead.

"It's hard, I know." He kissed the side of her neck and rocked her within his arms as if she were a child. "I have the luxury of three brothers, so the care of our parents and grandparents, and worries about children, have fallen onto more shoulders. But I'm here with you."

Leigh turned in his arms, desperate to be closer. "Nate, I'm so grateful that you were able to take off a few days." She pressed her face against his neck. "Thank you."

"Are you going to tell Chloe about your mom's surgery?"

Pulling away, Leigh rubbed her hands up and down her arms. "Mom insists I not tell Grandma until the surgery is over and the doctors know more about her condition. But should I do as she says?"

"Well, I think we should trust honesty."

The door behind them opened. "So do I, Nate. It's terrible when I have to resort to listening at keyholes in my own home to hear about my own daughter's health. Now what surgery is Bette having? Is it cancer?"

Saudi Arabia, January 17, 1991

Carly woke in the night, a siren blaring. She sat up. The other women in her tent did the same, some yawning and rubbing their eyes. "What is it?"

"War," one replied. "Could be an incoming."

"Incoming?" Carly parroted, fear ripping through her. "Has the war started?"

"Maybe. An incoming missile," the woman clarified. "A Scud."

"Then why are we just sitting here? It might be a chemical attack." Another woman nearer her jumped up. At this, they were all up and grabbing their NBC outfits and jerking them on over the sweats they wore to bed.

Carly fought the panic that sent her pulse through the

roof. She couldn't show her fear and perhaps stoke the qualms of others. She owed courage to her fellow soldiers. When they were all garbed, they hurried outside, joining the other soldiers in the walkways between tents. Everyone was looking up at the night sky. Huge, dirty-white clouds billowed on the far southeast horizon. Saddam Hussein had set the Kuwaiti oil fields alight and even at that distance the soldiers could see and smell the burning.

Then there were flashes of light above the far eastern horizon. "What was that?" Carly asked, her voice muffled by the choking mask. The NBC suit was heavy and hot and strangling her as usual.

"The war's started," Joe replied, appearing next to her, "Schwarzkopf is unleashing our air force. Bombing missions."

Everyone watched the intermittent lights that must be explosions—of what? What was blowing up in the skies over Iraq? *Their planes and missiles, or ours?*

Then, high above them, a brilliant burst of light shone and a blast shuddered through them all. In a spontaneous reflex, Carly ducked. "What was that?"

"Probably a Scud intercepted," Joe said, trying to sound unconcerned. "I read about the new Patriot missiles. They intercept and destroy incoming missiles."

Carly stared upward along with everyone else. Had one of theirs really taken out an incoming Iraqi Scud? Carly had never even heard of a Patriot missile. She tried to breathe normally through the confining mask, breathing in the smell of its rubber and the burning Kuwaiti oil.

A siren, the all-clear, sounded and everyone dragged off

his or her suffocating gas mask. Carly was the first to free herself. Breathing deeply, she led the women as they trooped back into their tent and shed the cumbersome gear. Then, as if they were all programmed, Carly and the others went back outside, sleep forgotten. An eerie quiet hovered over them—and again a dazzling flash to the east.

"This is like going to a major league game," a soldier groused nearby. "We'd be better off watching it at home on TV."

This garnered modest laughter. Carly wondered if she was the only one who felt as if she were in some other reality. *War. This is war*. She thought about the stories she'd heard from Kitty and Chloe about the two world wars, about doughboys and ration books. War happened in history, in movies, not in real life. *Not in my real life*.

"Carly." Bowie came alongside her.

She smiled up at him, but her lower lip trembled. Gooseflesh was crawling up the back of her neck.

"It's started," he said simply, and in the deep shadows, he took her hand.

She nodded and gripped his large hand. They had no choice but to face whatever came. *God, please protect me, Bowie, and our platoon. I don't know what may happen here or at home.*

She ended the silent prayer. Still, she didn't know what God and this war would demand of her. Did she have strength enough not to let her fellow soldiers and family down, faith and courage enough to face what would come and stand strong?

Ivy Manor, January 17, 1991

Nate nudged Leigh's shoulder. She turned over, blinking. "What is it? Does Grandma Chloe need—"

He shook his head, his bad news dragging his mood down. "It's started. The war's started."

"What's happening?" Leigh threw back the covers and slid out of bed, moving toward the door.

Nate stopped her, bracing her with his hands on her arms. "I got up to put on the coffee, and I turned on the radio. Schwarzkopf has started an air war with Iraq."

"No ground troops?" She pulled away and slipped on her robe.

"Not yet. Come on down. I've turned on the TV in the den." Hand in hand, they shuffled down the stairs in their fleece-lined bedroom slippers to the small room at the back of the first floor. The TV anchorman in khaki was standing in Saudi Arabia with the night sky behind him, discussing Scud missiles. A siren sounded, and a brilliant white eruption lit the desert sky behind him. He switched to talking about stealth bombers and Patriot missiles. He displayed the gas mask he had been given, the same kind the troops carried at all times.

To Nate, the gas mask looked like something from a horror movie. *Our daughter has to carry a gas mask with her at all times.* He urged Leigh onto the love seat. He sat down and put his arm around her shoulders to make sure she could feel his concern, his love. He gazed at her profile as she watched the TV screen. A station break came. She turned toward him. "I feel so close to the war, and yet so far away."

"It's strange to watch a war," Nate agreed, stroking her

upper arm. "It's kind of like the day in 1969 when I watched men step out onto the moon's surface and wondered not so much how they could do it, but how could I be sitting in my parents' living room watching it."

"You're right. It doesn't feel real." Leigh lowered her head to his shoulder. "Like it doesn't feel real that I have a daughter over there."

"*We* have a daughter over there."

"I'm glad you're here with me." Leigh turned in to him and burrowed her face into his shoulder. "How are we going to get through all this?"

He closed his arms around her. "We pray. And hope that our girl will come home safe."

"I'm glad you'll be going to the hospital with us today." She rubbed her face against him. "It's all too much."

He understood. "You're strong, and God hasn't forgotten us."

"I wish I had your faith." She sounded wistful.

"I have my faith, and you have yours. You just haven't relied on it in a while. But war is one of those situations that's too much for us humans. It's too big, too horrible."

"Yes," Leigh agreed. "Yes, it is too big." She stood up. "Let's get that coffee. We have to get off early. I want to be there when Mom wakes from the anesthesia."

Nate followed her out. When they entered the dining room, he breathed in the heartening aroma of fresh brewing coffee. "I think you were right to let Dan take her to the hospital this morning."

"I had to. I didn't want to be away from Grandma Chloe the night before Mom's surgery. I knew she'd be worried."

"The war's started." Grandma Chloe walked briskly into the dining room behind them. "My clock radio came on with the news."

Leigh turned back and hugged her grandmother. "Carly will be fine."

"She's in God's hands, and I trust him with her. Bette has me more worried." Grandma Chloe stroked Leigh's uncombed hair. "Does that make any sense?"

Nate watched silently. Leigh's golden hair caught the anemic morning sunlight. "Maybe it's because Bette's just closer. Today will be a rough day for a lot of people," he said. "Chloe, we'll call you often from the hospital—"

"I'm coming with you two. Michael told me he doesn't mind staying with Rose, and he doesn't want to go to the hospital." Chloe went on into the kitchen toward the cabinet of cups and saucers. "Rose will be here soon."

"Grandma, are you sure you're well enough to sit around the hospital most of the day?" Leigh asked, a plea in her tone.

"Bette's my daughter. If I can walk, I'm going. Period."

Nate patted Leigh's arm. Of course Chloe was coming with them. Rose walked in the back door and slammed it.

Nate felt the whoosh of cold wind swoop into the kitchen. He hurried forward to help Rose out of her coat.

"What a day, what a day," Rose said, walking into the kitchen and grabbing her apron from the hook. "I'm glad someone had the sense to put the coffee on. I called our pastor, Miss Chloe, and he's got the whole church praying for our soldiers, Carly, and Bette. So don't you be worried."

Nate leaned over and kissed Rose's full cheek. "You're a godsend."

"I always heard Irishmen knew how to charm the birds from the trees." Rose chuckled. "Who wants bacon and eggs?"

Later that day, Bette was moved from post-op to her room. The nurses lowered the sides of the gurney and moved her into her bed, and then Dan's face loomed above her—and her mother's, her daughter's, and Nate's. She smiled and tears welled up. They all looked so worried; she must be brave.

"Don't cry," Dan said. "The surgeon said you came through fine."

"I know," she mumbled. "Everything seems fuzzy."

Chloe stroked her hair. "The anesthetic is still in your system, and I'm sure they'll have you on painkillers for the next few days. But you'll feel more like yourself soon."

Bette blinked back tears. *Feel more like herself?* She'd not let herself think about the fact that her left breast had been taken from her today. When would she ever feel like herself again? "How's Carly? Has the ground war started?"

Nate came up behind Chloe and looked down at Bette. "No ground troops yet. Just bombing missions. We were watching it on the TV in the surgical waiting area."

"Yes," Dan added, "it must be the first *live* televised war—I can't decide if that's a good thing or not." He reached down and took Bette's hand in his, warming it.

Leigh stood just behind her husband, watching everything with her large, cornflower-blue eyes. *Does Leigh know how lovely she still is? Does she know how much I love her? I will have to let her know, make her believe me. I'm still alive*

*and there's still time to heal the rift. God, help me. And please
keep Carly safe.*

Saudi Arabia, February 23, 1991

In the smoggy winter twilight, Carly, Bowie, Joe, Sam, and
the rest of the company stood uneasily around their trucks,
waiting for those who were loading them to finish. After five
weeks of the air war, their orders had come down today.
Tonight, under cover of darkness, they would secretly cross
the border into Iraq. Her company wouldn't be fighting but
they were going ahead to set up the supplies, most especially
gasoline and water, that the ground troops would need as they
advanced toward Baghdad.

The general had decided to mislead Hussein into thinking
that the Americans would attack from their battleships in the
Gulf. Actually he would outflank the Iraq army on the north
and west and head straight for Baghdad. It was crucial to the
battle plan that the ground troops have the supplies they
needed on their way to Baghdad. This was what Carly and her
battalion had trained and prepared for.

There was one big catch. They were part of a support
company. Yet Carly and her platoon now faced advancing
ahead of the combat troops. Glacial fear like nothing Carly
had ever felt before wrapped her body in a tight, icy web. Her
face was stiff and frosted. She was very careful of whom she
looked at and how.

According to what they'd been told, the Iraqi army was
now blind and deaf since precision air strikes had taken out
their communication centers and destroyed their reconnais-

sance planes. The invasion of Iraqi territory should be undetected. But what if her company ran into a stray Iraqi force? They had once before, hadn't they? Evidently this thought had occurred not just to her. For once, the guys in her platoon didn't stand around grinning. Everyone looked very focused, very serious, and quiet. This was the real thing.

The last of the supplies was loaded; the trucks were closed and secured. Bowie got the signal, and he and Carly climbed into the lead truck. Once again, Carly had been given the map. Bowie started the engine growling and leading the company, they headed for the highway out of camp. On the seat beside Carly sat the pair of night-vision goggles she'd been issued. Their NBC warfare suits sat in two sacks on the floor between them. She tried to whisper a prayer, but her lips seemed frozen shut. Instead, she stared through the windshield, her hands fisted on top of the map.

Night came and the headlights ate up the black miles ahead of them. The *shammal* buffeted them as usual. Around midnight, they left Saudi soil and headed into the desert of Iraq. With intense concentration, Carly used her compass, binoculars, and goggles, trying to keep the platoon true to course. The supplies they carried must arrive at the right location on schedule. Ground troops couldn't waste precious time looking for them. Carly had no margin of error. None.

As they drove on, all she could hear were the powerful windstorm and their motors sounding so loud in the desert night. The smell of the burning oil wells, carried by the wind, became stronger and stronger. Was that thunder in the distance?

Her thoughts strayed to the most recent letter from

home. Her grandmother Bette was taking chemotherapy, and Chloe had gone to Florida with her friend Minnie to spend some time in the warm tropical sun to recover from pneumonia. Now, at least, she knew what they had been keeping from her: her grandmother's cancer. And that all explained why her mother hadn't turned up.

Being far from home when her family, her mother, needed her was hard. Carly wished she were closer so she could visit her grandmother. For a moment, Carly tried to imagine what life would have been like if she hadn't enlisted last May. Now she'd be in her second semester of college somewhere. She would have been watching the war in front of a TV set, not on this black chilly desert. What would that have felt like?

The wind picked up. Thunder rolled. The sand gusted against the truck, swishing away the finish, nearly shutting off their view. Suddenly, lightning struck the earth right in front of the truck. Thunder detonated around them. Carly screamed. What if one of the fuel trucks was hit by lightning? Hussein would see that fireball all the way to Baghdad and figure out the battle plan. Lightning struck again—just a breath away. More thunder jackhammered them.

Wind hit the truck's sides like boxer's punches. Blazing, brilliant lightning crackled and arced all around them. Carly held her breath and pressed her hands over her ears against the pounding, echoing thunder. Rain lashed their windshield, blinding them. Bowie stomped the brakes repeatedly as a signal to the truck behind him, then stopped the HEMTT. "We'll just have to ride it out!"

For the next uncounted minutes, gales of rain deluged. Lightning and thunder battered the supply train. Then the storm moved on, the thunder still exploding like bomb blasts on into the distance.

Both Carly and Bowie leaped out of the cab into the pouring rain and looked back over the supply train. Nothing was afire. Carly's knees weakened with relief. She caught hold of the truck and steadied herself, then swung back up into the cab. She was drenched and her heart pounded, but she sat back against the seat feeling grateful to be alive.

Bowie started up the motor and moved forward. "What was that?" he asked.

She looked over at him. "Don't you remember them warning us that this was the season for *haboob*?"

"What?"

"Bedouin word for the worst of all possible combinations. Vicious, fast-moving sandstorms with thunderstorms in them."

"Just what we needed for a little more excitement."

Her heart still racing, she tried to grin. "Hey," she said in a shaky voice and with a snap of her fingers, "piece of cake."

Bowie shook his head and wiped rain from his face with his sleeve. "Check the map, lady."

Holding her compass close to the dash light, she nodded. "You're fine. Just keep heading due east-northeast."

Sometime before dawn, they reached the point they'd been headed for. By the first few rays of sunrise, Carly gazed at the vast empty desert around them. She checked their location by the map, compass, and shadow-tip method, and she nodded to the drivers gathered around. Bowie stood beside her double-checking. Finally she confirmed, "This is it."

They all looked back at Bowie, at her. Carly took a deep breath. "Now we just wait for the army to catch up with us." *Wait for the war to catch up with us.*

One tense, interminable day passed and then another dawn. They slept in shifts. Leaning against and squatting near their vehicles, they ate their packaged MREs, drank bottled, luke-warm water, and swatted flies. Little happened to break the tedium except the flights of the airplanes and helicopters overhead. Periodically, some private who didn't know Carly would ask her to recheck their position, but finally Bowie put a stop to that, saying firmly, "We're where we're supposed to be. Chill."

The Iraqi army was blind and deaf, but so were the Americans. They weren't supposed to signal anyone unless they were unexpectedly attacked. The soldiers kept their weapons and NBC gear within reach and scanned the open skies and the vast, uncluttered horizon. They had no cover. Carly drew new significance from the saying "like a sitting duck."

If Iraqis came upon them, Carly's company was com-pletely on its own—a terrifying thought that no one voiced. Carly realized that war forced them to act in opposition to their natural desire to hide from danger. They must follow or-ders, do their duty, stand firm no matter what. Those weeks in boot camp had taught them all unquestioning obedience, and now she saw why. She could depend on the men and women around her to carry out their orders without fail. In this daunting situation, that was their strength.

Then came the faint, echoing, unnerving sounds of distant battle and the earth actually vibrated beneath her feet. "What is it, Bowie?"

"Must be artillery."

"Theirs or ours?"

He shrugged but took up his weapon. He scanned the horizon to the east and then the west.

After another sleepless, chilly night, at dawn on the third day Carly heard motors. At first she doubted her ears, but then the U.S. ground forces came over the west horizon and surrounded the supply train. Her relief drenched her in a cold sweat. Quickly and efficiently, Carly's company performed the duties it had been trained to do, filling gas and water tanks, unloading new ammunition. As she and the others worked without a wasted motion, the combat troops told them the little bit of the war they knew about. Then the re-supplying job was done.

As the combat troops rolled forward in tanks and Jeeps, part of the supply train followed them at a distance. But Carly's platoon had empty trucks to drive back to base. They all watched until the rest of their company vanished over the eastern horizon. Then they climbed into their trucks and turned west. Carly took her first easy breath in three days. Bowie said, "Whoo-ee." And Carly burst out laughing. *Thank you, Father. We made it.*

They reached the base in late afternoon and returned their

trucks to the garage. The next day they'd be busy cleaning out all the sand the *haboob* had gouged and packed into the HEMTTs. With light hearts, Joe, Sam, Bowie, and Carly—arm in arm—headed to the mess hall for their first hot meal in three days.

With her meal tray full of hot, fragrant beef and noodles, Carly sat down and took a long drink of cold milk. She felt effervescent, as if she could float to the ceiling of the tent and bob there like a stray balloon. She grinned across the table at Bowie. He grinned back at her. He mouthed, "I love you."

She beamed, she felt as if she were radiating light and warmth. She mouthed back, "I love you, too."

A siren sounded. Everyone froze. Disgusted, Carly reached for her NBC gear pouch at her feet. *Can't we have one meal in peace?*

"Another Scud warning," announced a soldier at the end of the table who had risen to suit up too. "Hey, where have you guys been? You look like you've been through about ten sandstorms."

Tugging on his mask, Bowie paused to grin. "You ever hear of a *haboob*?"

And then a shrill whistling, then screaming—an explosion devoured them alive.

CHAPTER FIFTEEN

Carly opened her eyes to glittering, blinding sunlight, but she couldn't seem to focus. She heard lots of loud voices. Footsteps shook, pounded through her. She was lying on her back on the sand. She tried to speak, but words wouldn't come. *I must be hurt.* She felt crumpled, but without pain. Her chest felt heavy and it was hard to breathe. What had happened . . . what was going on?

Then a face she knew hovered inches above her own. She tried to say, "Lorelle," but only garbled syllables came out of her gritty throat.

"Carly, you're going to be all right." Lorelle repeated the words twice more.

Carly swallowed the sand in her mouth and throat, then forced out a question, "What?"

"Scud attack," Lorelle said. "You've been injured—"

The voice of a stranger cut in, "We have to move her now. Triage deems her critical."

Critical? What does that . . . ? Carly felt herself being

lifted. She tried to reach for Lorelle, but there was something wrong with her arm. It was tied down. "No," she whimpered. "Lorelle."

"I can't go with you, Carly." Lorelle's voice followed her. "I'm praying! You'll be fine."

Carly stared at the grim soldier carrying the foot of her stretcher. Her carriers weren't walking—they were running with her, rattling her, waking the pain. The sound of helicopter blades whooped nearer and nearer and then she felt their wind beating against her face. She moaned. Agony began filtering in.

"Are you in pain?" the stretcher-bearer asked.

"Yes," she gasped. "Please. . . ."

"Don't worry," he assured her. "We'll get you on a morphine drip onboard."

She felt herself lifted and the swirling wind from the helicopter was like hands slapping, flogging her. Sand whirled up into her face. Choking, she moaned and closed her eyes. Her body tensed. Torture throbbed through her nerve endings. She moaned again. The noise and the pressure around the helicopter overwhelmed her. Tears trickled from her eyes. Helpless as a child, Carly silently said, *Mama, make it stop hurting*.

The helicopter lifted, and Carly couldn't bear the motion and stress on her limp body. She moaned louder. Someone was beside her, inserting a needle in her arm. Carly tried to focus on this, but the pain was eating her alive. Her head pounded, her stomach lurched, and then the noise and motion ebbed. She felt the arms of darkness claiming her. "Jesus," she whispered, "Jesus."

*   *   *

His tense hands gripping the steering wheel, Frank, with Cherise beside him, drove through the late winter Maryland countryside. Ivy Manor's many chimneys could be seen ahead over the tall oaks and barren maples. He'd called Nate at work and found that Leigh was staying with her grandmother and mother while Bette took chemo at the nearby hospital. He cursed silently. They had enough to contend with. *Why did this have to happen?*

"I didn't know her mother had cancer," Cherise said in a tight voice. "I've been so busy I haven't called in two months—"

"Don't start the guilt." Frank controlled his tone. This wasn't Cherise's fault or his. But it was hard to shake that feeling that he was responsible. "I'm the one who told Leigh to go ahead and let Carly enlist." *How did I know a war was going to start up?*

"Frank, I feel guilty for being glad that Lorelle wasn't with Carly."

"Bad things happen in wars. Lorelle isn't immune either. She's still in a combat zone."

"I wish you hadn't said that," his wife murmured.

"I just hope we get there before Leigh gets the news in an official telephone call." He turned up the lane to Ivy Manor. For a split second, it was August 1963 again and he was seeing—for the first time—his family's ancestral home, the one his family had shared with the Carlyles for centuries. He recalled how young and innocent Leigh had been that day. *Oh, Leigh, if only I could have spared you this.*

He parked by the back door. Hand in hand, he and

Cherise ran to it and knocked. He took a deep breath and waited, his heart still thudding.

His cousin, Rose, opened the door. "Frank? Cherise? What are you doin' here?"

"Is Leigh home?" Cherise asked.

"Sure. Come on in. I'll call for her."

Inside, Frank touched Rose's arm. "Don't call her. Bring her to the kitchen. We have news from Saudi. I . . . we want to tell her before Chloe or Bette."

Rose's smile slid from her face. "Oh, my, no." She hurried from the room.

After hanging up their coats, Frank put his arm around Cherise, and she lifted her face in her way of asking for a kiss. He kissed her and then tucked her closer. He couldn't give in to the urge to curse loud and long. Leigh needed his support, not his anguish.

Looking confused, Leigh walked into the kitchen. Rose hovered behind her. "Frank? Cherise? I didn't know you were coming."

"Leigh," Frank said, gathering his courage, "Lorelle called me about two hours ago. Carly has been wounded."

Leigh stared at him, her mouth opening and closing without a sound. *Carly has been wounded.* The words didn't sink in. "What?"

Cherise came to her and put her slender arms around Leigh. "Honey, it was a Scud attack. She's alive but in critical condition. She's been helicoptered to the USNC *Comfort,* a hospital ship stationed in the Gulf, for treatment."

"I've put a call through to the commander of the ship," Frank said. "And he or one of the Navy physicians will call here with Carly's diagnosis." Frank looked at his watch. "Anytime in the next few hours."

Leigh felt the life and strength being sucked out of her. She staggered, and Cherise helped her to a chair. "This can't be happening." *Frank, no. God, no.*

"We're so sorry," Cherise said as she stroked Leigh's hair. "Lorelle said that Carly was conscious and spoke to her. She's not dead, Leigh."

"And she's getting the best medical care in the world," Frank added.

Leigh's mind seemed to be frozen. *This hasn't happened. No.* "I thought the Patriot missiles were intercepting and destroying the Scuds." She looked to him.

"A few still get through," Frank admitted. "I talked to her sergeant after I spoke to the *Comfort.* Carly had just finished a dangerous supply mission and went to the mess tent for her first hot meal in three days. He said she'd been in charge of navigating the company to their supply position. He couldn't say enough about your girl."

Leigh tried to process what he was saying.

Frank sat down in the chair close to Leigh and took her hand in his. "He sounded sick over this. There were casualties in this attack, Leigh. He lost men and women. And Carly could have been killed. But she's still alive. We have to cling to that."

An unexpected moan sounded behind them. They all turned to see Chloe in the doorway sway and Rose caught her. "Frank!" she urged. "Help me. I can't hold her."

Frank leaped forward and took Chloe into his arms. He

lifted her and carried her through the dining room to the den. With Leigh at his heels, he laid her on the sofa there.

Bette, who'd been watching TV, jumped up. "What's wrong?"

Frank knelt beside Chloe, who lay silently upon the sofa. "Can you speak?"

Leigh sank to her knees at Frank's side and took her grandmother's hands in hers. "What are your symptoms, Grandma?"

Chloe's eyes looked frightened and she was gasping. "My chest . . . hurts, can't breathe."

Leigh squeezed her hands, her own breathing tight with fear. "Grandma, do you have pain in your arms, jaw?"

Chloe nodded. "Heart skipping."

Rising, Leigh rushed to the phone. "I'm calling 911," she said over her shoulder, her temples pounding. *She could be having a heart attack.*

Frank chafed Chloe's wrists trying to bring blood back into them. Bette looked to Cherise, who'd entered after Leigh. "What's happened?"

"Carly's been wounded," Cherise replied, coming to Bette's side. "We didn't know Chloe was listening. We were breaking it to Leigh first."

Bette sank down and put her hands over her face. "Oh, no, dear God, no. Not our little girl." Cherise sat down beside her and put an arm around her.

In a flurry of activity, the rescue squad came with the ambulance. Leigh watched helplessly as the medical personnel took

Chloe's vitals. Announcing Chloe could be in cardiac distress, they said they were taking her to the hospital.

Following the ambulance, Frank drove Bette and Leigh to the hospital. Rose stayed behind to watch for Michael, who had been at her daughter's house playing with Rose's grandson, and to be there to take the *Comfort*'s call about Carly's condition.

Leigh watched the ambulance ahead of them and tried to gather her scattered mind and put everything together. *Carly is wounded and Grandma Chloe may be having a heart attack. My mother is in the midst of her first round of chemo. Nate had to go back to work earlier this week. What more, Lord? What next? If you're trying to bring me to my knees, you've succeeded. No more, please. Please.*

Don't let Carly die. I haven't done what I ought. At first I didn't tell the truth about Trent being married and then when I did, I told it cruelly and in anger. No matter how much I pursue success, I always fail when it comes to my daughter. Don't let her die. Give me a second chance.

Groggy, Carly surfaced from oblivion. Airplane engines were idling nearby. She was being carried on another stretcher. She realized she wasn't in pain. "Where am I?"

Walking beside her, a nurse leaned close. "What?"

"Where am I?" Carly felt like she was talking with a mouth full of dried, brittle leaves.

"You're being put onto a flight to Germany for further treatment. You're stable. Don't worry."

"My mom—"

"Your family has been notified. They'll be permitted to see you if they come." The nurse patted her shoulder lightly. "Don't worry now. Everything is being done to help you. You're going to recover."

"Bowie?" Carly murmured, feeling the mindless fatigue roll over her again. She fought against it to ask her first clear thought. "I was with my friend Bowie. What's happened to him?"

"I really don't know. We had a lot of wounded in your attack. Over forty people. I haven't seen or spoken to all the nurses and doctors who worked on them. They'll tell you more in Germany.

"Are we keeping your pain level in check? We don't want you to get too deep into pain. It's harder to bring you back to relief then. If the pain starts again, let someone know, okay?"

Carly nodded, and then she was being carried up a ramp into the bowels of a large airplane. The nurse waved to her, and Carly closed her eyes. *Dear God, please let Bowie be okay. There were a lot more than forty people in that mess hall. Please let him know I'm going to be okay.*

Then a thought niggled at her. Had the nurse been honest or was she protecting Carly from the truth? *I have to be pretty bad for them to fly me to Germany for treatment. Maybe I'm not going to be okay.* Stunned by this thought, her spirit, shocked into mute terror, reached out wordlessly for the Infinite. God would have to pray for her. She closed her eyes, feeling a sob swell in her breast. A bump made her gasp and she lost consciousness.

*   *   *

Just past midnight, Leigh paced alone outside Chloe's hospital room, wanting to go home, but fearful at the same time. Before heading back to Washington, Frank and Cherise had driven Bette home to Ivy Manor to be with Michael and reassure him that everything would be all right. Leigh had called Nate right after Chloe had been admitted, told him all the news, and asked him to come. A doctor said that Chloe had suffered a mild heart attack. What else could go wrong? Would everything turn out right? Or would there be three deaths—Kitty, Chloe, and Carly?

Hearing confident footsteps, Leigh turned and Nate was striding toward her. Unwilling to break the sleepy silence of the hospital at night but needing him more than she could say, she ran on tiptoe to him.

Nate folded her into his arms and hugged her to him fiercely. "What's the news?"

She reveled in his reassuring strength but even more in his inexhaustible love for her. *Why have I been so angry with him? I'm the one at fault.* "Grandma Chloe is going home soon. They're watching her tonight and getting her heart medicine adjusted."

"Good. I stopped at Ivy Manor first and dropped off my stuff. Dan's there. He's staying in the cottage."

"I'm glad. He can help Mom while I concentrate on Grandma Chloe."

Nate murmured reassurance. "What about our Carly?"

She loved it that he called her daughter *"our* Carly." From the very first Nate had loved Carly. Leigh brushed away a tear. "Frank took the call from the hospital ship. Carly suffered a collapsed lung, a badly broken leg, a few broken ribs, a concussion." She drew in a deep, steadying breath. "Her right hand is the most critical. It was almost"—her voice broke—"severed. Carly has to have more surgery to put her hand back together so it will be functional."

Holding Leigh against him, Nate rubbed her taut back muscles with both palms. "What's the outlook?"

Leigh wanted to rest her head against his chest forever, just forget the terrible truth. But she couldn't give in to the weakness. She pulled back. "She's being airlifted to a military hospital in Germany for the hand surgery. Nate, I need to go to her. But how can I?" She heard the note of hysteria rising in her own voice.

He nodded and tugged her close again. "I know you can't leave," he murmured. "Bette, Chloe, and Michael need you. I think it was a good idea enrolling Michael here for the rest of kindergarten. He already knew a few kids from visits here, and he seems happy. Everything will be all right."

How could everything be all right? But Leigh didn't ask. "Michael's still clingy. I have to go home soon. I promised him over the phone that I'd be there when he woke up for breakfast." Never before in her life had Leigh felt so fractured, dragged in so many directions.

"Let's look in on your grandmother." Nate's voice soothed her. "And then we'll go home and see if we can snatch a few hours of sleep."

Leigh hugged him close once more, pressing her face close to his neck. "I don't know what I'd do without you."

"And I don't want you to find out."

*　　*　　*

Trent Kinnard hung up the phone and stared at the wall. His daughter had been seriously wounded and was on her way to a U.S. military hospital in Landstuhl, Germany. The fear that he might lose her, too, and before he'd ever spoken to her or touched her, burned through him like molten metal. He picked up the phone and dialed Lufthansa. Within minutes he'd secured a seat on a flight from Washington, D.C., to Germany in the early morning. He walked to his bedroom closet and pulled out his suitcase.

Then he sat on the bed without the strength to begin packing. He hadn't felt like crying for a long time. But tears started in his eyes, and since no one was there, he let them come. Would he see his daughter while she was yet alive? Would he be allowed to visit her? *She's my daughter, but I have no legal standing or rights to her. What will I do if I lose her, too?*

The next morning early, Nate had boarded a Lufthansa flight to Germany. Ten hours later, he was in a taxi on his way to the military base hospital. At the gate, he was held up while the sentry checked his bona fides. But Nate knew that Frank had already arranged for his visit in spite of the late hour. Soon Nate was waved through the gate, and the taxi took him to the hospital.

Within minutes, he was by Carly's bed. She was asleep in a room with three other slumbering soldiers behind white curtains. His first glimpse of her shocked him. She had a black eye. Cuts and abrasions covered her pale face. Her right arm was immobilized at her side and her right hand was swathed in bandages.

He stood gazing down at her, worried by the number of IVs she was hooked up to. He began to pray again for her life, for her complete recovery, for Chloe, for Bette, for his wife and son. He didn't think he'd stopped silently praying since he had received Leigh's initial phone call. He rubbed his tight forehead and gritty eyes. He wished Leigh could be there. He must call her soon.

A nurse came to the door and waved to him. Nate walked out to her. "The gate just called us. There is another man, a Trent Kinnard, at the gate who wants to see Carly Gallagher. He says he's her father, too. What's up?"

Nate digested this unwelcome and surprising news in a quick moment. How had Trent found out? He didn't want the man there. But he really had only one choice, didn't he? "I'm Carly's adoptive father. Trent Kinnard is her birth father." He hated saying this. *I'm her real father.* But he couldn't say that.

"Oh, okay then. You know him?"

"I know who he is."

She looked at him as if assessing the situation. "Do you want us to let him in? He has a valid passport and other ID, but we didn't receive word about him. But if you are willing to vouch for him . . ."

CHAPTER SIXTEEN

There is another man, a Trent Kinnard, at the gate who wants to see Carly Gallagher. Nate didn't want to answer the pretty nurse who watched him closely. He wanted to turn away and ignore her. Kinnard had hurt his Leigh, treated her with rank disrespect. Kinnard had been responsible for so much sadness and hurt for the two women he loved most. Savage anger—a violence Nate had never been aware of— roared to the surface of his consciousness.

"Sir?" the nurse prompted.

"Let him come up. He is her father," Nate conceded gruffly. He couldn't stop himself from sounding aggrieved.

The nurse gave him a questioning look. "Are you sure you want him up here?"

Nate wasn't sure, but he nodded. *Do good to those who despitefully use you.* He didn't want to recall that verse now, or to obey it. But this man was Carly's father. He must have some feeling for his daughter or he wouldn't have flown there right on Nate's heels. And Carly wanted to meet Kinnard.

The nurse turned away, went to the nurses' station, and picked up a phone. When she hung up, she gave him a nod. He remained in the doorway, watching the nurses quietly go about their duties. He wanted to talk to Kinnard before he entered Carly's room. Kinnard would have to abide by his rules or he'd send him packing. But Nate had time to deal with Kinnard. *Carly's asleep anyway.*

It didn't take long before a handsome, well-dressed though rumpled man got off the elevator, stopped at the nurses' station, and looked toward Nate.

Nate waited for him, a grim, silent sentinel at Carly's door. Kinnard walked slowly toward him, his dark trench coat over his arm. Nate detected the fatigue in the man's face and stride, and it stirred his sympathy in spite of the hostility he felt. *He must have been on my plane or right after it.*

"Trent Kinnard." The man eyed him warily but didn't offer his hand.

"Nate Gallagher." Nate recognized the unmistakable resemblance between the man and Carly. He made himself hold out his hand.

Kinnard gripped it and glanced into Nate's eyes and then away. "Thank you for telling them I am Carly's father."

"I didn't want to," Nate admitted, his gaze not wavering from Kinnard's face. "I think you treated the woman I love and married without respect. You've hurt both Leigh and Carly. To tell the truth, I'd like to take you outside and pound on you for a few minutes."

Kinnard looked as if he didn't know what to say to this candid declaration. Finally, he said, "I know I'm guilty of everything you've said. But I regret it, and that is the best thing I can say for myself. Regret is a dreadful place to live, but it's my home and has been for many years."

In the hushed hospital corridor, Nate digested this slowly, then turned. "Carly is unconscious." He walked into her room to her white-curtained area.

Kinnard followed him. When he glimpsed her, he gasped. "How bad is she?"

The man's concern sounded sincere. "Bad." Nate recited the list of Carly's injuries, a painful litany. "The worst is that hand." He indicated her right hand swathed in white bandages. "They did surgery on her before I arrived. It was nearly severed." The last word caught in his throat. The thought of Carly's losing a hand was too grisly to imagine.

Kinnard looked appalled. "Do they think they can save it?"

"Don't know." Nate rubbed his gritty eyes. "I haven't talked to any of her doctors. I just got here, too."

Kinnard looked into his face. "Flight 673 Lufthansa?"

Nate nodded. "Didn't see you."

"I always fly first-class," Kinnard admitted, looking ashamed.

It figures. Giving Kinnard another once-over, noticing his manicured hands and stylish haircut, Nate recalled that Leigh had told him that this man had set up a half-million-dollar trust fund for Carly, his illegitimate daughter. The wages of sin were evidently very good. Nate pushed aside this judgmental thought. Kinnard didn't look as if he'd gotten away with anything. He looked miserable. The rain fell on the just and the unjust, and this time it was a dark, painful downpour.

"I don't know if Carly should be told that you are here,"

Nate said, trying not to let his rampant possessiveness bleed through in his tone. *She's my daughter.* "It might be too much for her." And Leigh must be considered too. *My wife's carrying such burdens already.*

Kinnard frowned but then nodded. "I didn't come to upset her. I came because I was afraid that she might . . . I might lose her before I'd ever have had the chance to hear her voice or hold her hand."

Kinnard's bald confession blasted away Nate's self-righteousness and resentment. The man's love for his daughter glistened in his eyes moist with tears and resonated in his beleaguered tone. "I came because I was afraid it might be my last chance to do both of those." He paused, then drew a long, tortured breath. "Doesn't it seem that life," Kinnard muttered at last, "dishes out more than we can handle?"

Nate didn't reply, but yes, sometimes that was exactly what it felt like. It did at that moment.

Carly moaned and her eyelashes fluttered. She squinted as if trying to bring the room into focus.

Kinnard fell back behind the curtain.

Carly whimpered, "Hurt. Nurse."

Nate's heart lifted at her awakening. Quickly Nate located the call button. Then, feeling as if he'd just seen Carly reborn, he lightly stroked a small patch of unbandaged and unabraded skin on her face. "Hi, honey, I'm here. Daddy's here."

"Dad-dy," Carly said these two syllables as if they'd exhausted her. "Mom?"

"Mom had to stay with your Grandmother Bette and Michael." He spoke close to her face, not wanting to disturb the other sleeping soldiers. "She wanted to come but she couldn't leave them." He wouldn't mention Chloe's heart attack. Carly might feel guilty about it.

Carly tried to nod, then grimaced as if it had caused her more pain.

On soundless shoes, the nurse bustled up to the bed. "What's our patient need?"

"She says she's in pain," Nate said, ready to battle the nurse for his daughter.

"Woke me up," Carly mumbled.

The nurse consulted the IV bags hanging at Carly's bedside. "Did you forget," she said kindly, "that you have the morphine pump here?" She pointed out a line that had been secured to the bed near Carly's left hand. She slipped the control into Carly's hand. "Give it a push."

Carly obeyed. "I forgot."

"It would have been hard to give yourself an extra dose while you were asleep," the woman said with a gentle smile. "Wait about a half hour and if the pain hasn't ebbed, give yourself another dose. Then no more till morning, okay?"

"Thanks."

"No problem. This is my job. And I want to make you as comfortable as I'm able." The nurse straightened Carly's bed clothing and then left.

Aware that Kinnard stood nearby listening, Nate moved close to the bed again. "I'm here for the duration, honey. I'm not leaving until you're much better."

"Daddy, please find out about . . . Sam and Joe and . . . Bowie. We were . . . in . . . mess tent . . . together. No one . . . told me. . . ."

"I'll find out, honey. Is that morphine starting to kick in?" He tried to turn her attention away from those potentially disastrous concerns. *Dear God, let them all be fine.* "I'm going to watch the time for you." He glanced at his watch. "In case you need to give yourself another dose."

"Better," Carly said, closing her eyes. "Stay."

His love for her expanded inside him, filling him with the same tenderness that he'd felt for her the first time when as a little girl, she'd snuggled into his lap. "I will, honey. I'll be here all night." Nate kissed an unbandaged patch of forehead and then watched as Carly's features relaxed. Finally, he said, "She's asleep."

Kinnard stepped around the curtain. "She sounded really weak."

Nate nodded.

"She's so young. Only seventeen. She shouldn't have to go through this." Kinnard's voice roughened with outrage. "She should be at school somewhere, enjoying herself."

"That wasn't her choice," Nate said simply. "She's just like the rest of us. We make decisions and then we must live with the consequences." He looked Kinnard in the eye. *You have a lot to make up for.*

Kinnard said nothing, just stared down at his daughter who remained unaware he'd come.

Again, Nate went over in his mind the names that Carly had asked about. *I hope they're all alive and doing well.* He couldn't face adding to his daughter's burden. Kinnard was right. She was too young for this. But it had come anyway. *Dear Father, bless her and restore her. And help me know what to do about her meeting her real, I mean birth, father.*

Maybe he should consult her doctors about Kinnard first. *I'm not doing anything but what's best for Carly.*

Morning came finally. Though longing for sleep and a hot shower, Trent hovered near Gallagher, who still sat beside Carly. About seven o'clock, she opened her eyes and tried to smile. Trent fell back to his position behind the curtain, where his daughter wouldn't notice him. He watched with jealousy gnawing his insides as Gallagher touched her as carefully as if she were made of tissue paper. Trent hadn't gained the privilege of touching her yet, but he was hearing her voice. For that he was grateful. But would he, should he, be allowed to introduce himself to her today?

Trent saw Carly's breakfast tray being delivered. His own hunger awoke, but he stifled it while watching Nate help Carly swallow some oatmeal and scrambled eggs. Gallagher was helping her drink some milk through a straw when a tall, young doctor passed by Trent and entered the curtained area around Carly's bed. He carried what must have been her chart. The doctor paused at the end of her bed, reading, and then looked up with a very serious expression on his face.

Gallagher stood up. "I'm Carly's stepfather and her adoptive father. How is she doing?"

The doctor nodded but spoke to Carly. "I'm Law Henning, your primary physician. How are you doing, Private Gallagher?"

"I've been better," Carly said barely above a murmur. "How is my hand?"

"So far, so good. You might need further surgery, but

those of us in charge of your case have decided that we'll just wait and see how you bounce back before we do more."

"Are any of my friends here?"

Trent didn't like hearing the choked worry in Carly's voice.

"Who were you looking for?"

"Bowie Jenkin. Sam Washburn. Joe Connolly." She added mention of their battalion and company.

"I'll find out if they're here or not." The doctor jotted on the chart.

Nate asked, "How soon is she going to be able to go home, or at least Stateside?"

"She's going to have a long recovery time. And there will be some aftereffects." He turned to Carly. "You suffered a rather severe concussion, which is all too common in cases of explosions. I'm afraid that you will have periodic severe headaches and some memory lapses for up to a year."

Carly said in a rueful tone, "Thanks, I needed to hear that lovely bit of news."

Henning took a step closer and picked up her good hand, at last showing compassion. "I'll ask about those friends of yours. See if I can get news of them. If you need anything, tell the nurse." He turned and left the room.

Trent followed him and motioned for him to come farther away from the entrance. And then Gallagher joined them in the hallway. "What else can I do for you?" the doctor asked in a low voice.

Nate said, "This is Carly's birth father, Trent Kinnard. She has never met him."

Trent felt a hot flush suffuse his face.

The doctor looked him up and down. "And you are telling me this why?"

"We want to know," Trent replied roughly, unable to meet the doctor's gaze, "whether I should stay out of sight or let her know I'm here."

"Ah." The doctor folded his arms. "Does she want to see you?"

Trent looked to Carly's stepfather.

"I know she wants to," Nate replied, "but I hesitated to let her become aware of Kinnard because—even though it might be happy stress—I didn't know how much she could handle right now. I didn't want to—you know, upset the apple cart."

"I see. Later today, or tomorrow, a visit might be possible," Henning said. "She's been through a lot. Her body is really weak now. But fortunately, she's young and healthy, and she appears to have a supportive family."

"You don't think it would hurt her?" Trent asked, feeling as if this easy acceptance were almost too much to hope for.

"No, I don't. But don't do it if you're just going to say hi and then good-bye. After her physical wounds heal, she'll be dealing with the aftereffects of the concussion and also probably post-traumatic stress disorder for months to come. She's going to need a lot of care and support. Don't make her think you're going to be there if you're not." The doctor turned to leave.

Nate stopped him with a hand on his arm. "Did you mean it about checking on her friends?"

"If I said it, I meant it." The doctor looked disgruntled.

"No offense." Nate held up one hand. "Anyway, please

let me and Kinnard know first if anything happened to any of them, especially Bowie Jenkin. I don't know if he was a sweetheart or just a very good friend. If anything bad happened to him, or even to Sam or Joe, it will hit her hard. But Bowie would be the hardest loss."

The doctor nodded. "I'll let you know first. And if something did happen to them, it's best if you, rather than I, told her. She'll need your support to weather bad news." With that, the doctor left them.

Trent looked to Nate, his heart pounding with hope and fear. Would he get to speak to his daughter at long last that day? "What do you think?"

"I think we'll do it his way," Nate said. "You can talk to her later. Did you make reservations somewhere?"

Trent didn't understand why Nate was asking this but replied, after a pause, "Yes. I have a suite reserved in town."

"Well, maybe after you meet her, if it goes well, we should share the responsibility of being here with her. I'm not leaving until Carly is really on the mend, and that could be a while. But I can't stay here twenty-four hours a day. I need to shower and sleep and so do you."

"Right."

"How long can you stay in Germany? Don't they expect you back at work?"

"I'm retired from my law practice. What about you?"

Nate shoved his hands into his pockets. "I've taken a leave of absence. A lot of stuff has been happening with Leigh's family."

"I was told Leigh's aunt Kitty died last fall."

Nate eyed Trent. "And her mother has cancer, and her grandmother is recovering from a mild heart attack."

Trent let this collection of bad news echo through him. "Rough."

"Yeah, Leigh has been through the wringer. She took leave to help her mom, and then Carly was wounded and her grandmother had her attack. I decided I should be the one to come. Fortunately, I was between cases and was able to get leave."

Trent wondered if he should offer some financial assistance but instantly rejected the idea. Nate wouldn't appreciate it. Trent stifled a yawn.

"Well, do you want to leave and take your turn at a shower and a nap first?" Nate asked. "The doctor said to wait, and you've got a room."

One way of helping occurred to Trent. "Why don't you just stay at my suite? Suites usually can accommodate more than one and it sounds like we won't be there together often. I'll just let the hotel know." Trent wondered if even this offer would offend Nate.

Nate studied Trent for a long moment. "Thanks. We might as well."

Trent held out his hand in thanks.

Nate shook it. "Let's just hope that she doesn't get bad news about her friends. I don't know how she'll handle that."

Trent nodded. "Maybe having me here will help that."

Nate lifted his eyebrows.

"Give her something else to focus on," Trent said diffidently.

Nate shrugged. "Maybe. You go on to the hotel. I'll be

here. When you get back, we'll see if it's time for you to make yourself known."

Ivy Manor on the same night

In the upstairs bathroom, Leigh sat on the side of the cool porcelain tub while her mother, on her knees, wretched in dry heaves into the toilet. Leigh murmured soft encouraging sounds. She was in a warm nightgown, robe, and slippers, as was her mother. When Bette motioned for the glass of water on the sink, Leigh handed it to her. She couldn't remember the last time she'd had a full night's sleep. Every night either Bette or Chloe or Michael needed attention. But she was glad she had stayed.

Taking a leave of absence and right in the midst of the first war where women were serving as part of the U.S. armed services had been tough on her editor and on her. She rubbed the back of her neck and stretched it. Then she took the glass from her mother's trembling hand.

Panting, Bette pushed herself back and sat leaning against the bathroom wall. Her eyes were ringed with gray shadows and her face was gaunt, her cheeks hollow. "I think that might be it for a while. But I don't want to move right away and start everything up again."

"That's fine, Mom." Leigh said. Fatigue rolled through her like a bowling ball, taking down all her pins. She tried to swallow a yawn and failed. She wondered how long her mid-forties stamina would hold up.

"You should go back to bed."

Leigh shook her head. "No, I'll get you back to your

room and comfortable first. Don't worry about me. Dan's been a great help, letting me take a nap every afternoon. I don't know what I'd have done without him."

Her mother managed a wan smile. "Me, too. But I still wish you'd been able to go to be with Carly. I'm sorry all this has piled up on you."

"Mom," Leigh said, pausing to yawn again, "it's just life. Things seem to clump together. It's not your fault." *And I've never felt closer to you.* Still, the fact that her daughter was seriously wounded and in a military hospital shocked Leigh. She'd tried to imagine what her beautiful, young daughter had suffered. What did it feel like to be in the midst of a missile explosion? Perhaps see friends die?

Leigh recalled the riot in Chicago that she'd been a part of in 1968. It had shaken her badly and changed the course of her life. What would the aftermath of this experience be in Carly's life? "Don't worry about Carly," she said to reassure her mother and herself. "I believe Nate. When he called, he said that Carly is in bad shape, but she's recovering."

Bette nodded. "That's a blessing. I was so frightened that we might have lost her."

Me, too. Dear God, I've been so stubborn. You preserved Carly's life. Bring her home safely, and I'll tell her the truth. I will. I won't hide from the past anymore. Please bless my mother and grandmother and help them recover, too. I have given up trying to do it my way. I want you to lead me out of the tortuous maze I've trapped myself within, where I keep hurting the ones I love.

Landstuhl, Germany

That evening, Nate had wandered over to the TV in the waiting area at the end of the floor. Schwarzkopf was answering questions about the end of the Gulf War. Five weeks of air strikes and four days of a ground war and it was over. Saddam Hussein's famous Republican Guard had melted away into the desert. If the war had ended a few days earlier, his girl wouldn't have been wounded.

For a moment, Nate wished he had Hussein alone in a room for about an hour. But that was pointless. From jet lag, he felt dragged out and almost dead. He wanted to get out of his wrinkled clothes and shower. He turned to see Kinnard getting off the elevator—an unexpectedly welcome sight.

They met in the hallway. "I actually fell asleep for a couple hours," Kinnard said. "I didn't think I would. Did I stay away too long? How are you? Carly?"

Nate held up a hand in greeting. Fatigue clawed his stamina. Each step, each word depleted him. "I'm fine. No change in Carly. Did you watch the news?"

"No, I don't speak German so I didn't bother."

"The war's over."

Kinnard's mouth became a straight tight line. "Why couldn't it have ended just a few days earlier?"

Nate shrugged. "I can't stay here much longer. I'm about asleep on my feet, and I need a shower. I think we better just take the plunge. Are you ready to meet Carly?"

CHAPTER SEVENTEEN

Trent felt his pulse race. Gallagher was offering him access to Carly, something that had been denied him for nearly eighteen years. It was almost too wonderful to contemplate, too exquisite a hope and fear combined. But he managed to nod. "Maybe. . . ." He cleared his dry, constricted throat. "Maybe you should go in and prepare her . . . ask her."

"No," Nate said with a certainty that Trent coveted, "let's just do it. She's waited long enough, and she wants to meet you." He turned to go back into Carly's room.

Trent stopped him by gripping his arm. A tardy concern intruded. "Won't Leigh be angry with you that you let me see Carly? I don't want to cause trouble between you two."

"Let me worry about Leigh," Nate said gruffly. "Carly is determined to see you with or without her mother's permission." He frowned. "This has caused a lot of conflict between them. I've tried to get Leigh to tell Carly, explain how—"

"How I seduced her mother while I was in a marriage of strictly political convenience," Trent forced out the words. "I know that Leigh would never believe this, but I realized after I lost her and my wife, that she was the one I could have loved."

Trent stopped there. After all, Nate was Leigh's husband. "Don't misunderstand me. I want to see my daughter, have wanted to since I learned I'd fathered her. That has only intensified as the years have passed. Carly is all that I have of my brief time with Leigh." Trent felt his heart pounding as he stripped away his pride. "I've regretted treating Leigh so cavalierly, and I've paid for my sin."

Nate listened but said nothing. His quiet acceptance had uncapped Trent's reserve. Nate Gallagher gave the impression that he was the kind of man one could confide in, a man not easily shocked. No doubt as a detective he was practiced in the technique of subtly encouraging confidences. And no doubt Gallagher was used to hearing confessions of all the unconscionable things people did to one another.

Trent stilled himself, slowing his breathing. "Five years after my one-night stand with Leigh, my wife left me. She decided she could no longer live in a loveless marriage, and she'd found someone she loved. I tried to act like it didn't bother me. But it did. My neat plan for a prominent and successful life was starting to unravel. And then two years ago, our only son died in a drunk-driving accident. The last traces of the cocky guy I was, the one who had all the answers during McGovern's 1972 presidential campaign, died a fiery death that night." Trent felt purged, stripped naked. He waited for Gallagher, the man who'd had enough sense to win both Leigh and Carly's love, to reply, to condemn him.

Gallagher stared at him. "I'm sorry about your losing a

son." Nate's genuine sympathy showed in his dour expression. "But no one gets through this life free and easy—whether they've been good or not. You say you've paid for your sins. Not really. You've suffered the consequences. I think you need to talk to God about your sins. He paid for them. You don't have to." He took a deep breath.

"Now let's go meet Carly. She needs you. And that's what's important now. She needs all the love she can get. And she deserves it, too. She's a great kid, and I love her with all my heart."

Nate's sincerity came through to Trent like pure, chilled mountain air. Mute before it, Trent couldn't reply so he nodded. *What if I can't speak—can't say a word to my daughter?* But he put one foot in front of the other, and then he and Gallagher were side by side next to Carly's bed.

She opened her eyes and looked up.

Gallagher took her good hand. "Carly, someone else has come to visit you. This is your father, Trent Kinnard."

Carly gazed up into Trent's face. He saw his own gray eyes looking back at him, and he felt as if he could stand there, gazing at her for centuries. He tried to read her expression but was unable to. Tears welled up in his eyes; he couldn't stop them. He attempted to put together some words of greeting, but he failed.

"Father?" she said.

He nodded. And at her innocent greeting, he felt his tears release. He sucked them in, down into his throat.

Gallagher took their daughter's uninjured hand and gave it to Trent. And then Trent's daughter, his Carly, his living child, squeezed his hand—and began to cry, too.

Nate leaned down and kissed Carly's cheek, then left them.

"Father?" Carly said again to Trent. "You came?"

"I was here last night." Shaking, Trent wiped the moisture from his eyes with his free hand. He felt compelled to let her know how much he owed her stepfather. "We didn't know it but Gallagher and I flew over on the same flight. Your stepfather told them to let me through the gate to get to you. Your mother's friend, Frank Dawson, had set it up for Gallagher to visit you. But of course I wasn't listed as family. If your stepdad hadn't vouched for me, I wouldn't have been let in. I can't thank him enough."

"Nate's great. He loves me and I love him. Oh, Father, I can't believe I'm finally seeing you." Free, unabashed tears flowed down the sides of her face onto her pillow. "I've missed you . . . *so*."

Weak in the knees, Trent dropped into the chair beside her bed and clung to her hand. "Don't cry. Please don't cry." But his silent tears continued pouring down. Finally, he took a deep breath. "I'm so sorry I missed your childhood."

"Why didn't my mom ever let you visit me?"

"Carly, don't blame your mother." With his palm, he rubbed his taut forehead. "I put her in a terrible position. I was a selfish man who wanted her, *used* her, when I didn't have any right to her."

"You were married," Carly said in a soft, hurt voice.

"Leigh told you?" The truth, a sharp razor, sliced Trent's heart.

Carly nodded solemnly. "When I told her you'd started writing to me while I was in boot camp, it made her so angry."

"I didn't mean to cause trouble between you and Leigh. Never." His guilt stung him. "But I knowingly took advantage of your mother. She didn't know I was married until after . . . until after we'd spent the night together. I acted like I didn't know she might be unaware that I was married, but I never gave her the slightest hint that I wasn't free."

"Did you . . . did you ever try to see me before?" His daughter looked fearful.

"Yes, twice. Right after you were born and right after you were kidnapped. Indirectly, you suffered that awful experience because of me, too."

"How?"

"A man wanted to hurt me. He found out and used you to get at me." Trent swallowed a sob. "I've hurt you in so many ways."

"It's all right." Her voice caught, and then she went on, "You're here now."

Her easy, innocent forgiveness and acceptance stunned him. Trent bent and kissed her good hand.

She reached up and stroked his wet cheek. "It will be okay, Father. We'll work it all out."

"I don't deserve you." He wasn't able to say more. He wept silently, sobs shaking his shoulders.

Carly stroked his cheek and softly murmured comforting words.

This is Leigh's child, my daughter, my beautiful child. I don't deserve her. Nate's words about God had touched him. But God was only for good men, not foolish men like him who made messes of their lives and scarred those that warranted their love.

Nate walked back into Carly's room. He watched the tableau of the weeping prodigal father and Carly's gentle loving ways. He didn't want to tell her the news he'd just gotten. But it was no good waiting. Carly would keep asking till she got an answer. Trent's presence might soften the blow. But most important of all, Carly hated it when secrets were kept from her. He wouldn't treat her like a child. She was a woman, a soldier.

"Carly, I'm sorry," he said softly. "Joe and Sam survived the attack, but Bowie Jenkin was killed instantly."

Much later, Carly lay in her hospital bed in the dim light and hush of evening. Most guests had left, and she'd insisted that both her fathers go back to the hotel for a late supper. They'd insisted that she needed them, but she'd overruled. She needed time alone to mourn for her . . . for Bowie, her best friend, her first love.

Nate and Trent had wanted so much to comfort her. But just having her two fathers with her had been a blessing she could only have guessed at before today. Her two fathers. . . .

God, I'm so happy that I finally met my real . . . my biological father. I was so happy and now . . . I can't bear it. Bowie . . . I can't believe he's gone.

She pictured herself on that fatal final day, across the table from Bowie in the mess tent. Would the image of Bowie mouthing the words "I love you" stay with her, torture her forever? She heard again the whistling and screaming of the attack, but that was all. She remembered nothing afterward except Lorelle's face above hers and then being wheeled into the hospital.

Tears streamed from her eyes in a steady but unhurried flow. Would she run out of them eventually—but continue to weep without tears?

I don't know what to pray, God. You felt so near to me in Saudi when I stood beside Bowie in church each Sunday. The hymn she'd sung with Bowie in Saudi replayed in her memory, "Child of weakness, watch and pray, / Find in Me thine all in all." *I know you haven't left me, but I must have moved away from you. Is that how it is when a person loses someone—as though in some way, I've died, too? I almost feel like I don't care if I get well or not. And I know that's not right. I know my family . . .*

The phone beside her bed rang. She jerked in surprise. Nate had positioned it so she could get it with her good hand. He was probably calling to see if she wanted them to come back. Carly tried to stop crying and picked up the receiver. She felt as if she hadn't held a phone for a long time. With a rush of poignant memory, she realized that the last time had been at Christmas with Bowie beside her. "Hello," she murmured.

"Carly, it's your great-grandmother."

Fresh tears flooded Carly's face and throat. "Grandma Chloe."

"Oh, my darling child, how I wish I could be there with you. Nate called us about your friend Bowie."

Carly couldn't speak. She tried and the only word that came out was, "Loved." *I loved him, Grandma.*

"I know, dear. It's so hard. It's been around sixty years, but

263

I still remember how lost I felt when your great-grandfather Theran died in World War I. It's so horrible, and yet it doesn't feel real, feel possible at first."

"I know," Carly managed to respond.

"I'm so glad that Nate is there with you."

Carly took a deep breath. "I made him go back to the hotel. He's so tired."

"He's a good man. Here, I'm going to hand the phone to your Grandma Bette."

"Sweetheart," Bette said, coming on the line, "we miss you so, love you so."

Her grandmother's fight with cancer roared in Carly's head. *I don't want to lose her too, God. Please.* "Grandma, how are you?"

"Well, pretty miserable, just like you, I suspect. But I think I'm going to win, and you will, too, darling. You are so precious to us."

"Daddy says you have a boyfriend." Carly couldn't quite believe it, but her mouth lifted in a smile as she said this even though tears still wet her face.

"I don't know if I'd call Dan my *boy*friend"—Grandma Bette's usual good humor came through—"but yes, I have Dan in my life now. I think you'll like him. He's very dashing."

Carly giggled in the midst of tears. "It's so good to hear your voice. Is Mom there?"

"Yes, sweetheart, here she is."

"Honey," Leigh said, sounding as if she'd been crying, too, "I wish I could be with you. I'm so sad for you, but so glad you're alive."

Then Carly recalled wishing for her mother as she lay wounded. "Mom, I loved him."

"I know." Her mother tried to muffle her sympathetic weeping. "It's all so hard. If I could have spared you this, I would. But mothers can't do that. Life happens to our children, and we can't stop it."

"Mom, I've been praying." Carly's heart sped up. She'd never talked to her mother about God. It was one of those topics her mother wouldn't respond to. Nate had always been the one to take Carly to church and Sunday school. "I feel like I have to cling to God as if my life is melting away beneath me."

"I've experienced that feeling, too. It's awful. I won't insult you with any platitudes. But I'm glad you're clinging to God." Leigh lowered her voice. "I've been doing that lately myself."

Her mother's admission took Carly by surprise, but then she thought, *Maybe that's what it means: "Find in Me thine all in all." Is it just clinging to you, Lord, through every loss, every sorrow, everything?*

Ivy Manor, March 1991

Nate waved good-bye to Rose's grandson, who'd collected him at the airport. In the chill gray afternoon light, Nate looked at the venerable home and wondered when he'd go back to his and Leigh's flat in New York City. He'd spent two weeks in Germany with his daughter and her birth father. And finally, Carly had told both of them to go home. She would be flown Stateside sometime in the next two weeks, and she'd be given leave soon after to come home to convalesce.

In all that time, no one had ever revealed to Leigh that Trent had also spent the two weeks with Carly. Nate had appreciated having someone to share the visitation with. It was hard seeing his little girl suffer. And Carly had been so happy to be with Trent—Nate hadn't been able to drum up much jealousy. More and more, he valued seeing Carly holding Kinnard's hand and listening to her tell him about her childhood. To Nate, it had been like reliving those fun hours and days. *But now I have to tell Leigh.* He knew she would be angry, but how angry? What effect would it have on their already rocky marriage?

And he hated hitting her with this now. Chloe had evidently come through all right and was doing well on heart medication. But Bette was still waiting for further testing to see if her cancer had gone into remission. Why did life only get harder as one aged? Shouldn't life experience and the ease of more material wealth after years of hard work make it easier? In a word or two, evidently not.

The back door swung open and Leigh, looking fabulous in a soft blue sweater and slacks, threw herself into his arms. "Oh, I've missed you so!" She clung to him as he held her close and kissed her. It was as if he hadn't seen her for years. Passion for her burst over him afresh, and he breathed in her unique scent. She pulled away to look at him. "You don't know how glad I am to see you."

"I have a feeling I do. I've missed you." He held the back of her silken head in one hand and began another long kiss of reunion.

With a quick hug, she pulled from him and drew him in-side. "Michael's at school. Grandma Chloe's napping and Mother's out with Dan. He drove her to Arlington—some-thing came up at the CIA, and they wanted her to drop by."

In the warm kitchen, fragrant with roasting beef, Rose greeted Nate with a hug. She insisted on making him a snack right away, and then Leigh drew him to the den at the back of the first floor as if eager to have him alone. For a long mo-ment, they just stood holding one another. She was softer than he'd remembered and much, much thinner.

Then Leigh drew Nate down to sit beside her on the sofa, clutching his rough hand in hers. He looked so handsome, so good to her. It was like seeing him again for the first time, his rich auburn waves and clear blue eyes. "I love you, Nate," she whispered and bent to kiss the back of his hand. "With every-thing happening here and worrying about Carly over there, I feel like I've been forced through a long, narrow tube. But now you're here and Carly will be coming home soon. I can relax for a bit."

Nate looked funny, frozen.

"What's wrong? Is there something I don't know about Carly?" She moved toward him, her heart speeding up.

"No, I've told you everything about Carly's health. She'll be home just like we told you. It's about her father, about Kinnard."

Leigh could only stare at him.

"Kinnard flew to Germany on the same flight I did."

"So. . . ." Bewildered, she couldn't think what to say, to ask.

"I vouched for him, and he met Carly."

Leigh's mouth dropped open. Waves of shock vibrated through her flesh. Her head drooped, becoming heavier and heavier until she had to hold it up with both hands.

"Are you all right?" Nate gripped her shoulder. "I didn't tell you because I knew you had enough on your plate here. Are you very angry with me? I didn't do it to hurt you. I did it because Carly needed him."

Leigh struggled with an amazing free fall of emotions—each one ramming her with astounding force. Anger. Shock. Hurt. Guilt. Jealousy. Horror.

"Leigh, speak to me." Nate shook her slightly.

"I don't know what to say." She stared downward. "It's all too much—"

Rose entered with a tray of sandwiches and a pot of coffee. "Here you go." She looked at Nate and said, "Your wife's been eating like a fly. Make her snack along with you. She'll be a size zero if this keeps up. And after that, I don't know what she'll wear. Minus-zero?"

"I'll take care of it, Rose," Nate said. After the housekeeper had left, closing the door behind her, Nate lifted Leigh's chin. He handed her a sandwich, forced her to take it in hand, and then he took a bite of his.

Leigh stared at the ham and cheese on rye. "I can't eat."

"Rose is right. You look as if you could blow away on the wind. Just take a bite and start chewing."

The idea of eating felt repugnant, but she had to do something to make the unreality go away. "What did . . . what did Carly say when she met her father?" Leigh forced herself to bite into the soft bread.

"I didn't know what to say when the nurse told me, the

night I arrived at the hospital, that there was *another* father wanting to see Carly." He paused to chew. "But I decided if he'd flown all the way to Germany, he must want to see her very badly. Don't you think?"

She nodded, her mind still numb at the mention of Trent. She chewed, and the tang of the sharp cheddar burst in her mouth.

"I left them alone after I introduced Kinnard to her. Anyway," Nate continued, "it did Carly good, I think. Especially when I had to tell her about Bowie—"

She understood what he was saying, but had it been necessary? "Couldn't that have waited?" she implored him.

"No. Carly doesn't like secrets. She wants to know and face stuff in her way. You know that."

"I know." Defying her trembling hand, she picked up the mug of black coffee Nate had poured her and sipped the hot brew. "I wish I'd been more open with her. You were right, and I was wrong."

Her mind took her back to the day she'd first told Nate she loved him. She'd been listening to "Amazing Grace" at the NYPD funeral for Nate's grandfather. *If only I'd carried out all that I'd promised God that day, Carly and I wouldn't have been at odds. Maybe she wouldn't have enlisted, wouldn't have been wounded.*

"Hey, I can tell from your expression that you're busy blaming yourself for everything." Nate nudged her shoulder. "Just remember that you're human. You make mistakes. You can't control what happens to anyone or how anyone is going to react to what happens to them. Carly was wounded because Saddam Hussein is a nutcase, a murderous one. You didn't do it. Carly will be home soon—what you must decide is how *you* are going to react to the fact that she's let her father into her life."

"I know I should have let her meet him." The words were shards of glass in her throat. "I should have years ago."

"Maybe. Maybe not. We can't know how meeting Kinnard earlier would have affected her. From what he told me, he has changed a lot over the past few years. His wife divorced him, and two years ago, he lost his son in an auto accident."

"Oh, no." Leigh hadn't realized that she could feel sympathy for Trent. But she'd nearly lost her daughter. "That's dreadful."

"He's not the man who seduced you in 1972. I'd say he's learned that life isn't his to manipulate for his own purposes." Nate massaged her shoulder, releasing warmth through her flesh. "Just let it be."

"I know I must." She steadied her nerves. "I don't want to do more damage to my relationship with Carly and you. But I can't see him. It hurts too much."

"I don't think he's going to force his way into our family. I think he will be content merely to be in touch with Carly. And she's not about to wave him in your face."

Leigh took a deep breath and then took another bite as if it were her duty to eat, to go on living. "Nate, I still want us to go to counseling. I feel the need to talk all of this over with someone, and I want us to be the way we were when we were first married."

"Sounds like a good plan. Only I want us to be better."

As Leigh finished her half-sandwich and reached for another, she'd actually begun to taste the salty ham, the sharp cheese, the mellow rye, the tangy mustard. Nate had brought her back to herself, to life. "I love you, Nate."

He leaned over and kissed her below her left ear, right where he knew she loved to be kissed. Desire for him tingled through her, and she smiled. *It's not too late to make things right. We'll make it together. Oh, Lord, prepare me to show Carly how much I love her. With honesty.*

That evening, the phone rang at Ivy Manor and Chloe picked it up. She listened to the hesitant woman at the other end, her sympathy stirring. "You must come. Please. When Carly comes home, you must come and be our guests. I insist."

CHAPTER EIGHTEEN

Two weeks later, April 1991

*I*n her bedroom at Ivy Manor, Carly stood, looking out the windows down onto the lawn of green grass dotted with yellow dandelions. In the two days she'd been home, she felt as though she'd never left—until she looked down at her bandaged hand and walking cast. She had been to war, and now she was home. She gazed down at the green grass and saw umber desert sand superimposed over it until she blinked again. She was Carly, and she wasn't.

On the unusually warm April day, the house was quiet. Nate and Michael had gone fishing on the nearby creek. Rose had the day off, and Carly planned to spend the afternoon reading. The next day, Nate was going to drive her to Walter Reed for physical therapy. A knock came at her door. "Come in," Carly called.

Wearing a new spring dress of blue chambray, Grandma

Chloe peered inside. "Will you come down with me? Bette wants us to drop into the cottage for a few minutes."

"Sure. Grandma Bette really looks thinner."

"Yes, the chemo kept her from eating enough."

Carly finally had enough courage to ask, "Is she going to be all right?"

Chloe made eye contact with her. "She may have another round of chemo. But the doctor was pleased with her progress. She has a chance, a good one."

Carly felt suddenly full inside, as if she'd eaten a feast. It was a good feeling. "I'm glad."

"Me, too." Chloe held out her hand. "Come with me."

Using cast and cane, Carly turned and slowly swung across the hardwood floor. Grandma Chloe had banished all throw rugs from Ivy Manor until Carly put away her cane. Slowly, Carly made it down the steps to the first floor. She'd insisted on staying in her upstairs bedroom. It was good for her to exercise. And she didn't want to stay in the den where Aunt Kitty had died. That grief was still too fresh.

At the bottom, Chloe led her out the front door into the balmy day with blue sky overhead and fluffy cotton clouds. Carly had switched to wearing dresses, so much easier than slacks because of the cast. The spring breeze felt good as it wafted against the back of her knees. Still, images of the stark desert with its hot days and chill nights and the burning oil fields flowed in and out of her mind.

Carly made herself concentrate on the here and now. Slowly they made their way down the familiar rutted lane to the cottage. From the far side of the house, they heard the painters scraping away the old paint, preparing Ivy Manor for a new coat of white. Chloe and Carly stepped inside the cottage's back door, into its cozy kitchen. There a fresh coat of light yellow paint brightened the walls.

Around the old kitchen table sat Leigh in jeans and one of Kitty's Mets T-shirts and Bette in pressed black slacks and a flattering royal-blue georgette blouse. Her mother was as beautiful as ever, her golden hair falling loose around her shoulders. Bette looked sophisticated with her upswept do and a string of pearls at her neck.

"What's this all about, Mother?" Bette looked up.

Chloe helped Carly settle in a chair, then took her place at the head of the table. "Today we are going to tell the truth and set each other and ourselves free. Today, our family secrets and guilt will be exposed and disposed of."

Leigh and Bette stared at her openmouthed. Whatever Carly had expected, this wasn't it. She gazed from face to face. The truth? *I already know the truth, my truth.* Even if her mother finally told the truth, the truth that Trent had already revealed to Carly, what other secrets were there?

"And since I've decided this should happen, I'll go first." Chloe looked at each of them in turn. "I know that you all love me, but even all these years later, I still carry guilt over the way I treated my daughter when she was a little girl."

Bette looked startled. "Mother, you've always been wonderful to me. I couldn't have asked for a better mother."

Chloe covered Bette's hand with hers. "I thank you for that, dear, but what you've never questioned and never blamed me for is this: where was I for the first eleven years of your life?"

There was silence then. Carly had never heard about this. Why not?

Bette stared at her mother. "I . . . just always accepted that you had to be away helping Grandpa with his work in Washington, D.C." Bette smiled almost shyly, suddenly giving Carly a glimpse of her grandmother as a girl. "You were like a fairy princess when you visited me. I didn't know how to speak to you. You were too beautiful, and in your diamonds and furs—too grand for me."

Chloe looked surprised. "I didn't realize that was why you never seemed able to talk to me, Bette. It used to tear at my heart when I'd see you and want you to run into my arms. But you wouldn't even speak to me. I thought you blamed me for not being with you."

"I didn't know, Mama," Bette murmured and then leaned over and kissed her mother's cheek. "I never blamed you for anything."

Carly tried to imagine this new concept of Chloe, a glamorous woman who stayed away from her own child and merely visited like a queen. Carly couldn't make it fit with the woman who'd loved her unconditionally her whole life. No.

Tears moistened Chloe's eyes. She took out a frilled hankie and dabbed her eyes as she began again. "After the stock market crash in '29, you can't know how fearful I was when I came home to stay at long last. I was frightened that I wouldn't be able to gain your love, be a mother to you. When you were born, I'd wanted to be close to you, care for you. But I had been weak, so insecure. My mother wanted you for herself and you were a difficult baby. I didn't feel able to do what a mother should. All those lost years." Chloe shook her head. "Forgive me, Bette."

Bette squeezed her mother's hand. "There's nothing to forgive."

Chloe smiled sadly. Then she took a deep breath. "I'm grateful for your understanding. But now you have a secret you must tell your daughter."

Carly became instantly alert. Bette had kept a secret from Leigh?

Bette looked to her daughter and then back to Chloe. "I promised Curt—why does she need to know?"

"The truth will not hurt her," Chloe said. "And she already knows that you've held something back about her father."

"Yes," Leigh agreed, but gently, without any accusation in her voice. "I want to know the truth. I want to know why you never spoke about my real father. What happened?"

Carly waited, wondering if this was why her own mother always ignored her questions about her father. Had she learned avoidance and deception from her own mother?

Fingering the pearls at her neck, Bette stared down at the tabletop for several minutes. The silence gathered around them. The wall clock ticked and outside a robin chirped. The painters scraped and turned a radio to a country station. Someone was singing, "Tie a Yellow Ribbon." "Your father didn't die in an accident," Bette admitted, "he committed suicide."

Carly couldn't believe her ears. No wonder Bette didn't want to tell Leigh that.

Leigh's mouth dropped open. "Why?"

Chloe answered for Bette, who'd put her face into her

hands. "He carried terrible guilt over being unfaithful to your mother during the war. He couldn't live with himself."

"While he was dying, he asked me to promise never to tell you," Bette said, still not looking up. "He loved you. He felt that he'd failed you."

"So that's why you'd never talk about my father," Leigh said. "I always knew there was something." Leigh stood and put her arms around Bette's shoulders. "Oh, Mother, how awful for you."

Bette looked startled. "You understand why I couldn't tell you?"

"Of course," Leigh said and sat back down. She reached for her mother's hands. "He asked you to promise. And you gave me such a wonderful stepfather. I never felt cheated. I loved Ted. He was my dad."

Bette smiled through tears. "Ted loved you as if you were his own. From the first time he saw you."

Another moment passed in silence while Carly put all this information together in her mind. *Lord, I won't keep secrets from my child. Or I'll try not to.*

Her chin down, her cheeks pink, Leigh smoothed stray hair back from her face and then looked at Carly. "I'm afraid I already blurted out most of my secret to my daughter." Leigh reached for Carly's hand. "I hope you'll accept my apology. It was awful the way I threw the fact that Trent was married when we . . . when . . ."

"When I was conceived?" Carly supplied bravely. "You know I talked to him in Germany? He's going to be in my life from now on. I feel so sorry for him. He's so alone."

Leigh nodded and lightly stroked Carly's arm, gazing

down at it, not into Carly's eyes. "Nate told me. I don't think I want to see him again. But I don't begrudge you or him time together. And Carly—" Leigh hesitated "—I'm sorry I couldn't see how much harm I was doing to you by not telling you about Trent. But it always came down to this." Leigh looked directly into Carly's eyes. "How could I make you understand that while I regretted . . . being with Trent, I didn't regret you?"

Carly turned this over in her mind. How would she have reacted to hearing the bald truth as a child? She had no answer. She kissed her mother, letting that show her love.

"And I didn't help the situation," Bette added, sounding ashamed. "I've regretted over and over how I treated your mother, Carly. I should have supported her in her time of need. I should have done better."

Chloe placed her hand over Bette's. "You were suffering from losing both your stepfather and your husband and grieving over Leigh's loss. No one in this world makes the right choices all the time. Evil knows just when to hit us. Evil knows to strike when we are weak."

"Mom," Carly said, "I'm not mad at you anymore. Trent told me how it was. He said he wasn't . . . a very good person then. He used you. But he does love me. And now that I have him in my life, I'm not angry with you anymore. I'm older now, too. I know that sounds funny because I'm still only seventeen. But I understand now. Life hits you with things you . . ." Carly brushed away tears. "You don't see coming, and it can hurt so much."

Leigh took Carly's good hand in hers. "I wish I could have saved you from all that's happened to you."

"I don't." Carly faced them fiercely. "All my life I've been afraid, uncertain about who I was. I see now that I enlisted in order to put myself to the test and either conquer my fear or go down once and for all." Carly felt her heart pounding, but it felt wonderful to say the words, the words that were freeing her.

"This past year, I've been pushed to my limits and survived." Carly thought of Alex and boot camp and of the first trip into the Saudi desert, and her chin trembled. "I've faced paralyzing, overwhelming fear, fear of capture, of pain, of death. I've lost someone I loved, too. So maybe I can understand how it is to love and . . . lose. But I learned I can survive." She cleared her throat and let the words she'd held back flow out. "Through it all, I've found that I can go through hell and then come back again with the help of God. I'm trying to find in him my all in all. I've started." Beaming at them, she burst into tears.

The other three gathered around her, stroking her hair, kissing her, speaking words of love. She looked into each of their faces and thanked God for them. Finally, all their tears had fallen, and they sat around the table quiet, drained but uplifted by love for each other.

"There's more, Bette," Chloe prompted briskly, tucking her hankie into her sweater pocket. "Now you need to tell them. The ceremony will take place in just two months."

"What ceremony?" Leigh asked, glancing from face to face.

"I'm going to be honored for my service in World War II," Bette said, looking at her lap.

With a wry smile, Leigh studied her mother. "Yes? What else haven't you told us?"

Carly watched both of them, anticipation tingling through her.

"Well, dear," Bette said without looking up, "you know how you always thought I was just a secretary at the CIA?"

Leigh nodded.

"I wasn't a secretary. I was a spy."

Carly gawked at her grandmother, and Leigh's mouth dropped open.

"Your mother," Chloe added, sounding proud, "worked against the Nazis before and during the war and then joined the new CIA after the war."

"Mom," Leigh said with eyes wide, "why didn't you ever tell me?"

Bette shrugged. "Part of being a spy is not letting anyone know."

"Did Daddy know?" Leigh asked.

Finally, Bette looked up with a smile. "Your stepfather, Ted, trained me, and we worked together."

"What?" Leigh gasped. "Daddy was a spy, too?"

Bette nodded and grinned. "And what a spy he was. I have so much to tell you."

"And I want to hear it, too," Carly interjected. "Grandma—a spy. Wow."

Through the open windows, the sound of a vehicle pulling up to the side of Ivy Manor interrupted them. Carly swiveled on her seat. And the other three rose and went to look out the back door. "Who is it?" Carly asked, gripping her cane and rising to join the others.

"They're here early," Chloe replied. "I thought they'd be here by dinnertime tonight."

"Who are they, Mother?" Bette asked.

Chloe didn't reply but opened the door and called, "We're here." She motioned toward the middle-aged couple getting out of a somewhat battered blue pickup.

The two strangers walked toward them. Both wore blue jeans and jean jackets. Carly studied them and suddenly she knew who they were. She'd seen a family photo of them. She pushed her way out the door. "You're Bowie's parents!"

Nodding, Mrs. Jenkin hurried forward. "Your great-grandmother invited us. You're Carly. Bowie sent us a photo of you two together." The plump woman with graying blond hair burst into tears.

Carly put her arms around Mrs. Jenkin's neck and wept with her. "I'm so glad you came. I've been wanting to talk about Bowie to someone who knew him. I loved him and he loved me."

"We had a memorial service at our church for him." Mr. Jenkin came up behind his wife. "But we needed to see you, talk to you. You were with him, weren't you? When it happened."

Carly nodded, the great grief welling up inside fresh, dragging her down once more. "I'm so sorry."

"You don't be sorry, honey," Mrs. Jenkin soothed her. "We're glad you're alive. We lost Bowie. But we know he was so happy to have you in his life." Bowie's mom broke down again. Mr. Jenkin wiped tears from his lined, sunburned cheeks and put a comforting arm on his wife's shoulder.

Carly hugged Mrs. Jenkin and whispered a prayer that

God would let Bowie know about this meeting. Bowie had thought them so different, but that had been all about this world, and Bowie was beyond that now. "I know he's with Jesus," Carly whispered to his mother. "I know I'll see him again."

Mrs. Jenkin stroked Carly's moist cheek. "If we have Christ, we have hope."

Carly could only nod.

Chloe drew them all inside to the cottage's living room. Bette and Leigh bustled around, brewing coffee and making sandwiches. Carly looked at her great-grandmother and mouthed, "Thank you. I love you."

Chloe mouthed back to her, "I love you. Always."

Washington, D.C.

Two months later, Carly sat in the front row in the Rose Garden at the White House to witness her grandmother receiving the Medal of Freedom. Warm summer sun beat down on them, but a breeze made the day bearable. On Carly's one side sat a happy-looking Alex Reseda, who'd gotten leave to spend time with Carly as she convalesced at Ivy Manor. On the other was Lorelle, home from the Gulf and on leave, too. Carly's cast was off and her hand was without bandages, but she still needed a cane. Lorelle, Alex, and Carly wore their dress uniforms. "This is so cool," Alex whispered into Carly's ear. "I never thought I'd see the president in person at the White House."

Carly grinned. In the same row sat her mother and stepfather, her great-grandmother, and Chloe's friend Minnie

Dawson, Lorelle's great-grandmother. Gretel Sachs, her grandmother Bette's lifelong friend, had flown all the way from Israel to attend. And Dan proudly sat beside Bette. All of them were dressed in their best and looking excited. Bette looked stunning in a crisp linen dress in her favorite shade of deep purple. Dan had sent her a dozen red sweetheart roses and Bette had insisted on his wearing one bud as a boutonniere. Dan was holding Bette's hand, and Carly loved it.

The president was announced and appeared. Everyone rose. At his motion, everyone sat. He began speaking about the cost of liberty in each generation and the brave men and women who gave their talents, and even sometimes their lives, to defend freedom for all Americans. He said that the World War II generation was vanishing and that their nation must take the opportunity to proffer those veterans gratitude. "Among the services that are being recognized today are the first of Ms. Bette McCaslin Gaston's intelligence career. If it hadn't been for the efforts of young Bette McCaslin in the 1930s, the U.S. would have entered World War II with the Nazis knowing all our weapons secrets. This was only the first of a career crowned with success." The president listed the ways Bette had aided the cause against Nazi Germany. Then he concluded, "Several times young Bette McCaslin received private thanks and commendations from President Franklin Roosevelt. I'm happy to be able to thank this woman publicly today."

Awed by these words, Carly felt her whole being filled with pride, a glowing, expanding warmth. *This is my grandmother.* Then Bette was called forward and the Medal of Freedom was presented to her. The president shook her hand and then motioned her to the microphone.

Near tears, Bette thought of those events of all those years ago and also of Ted, her intelligence partner and later husband. Bette pulled herself together and looked out at the audience and cleared her throat. She had something important to say, and she'd been given a golden opportunity to say it.

"Mr. President, honored guests, I never imagined that I would receive this honor from the country I love. I was privileged to work against Hitler and later against Stalin, both cruel dictators. Due to wartime necessity, I served in the FBI unofficially thirty years before women were allowed to enter the FBI. The work I did was exciting and at times dangerous. But I was able to meet the demands because of who I am, because of those whose love made me the woman I was, and because of what they'd taught me about courage. I am a woman of Ivy Manor, my family's ancestral home in Maryland. But I'm not the first strong woman to come from Ivy Manor.

"First of all, I'd like to thank my mother for her example of courage. In the midst of the Great Depression and in spite of the anti-Semitism of her neighbors, my mother took in a young Jewish immigrant girl in the 1930s. Mother, will you and Gretel join me up here?"

Chloe looked reluctant, but a beaming Gretel took her arm and marched her up to the microphone.

"Next, my mother and, I hope in some small way, I influenced my daughter Leigh. As part of her iconoclastic generation, Leigh took part in the women's movement of the 1970s. And even before that, passionate in her support of equal rights as a high-school girl, attended Dr. King's march here in Washington in 1963. Come up, Leigh."

Looking surprised, Leigh joined her great-grandmother at the front near Bette.

"Now, I commend to you my granddaughter, Carly, who has continued the tradition of service to her country. She has just served in the Gulf War and was recently presented the Purple Heart. Come up, Carly."

Applause surrounded Carly as she walked with her cane to stand beside her mother.

"Also, I'd like Minnie Dawson and her great-granddaughter, also a Gulf War veteran, to come forward."

Looking puzzled, Minnie and Lorelle joined the others grouped around Bette.

"Minnie and my mother ran away together in 1917 to New York City. Minnie Dawson nee Carlyle became Mimi Carlyle, who appeared on Broadway and later in supporting roles in several of Dorothy Dandridge's films in the 1950s."

Minnie lifted one eyebrow as if to ask, *What are you leading up to?*

Bette winked at Minnie. Then she faced the audience, pride pulsing in her heart. "All these women had a part in my life and more importantly, in the greater life of this nation in the twentieth century.

"When I look at them, I see how the role of women in America and in the world has changed over this century." Bette paused to compose herself to voice the tribute she'd planned. "It makes me proud of them and proud to be a part of them. This medal not only honors me, but it honors all these women. Ladies and gentlemen, I give you the women of Ivy Manor."

HISTORICAL NOTE

*O*nce again, *Carly* (as the previous book in the series, *Leigh*) involved researching more current history. My memories of the First Gulf War are vivid but civilian. Fortunately, I was able to tap into the military memories of women who'd served in the First Gulf War or soon after. But I found a couple of pitfalls in writing current history.

First, people were likely to contradict me if their individual experiences didn't match those of my characters. Second, it is difficult to get eyewitness reports. Many people don't like to share their memories for various reasons, so it's difficult to find written sources on this war. Most of the sources were written for children and teenagers, not adults. It's as if the accepted historical perspective on the event hasn't been settled yet.

Since I have no firsthand military recollections, I have based all the events depicted in *Carly* on personal experiences of former soldiers, male and female. If you're a veteran and your experiences in the military and in the First Gulf War don't jibe with Carly's, please don't discount what I have written. When I tailored those recollections of other soldiers and portrayed them in Carly's life, I hope I did so both accurately and vividly.

Finally, *Carly*—unlike the first three books of the series—covers only one very eventful year in my heroine's life. Carly is just seventeen throughout the book. Therefore, she has time only to experience her first bittersweet love. I'd already begun imagining Carly's future, but I ran out of pages!

I hope you've enjoyed this series, The Women of Ivy Manor, as much as I have enjoyed researching and writing it. Please let me hear from you at: l.cote@juno.com or P.O. Box 864, Woodruff, WI 54568. Drop by my Web site: www.BooksbyLynCote.com.

Postscript

Just a correction for those who read *Bette:* On the dedication page, my father-in-law's name was misspelled. He was Orville "Jum" [sic] Cote, not "Jim." "Jum" was short for "Jumbo," his childhood nickname.

Sorry, Jum.

READING GROUP GUIDE

1. The effect of truth versus secrets is a forceful theme in *Carly*. Should Leigh have told her daughter the unvarnished truth about her biological father? If so, how and when?

2. My generation, the baby boomers, has also often been called the "sandwich generation." Why do you think this situation has evolved? (A hint: think life expectancy.) Was this true for Leigh—was she "sandwiched"?

3. Have you ever been in a situation like Carly's in boot camp? Did anyone ever make you the target of bullying or gossip? How did you handle it—or wish you'd handled it?

4. If you've read all four books, compare and contrast how each generation, starting with Lily Leigh and Chloe, clashed with the next. What caused problems between mothers and daughters? What created harmony?

5. Every action brings consequences. What consequences

did Carly experience from her kidnapping? How did she try to deal with those consequences?

6. Why do you think Carly enlisted? Explain your reasons.

7. In my humble opinion, the way to true peace is to be honest with yourself, genuine with others, and open and humble with God. Consider each of the Women of Ivy Manor: what resulted when each lived up to this—or didn't?

8. How did Lorelle's life differ from her father Frank's and her great-grandmother Minnie's?

9. Besides the heroine, which of the characters in this book did you enjoy most? Discuss the same for each previous book.

10. Are there any characters in the previous books that you wished you'd read more about? Why?

THE WOMEN OF IVY MANOR

Meet the women of Ivy Manor—four
strong and independent ladies who live
and love throughout the decades of the
twentieth century. Each has experiences
unique to herself; each must learn to
grow and succeed on her own terms.

Chloe

Born in the early
days of the new century, she gives up
her old life for a new one—before
realizing that perhaps what she's
always wanted was right in front of her.

Bette

Coming into her own during World
War II, Bette learns that dreams and
expectations often change, hopefully for the better. Can
she give up her childish hopes and
embrace real life?

Leigh

A child of the civil rights movement,
Leigh lives and breathes the exploration of
new ideas and thoughts. But independence
isn't always easy, and mistakes are made.
Can she learn to accept who she is before
it's too late?

Carly

Carly longs for independence, and finds it in the
military. But when all that is stripped away, will she
realize that her sense of identity comes from within, not
from anything or anyone else?